"I'm losing patience. Don't make me get nasty. You won't like me if I get nasty."

She thrust her chin out, pushed away from the desk, and stood with arms akimbo. "I don't like you now, and I'm not scared. If you planned to kill or knock me over the head for it, you'd have done so Friday night."

He leaned his head back and sighed. "Why are you being so stubborn? Can't you see how much this means to me? Besides, you don't look like the type to go off chasing after buried treasure. It's not your style. Okay, five thousand. That's my final offer. Just let me have the map."

Alex walked behind the desk and sat slumped, biting her lip. If he didn't have the map, that left only one other person who could have taken it, because only one other person knew of the map's existence *and* had the combination to the safe—Rod.

Rod! Shit, in the excitement over the missing map, I forgot all about him.

She straightened as a horrible thought raced through her mind. Oh, God! Could this Victoria person have come into the shop on Friday and forced Rod to open the safe? And where was Rod now? Hurt—or dead? She needed to check his apartment. If he wasn't there, she'd call the cops regardless of how much Quinn Rafferty objected.

Along Came Quinn...

...finaled in the 2006 CTRW CONNections Contest.

Along Came Quinn

by

Suzanne Rossi

This is a work of fiction. Names, characters, places, and incidents are either the product of the author's imagination or are used fictitiously, and any resemblance to actual persons living or dead, business establishments, events, or locales, is entirely coincidental.

Along Came Quinn

Cover Art by *Kim Mendoza*

The Wild Rose Press
PO Box 706
Adams Basin, NY 14410-0706
Visit us at www.thewildrosepress.com

Publishing History
First Crimson Rose Edition, 2010
Print ISBN 1-60154-599-1

Published in the United States of America

Dedication

I've had many critique partners over the years, and each had one thing in common. They improved my work. To Toni Andrews, Sharon Hartley, Vonnie Kennedy, Anne Marie Maghee, Aleka Nakis, Mona Risk, and Tina Stitzer, my heartfelt thanks for helping to get me here.

Thank you to my editor, Johanna Melaragno, who made the whole process easy and pain free.

And special thanks to my husband, Bruce Peek. Without his love, support and understanding, I'd have never succeeded. Love ya, babe!

Thank you one and all for making this happen.

Chapter One

Alexandria Montgomery awoke with a start, blinked several times, and sat upright trying to figure out what had disturbed her. The clock on the nightstand read eleven-thirty. She had fallen asleep with a romance novel open on her lap, a bedside lamp the only source of illumination.

She cocked her head and listened. Silence.

I must have been dreaming.

Her hand reached to turn off the lamp when she heard a faint tinkling, as though someone had bumped into the curio cabinet along the back wall of her antique store downstairs. Alex froze and held her breath. Footsteps trod along the worn wooden floors. Whoever was down there wasn't concerned about being quiet.

Maybe it's Rod.

No, her boyfriend would have called to let her know he'd changed his mind about leaving for Detroit, not scare her half to death like this.

Alex slid out of bed and stood on trembling legs, then picked up the phone. Clenching it in a sweat-dampened palm, she dialed nine-one-one.

"What is your emergency?"

"There's a burglar in my antique store at 752 North Main in Waukegan," she said, speaking softly.

"Yes, ma'am, please stay on the line."

She jumped at a crash from below. *Oh God, he's seen the stairs and coming to get me.*

The thought of someone creeping up the steps spurred her into action. She placed the phone on the nightstand, padded to her bureau, opened one of the

1

drawers, and pawed through the hosiery and scarves.

Where is it? Where's that stupid gun I found at Grandfather's?

Her hand closed around the cold plastic grip. Pulling it free, she took a few seconds to inspect the damned thing. She had no idea what kind of a gun it was and couldn't remember if it was even loaded, but presumably all she had to do was point and pull the trigger.

If it comes to that, at least I'll go down fighting.

She tiptoed on bare feet through the apartment to the door at the top of the stairs and opened it a crack. Another crash signified more breaking china, this time followed by a not so muffled curse.

Dammit! If I have to be robbed, why is it by some clumsy oaf? He's wrecking my store.

Alex descended the stairs, not the smartest thing to do, but she was too angry to care. She'd hold him until the cops showed up. A quick peek over the banister showed the burglar probing the bookshelves of classics with a pencil flashlight. A literary burglar?

Her cold, shaking fingers fumbled along the wall, found, and then flipped on the light switch.

"Freeze! Get your hands up now!"

Hey, that was pretty good. I sounded just like they do on TV.

Unfortunately, the sudden glare blinded her. While advancing further into the room, she stubbed her toe on the leg of a Victorian loveseat. The roar of the gun going off when her finger accidentally tightened on the trigger drowned out her yelp of pain.

"Ow! Goddamn it!" the intruder yelled.

Startled, Alex squeezed again. A second shot discharged. She dropped the gun.

"Jesus Christ!" the man swore.

In her panic to retrieve the weapon, she rushed forward inadvertently kicking it straight at the feet of the thief, who scooped it up.

Alex reached for the ceiling and declared, "I…I've called the police! They'll be here any second."

She hoped her facial expression oozed confidence. Her pounding heart and wobbling legs certainly didn't. With insides quivering and knees ready to collapse, she thrust her chin up hoping the burglar took it as a sign *she* was in control.

"For Pete's sake, put your hands down. I won't shoot. I wish *you* hadn't."

His voice held a rasping note and his face contorted as if in pain. Then, she noticed the dark wetness against the sleeve on the upper left arm of his black sweater, and the bright red drops slowly splattering onto her floor.

"Oh, my God! I shot you?" She groaned and shook.

Oh, shit! I've killed a man and I don't even know his name.

"It just nicked me. I'm lucky to be alive. Lady, what are you doing with a gun if you don't know how to use it?" He looked and sounded furious. His brows drew together in a scowl, his narrowed eyes emphasizing high cheekbones. A strong jaw clenched against the pain gave him a dangerous appearance. He stepped closer.

Alex didn't like being intimidated. Since she hadn't fatally wounded him, his attitude—like somehow this was all her fault—pissed her off.

"Excuse me, but this is *my* store, and I believe *you* are the burglar."

"Sweetheart, you are a menace. And why are you even here? You and your boyfriend should be at some dance club by now."

He towered over her five-foot-four-inch frame by a good six or seven inches. She backed up a step, irritated that she did so.

"How do you know about Rod?" she asked in amazement. Then comprehension dawned. "You've been casing the place."

"Let's just say I've kept my eye on things."

"Well, why are you making such a mess? The cash register is over there behind the counter. A-r-r-r-g-h!" she cried, spying the shattered vase on the floor. "You klutz, that was a Lalique!"

The sound of approaching sirens cut off any further remarks she could have made. *God bless the Waukegan Police Department.*

The man glanced toward the front of the shop. "That's my exit cue. If you don't mind, I'll keep this," he said, slipping the gun into his pants pocket. "It is registered in your name, isn't it?"

"Uh..."

"I thought not. If I were you, I'd make up a story to tell the cops. I'm sure there must be some kind of ordinance against discharging a firearm within the city limits. Now, if you'll excuse me..."

Before she could protest, he slid past her, through a kitchen in the back of the store, and then out the door. Ten seconds later, two police cars pulled up. She forced her trembling legs toward the entrance and tried to get her shaking fingers to unlock the door, succeeding on the third attempt.

Her mind lapsed into a total brain freeze. Cops made her nervous. She didn't know why; they just did. A simple speeding ticket always made her feel like a bank robber on the lam.

Did Waukegan, Illinois, have an ordinance against shooting guns inside the city? She had no idea. If she told them about the burglar, they'd be here for hours. And if they searched and found him, how would he explain the wound? Worse yet, they'd find the gun in his pocket with her fingerprints on it. Plus, she had no clue as to the laws concerning gun ownership. *Had* her grandfather registered the damned thing?

Oh, crap, why me?

Logic demanded the thief would be long gone and not skulking around waiting for another crack at robbing her.

Having no idea of the legal ramifications to any of this, Alex did what made the most sense—she lied.

"Oh, officers, I'm so sorry. This has all been a dreadful mistake. I feel like such a fool," she gushed and babbled. "You see, I was asleep when a noise woke me and at first I thought I was hearing things, and then I heard it again and called nine-one-one, and I know the lady said to stay on the line, but then I heard a crash followed by another crash, so I ran downstairs, and when I flipped on the lights, I saw it was a...um...a cat."

Alex took a deep breath after the longest sentence she'd ever uttered. Having never been able to think on her feet, she wasn't very good at this. She preferred using a logical, practical response to a situation, but then she'd never been in this type of situation before. She knew she looked guilty as hell about something.

Face it Montgomery, you are a lousy liar.

She shivered, imagining the cold steel of handcuffs on her wrists.

"A cat, ma'am?" the first officer asked. His lips twitched, and his gaze slid away to look around the shop.

Good grief, they'd bought it. She stared for an instant before blurting, "Yes, a cat. It must have...ah...gotten in when I...um...ah...emptied the trash tonight. There are a lot of them around. Cats, I mean. Strays, you know. At any rate, I managed to chase it out."

"Ma'am, you shouldn't have come downstairs to

confront a possible burglar. You could have been hurt," the second officer admonished.

"Oh, well, yes. I guess I can see that. You're absolutely right. I acted very foolishly. I'm afraid I just didn't think." She gently smacked her forehead with her hand. "Oh, silly me."

Who gave a rat's ass if they thought she was a ditz? As long as they would *just leave*.

"Would you like us to check around for you?"

"No, no, that won't be necessary. Everything's fine. I just shooed the cat out the back door."

"Is that blood?" the first cop asked.

Shit! She gazed in horror at the telltale drip of red drops all the way to the back door. Those imaginary handcuffs tightened.

"Oh, dear, the cat must have hurt itself when the vase shattered," she explained, swallowing hard. Maybe it was her imagination, but that sounded convincing.

"Are you sure you're all right?" the second man asked, his hand on the gun in his holster. His gaze swept the room.

"Oh, I'm fine. In fact, I'm going to get a broom, sweep up this mess right now, and then go back to bed. I can only apologize to you once again. I'm not in any trouble for calling nine-one-one about a cat, am I?"

Please, just think I'm a dumb ass and get the hell out of here.

"No, ma'am, but we'll just have a quick look around anyway." They finished their inspection in less than ten minutes, including her apartment, and then returned.

"If you're sure you're okay, we'll be going. I hung up on the nine-one-one operator and told her everything was all right. She said she thought she heard shouting and shots fired."

Alex's heart lurched. She saw bars in her future.

"Shots? Good heavens, no. Maybe she heard me slamming the back door when the cat left, and I did yell a lot."

"All right, but just remember, no more investigating on your own." He shook a finger under her nose, but smiled anyway, glanced down, and then averted his gaze.

"I won't, I promise," she said, practically pushing them out the door.

The policemen returned to their cars. Alex even remembered to wave as they drove off. When their cruisers disappeared around the corner, she turned and sagged against the door.

Oh, brother, what a night.

Avoiding the smashed china, she made her way into the kitchen, returning to sweep the pieces into a dustpan, and then the wastebasket. Finished with that task, she wet a towel to clean up the blood. As she tossed the towel on top of the shards, her temper rose.

Dammit! That Lalique vase was worth eight hundred dollars, and I could have gotten nearly five hundred for the Staffordshire figurine. Why on earth did I lie to the police? I should have told them the truth, gun and all. Dumb ass, it's too late now.

She picked up the wastebasket and opened the back door wrinkling her nose at the damp, dank smell of the alley, then cursed when her bare feet hit the cold pavement still wet from the rain during the day.

How did the bastard get in anyway?

She had locked the doors when she'd come home with dinner. Since she noticed no sign of forced entry, she assumed he was proficient at picking locks, including deadbolts.

Alex tossed the trash in the nearest dumpster and turned toward the door when a shadow detached itself from an alcove and stepped in front of her.

"Shit!" she yelped in fright, dropping the wastebasket with a clatter. She faced her intruder.

Before she could move, he grabbed her arm and shoved her into the kitchen, closing and locking the door behind him. Backing up until the refrigerator stopped her, Alex stared, unable to utter another word.

"Lose that deer in the headlights look, would you?" he said in an exasperated voice. "I'm not going to hurt you. You hurt me, remember? It's time you took care of it."

"Wh…what are you talking about?"

"You shot me. I can't go to a doctor or a hospital without questions being asked, so find some bandages and fix the damned thing."

Her shock wore off. "What? Are you crazy?"

She should be scared out of her wits, but that particular emotion was curiously lacking. She had no clue as to why. After all, he still had her gun. On the other hand, throughout this entire ordeal, he had shown no inclination to use it.

He grabbed her arm again, marched her through the store, and up the stairs to her apartment where he stripped off his sweater.

The bullet had gouged a two-inch furrow in his upper left arm. While the bleeding had slowed, blood still welled and flowed sluggishly down his arm.

Shaken, Alex pushed him toward the dining area. *Why am I doing this?*

She had no explanation for *that* either, further pissing her off.

"Sit down while I get the first aid kit and some towels. I don't want you bleeding all over my carpet. It's an Aubusson," she stated through gritted teeth. She'd never seen a bullet wound before and felt a trifle lightheaded.

"For God's sake, don't faint!"

"I won't, just sit down. I'll only be a minute."

Irritating man.

While she cleaned, and then bandaged the injury, Alex took the time to covertly study this man who had burst into her life in such an unsettling manner.

His shoulders, chest, and arms were well-muscled and the chest covered with dark hair that ran straight as an arrow beneath the waistband of his jeans—a place she shouldn't be concerned with, but about which she speculated anyway.

She supposed some women would consider him good looking in a rugged sort of way. All in all, he was a prime specimen.

If you like that type, which I don't.

She continued to clean his wound and wondered what he would do when she finished. Tie her up and gag her so she couldn't call the police again? Drag her along as a hostage? Or just kill her? It occurred to her that maybe, she *should* be afraid.

****

Quinn Rafferty watched Alexandria wash his arm, clenching his jaw as frequent jabs of pain shot through him. Switching his gaze away from his wound, he eyed his nurse.

What would she do now that she'd caught him? Breaking in had sounded like a good idea this morning. He was willing to pay to get his map back, but the temptation of retrieving it free of charge had won out over common sense.

Quinn cursed silently. Damn it, she and that slimy con artist, Rod Halston, should have been whooping it up somewhere. They always went out on Friday nights. He'd invested three weeks of surveillance before coming to that conclusion.

Where did it all go wrong? I should have made sure she'd left before picking the locks.

He sneaked another glance at the top of her head, the curly black hair just inches from his nose.

She fussed with the dressing and in spite of the pain, his hormones kicked it up a notch. His gaze dropped to her breasts, and then back up.

Definitely good to look at and sexy as hell, with lips made for kissing.

He contemplated exploring that avenue of thought a little further when another shot of pain had him sucking in his breath. It also served as a reminder for him to stay focused on other matters.

Owning her own business showed she had to have some intelligence, so it mystified him as to how Alexandria Montgomery could have been taken in by a cheap piece of work like Halston.

"There," she said, taping the bandage into place. "You should have penicillin or something in case of infection, but I'm fresh out."

He didn't begrudge her the sarcasm. This probably hadn't been her best night of the week either.

"What's this all about? You should still be running like a deer and tending your own injuries. It's not logical."

"What did you tell the cops?" he countered.

"I said a cat got in. Who are you, and why were you sneaking around my shop?"

He ignored her questions, not yet ready to give any answers. "Very inventive. I don't suppose you have a bottle of brandy nearby, do you? Just to ward off germs."

She glared, but brought him the bottle and a glass. "What happens now?" Her voice shook.

He gazed into her face easily reading the uncertainty. "Relax. I said I wasn't going to hurt you."

The tense expression eased.

"Hmm, Cognac," he murmured pouring a glass, and then taking a swallow. "You have great taste. Or does this belong to the boyfriend?"

"Leave Rod out of this. Now, who the hell are you?"

"All right," he said, taking another drink. He looked her in the eye. "I guess you deserve an explanation. My name is Quinn Rafferty, and you have something that belongs to me. I want it back."

The implication of his insinuation brought an immediate, indignant reaction. Her brows meeting over her nose crinkled her forehead. She inhaled with a sharp hissing breath, widened her stance, and stood with her fists on her hips.

"Are you accusing me of being a thief? *You?* That's the most ridiculous statement I've ever heard considering the circumstances. I'll have you know every item in this store is either from my grandfather's home or purchased legitimately at estate sales. Of all the nerve!"

"Chill out, Miss Montgomery. You're in possession of something that belonged to my late grandfather and is now mine. I want it back. It's as simple as that."

"What could I possibly have that belongs to you?"

"How about a map showing the location of The Treasure of the Mayan Kings?"

****

He had taken a deep breath before uttering those words, which drew her focus to his muscular, hair-covered chest.

Now, her attention snapped away from his torso, and her breath caught in her throat. How did he know about the map? She hadn't even known of its existence until a month ago. A little thrill of fear rushed through her and, this time, not for her life.

"I don't know what you're talking about." She hoped her face looked impassive.

"Don't insult my intelligence, honey. You know you have it, and so do I. It's mine, but I'm willing to pay. How much do you want?"

"How do I know what you're telling me is true? What proof do you have that this item, which by the way I'm not admitting I have, belongs to you?"

Her eyes fixed on his face, but her mind once again moved south. *Damn all sexy men to hell.*

"Almost three years ago, my grandfather got a hold of an old map. He suspected the thing was legit and began authenticating it. Before he could finish, he caught his secretary in the act of stealing it. She's also responsible for his death."

"She killed him? That's awful," she said with a gasp, her indignation momentarily forgotten.

"Damned straight. Not long after, she lost possession of it. The map went through several owners until coming to you. As I said, even though it's mine, I'll be willing to pay five hundred dollars for it."

"And if I say no?"

"That would make you the recipient of stolen goods, wouldn't it?"

This time her gasp was one of anger. "I wouldn't take one red cent from you! How do I know what you're telling me isn't a pack of lies? Do I look like I was born yesterday?"

He rose and pulled the sweater back over his head. "It's been a long day. I'm tired, in pain, and out of patience."

Thank you, Mr. Rafferty, for covering up the distraction. Distractions she didn't need. What she needed was time to analyze what he'd said.

"Think about it over the weekend. I'll be in touch." He looked into her eyes. "I'm not lying. The map really does belong to me."

His gray-blue gaze caused her heart to beat faster and her breathing to quicken. A strange, nervous fluttering grew in the pit of her stomach and somehow, that was more disturbing than any other event of this crazy night.

"All I'm asking is for you to think about it, Miss Montgomery. It's after one and I'm exhausted. Why don't you call me a cab so I can get out of your hair?"

"A cab? You break into my store, destroy thirteen hundred dollars worth of merchandise, scare me to death twice, encourage me to lie to the police, demand I dress your wound, and now want me to call you a cab?"

"If it's not too much trouble."

"You're not serious." The expression on his face indicated he was.

"In case you haven't noticed, it's raining again. Since I'm in a weakened condition because of a gunshot wound inflicted by you, I'd hate to have to walk all the way home in the rain risking pneumonia," he replied, an innocent look on his face.

Making a noise of pure exasperation, she grabbed the phone, riffled through the pages of her address book, and punched in the numbers all the while muttering, "I don't believe this."

"You have the cab company in your address book?" He looked amused.

"Of course. You never know when it might come in handy." Did he notice the irony of those words?

Five minutes later, the cab pulled up in the alley at the foot of her outside stairs. Quinn stopped in the doorway, glanced down her body, and then up again.

"Thanks for everything."

He dropped a brief, hard kiss on her mouth, trotted down the steps, and into the cab.

Alex stood in the open entryway, her jaw unhinged, too shocked to react. With her heart hammering and her breath catching somewhere in her chest, she continued to stare as the taxi pulled away. Raindrops splashed onto her face bringing her out of the daze. Alex closed and locked the door.

She looked down at herself and noticed that

throughout the entire evening's ordeal, she'd been wearing a flimsy silk nightgown, her breasts and nipples clearly outlined.

Geez, no wonder he kissed me. It must look like I'm advertising.

Then she remembered how the cops had also avoided looking at her. Embarrassment burned her cheeks and the tips of her ears.

She scrunched up her eyes and shouted to the walls, "Oh, crap!"

Feeling like a fool, she cleaned up the remains of the antiseptic and bandages, then went to bed again and stared at the ceiling. Did she believe that ridiculous story of his? She had no answer.

But Alexandria Montgomery was nobody's fool. The instant she'd clapped eyes on that treasure map she just knew it had to be real. Today, her trip to Downer's Grove had confirmed her hopes. The map was authentic, and she would be damned if she'd just give it up on his say-so.

A sudden noise outside made her jump. "Knock it off, dummy. It's just a cat—a real one this time. Go to sleep."

She closed her eyes and channeled her thoughts toward a more pleasant subject matter—Rod, her current boyfriend and shop assistant. Lord, she could have used him here tonight. What a time to go out of town for a family reunion. Why couldn't he have stuck around for at least one more day? Maybe then, she wouldn't have met Quinn Rafferty.

Quinn Rafferty—sexy Quinn Rafferty. She gave herself a mental kick. *No, don't think about him. Think about Rod.*

How had she managed before Rod Halston came into her life? It had taken her less than a week to realize she wanted to see more of him, and what better way than to offer him a job as her assistant? Rod met all the requirements on her matrimonial checklist. He'd proven dependable in the shop, too. She trusted him.

Dependability—that's what it all boils down to.

Dependability topped her list. She'd searched for a man like him for years.

Alex first compiled the list on her sixteenth birthday and added to it on a regular basis ever since, although football player and Mel Gibson look-alike had been dropped as she matured.

Since hiring Rod, her clientele had almost doubled and he'd sold several expensive items to middle-aged women who giggled at his mild flirting, after which he'd catch her eye and wink. It might not be professional, but she couldn't get mad. He was devilishly charming and irresistible.

Thinking pleasant thoughts about Rod did not help. Her dreams were anything but restful, centering on a bare-chested Quinn Rafferty.

****

Alex overslept, and then scrambled to dress and open the store. She barely had time for a cup of coffee and some extra-strength aspirin to relieve a pounding headache before her first customer came through the door.

The previous day's rain had moved on, leaving a perfect morning of bright sunshine and reasonably warm temperatures, which in turn, brought out the shoppers. At one point, Alex thought it had been declared National Buy-An-Antique Day. Upon closing, she opted for the bank's night deposit box rather than the safe in her office. It seemed prudent after the events of the previous evening.

She knew Rafferty hadn't entered her office because the door was locked this morning and nothing had been disturbed in or on her desk. The safe was well hidden in the floor in a corner of the room, an antique Louis XIV chair over it. Thieves could have removed every painting or picture on the wall and come up dry. A small box of petty cash containing less than a hundred dollars stayed in a lower desk drawer as a decoy.

Alex couldn't keep Quinn's words out of her mind. That evening she paced about her apartment until stopping in front of a large antique bookcase. Running her finger along the spines of the books, she hesitated, and then pulled out a slim volume printed with very small type in a font used almost a century ago.

Alex opened the book and extracted a sheet of white paper. Unfolding it, she studied the marks printed along the border in a long forgotten language, then looked at the Spanish words in the center. Handwritten and badly faded in places, they predated the book by at least three and a half, perhaps four centuries. Finished, she replaced everything and sat down to think things out logically.

She had come into possession of the map about ten months ago while at an estate sale. She'd spied a large box of old books and an inspection of the contents had surprised her. While she didn't care a fig about the Maya, her grandfather did—it had been his field of expertise. She'd acquired it for a song, given it to him, and then forgotten about it.

After he died, she'd found the map tucked between two pages of a small book about the Maya in the 12th century. It was then she had begun to authenticate it. A few weeks later, she'd copied the map. The original now lay in her office safe.

So, I don't see how Mr. Rafferty can claim my map is his. Where's the proof his grandfather ever owned it?

Before retiring, Alex double-checked the locks on the store, then returned upstairs and slid into bed where she lay wide-awake, listening to the creaks and groans of the old building.

She pounded the pillow into a more comfortable shape and burrowed her head into it, determined not to let bumps in the night rob her of a much-needed sleep.

She awoke on Sunday morning just as tired as when she'd gone to bed. Alex dressed and headed for her grandfather's. Today would be a good day to go through the rest of his things.

Sunday night's sleep turned out to be no better than the last two. She dreamed not of Rod, but of Quinn Rafferty, his light-brown hair sparkling with golden highlights, and dwelling on a kiss she couldn't forget.

Proud Mary blaring from the radio at eight o'clock awakened her. Alex slammed her fist down on the off button, silencing Tina Turner in mid-scream.

She sat up and ran a hand through her tangled hair. She had survived the weekend without having to think too much. Now, she could no longer avoid it. Rod would be back today, and then—and then there was Quinn.

Chapter Two

Alex clamored out of bed, showered and dressed, then hurried downstairs to the store's kitchen wondering what would happen when Rod and Quinn Rafferty met.

She'd told Rod about finding the map, of course, and his enthusiasm had matched hers. He wouldn't let some good-looking quasi-burglar walk out with it no matter how much money hit the table.

Quinn may be bigger and probably ten times more athletic, but Rod will defend me.

She enjoyed the fantasy of the two men grappling over her and the map.

She made a full pot of coffee and in an uncharacteristic burst of domesticity, grabbed a box of muffin mix out of the pantry. Forty-five minutes later, the inviting aromas of freshly brewed coffee along with banana nut muffins filled the air.

Alex opened the shop at ten o'clock disappointed Rod hadn't yet arrived. She rationalized his absence.

He's tired and taking it easy this morning. Mondays are slow and no big deal anyway.

Still absent at eleven-forty, she dialed his cell. When he didn't answer, she left a message. "Rod, it's me. It's been a hell of a weekend, and I need to talk to you about something."

By twelve-thirty, her worry had increased to high anxiety.

Good grief, maybe he's been in an accident. Hospitals. I need to contact hospitals.

She retreated to her office, her hand paused inches from the phone, when something caught her eye. She'd been in the office briefly on Saturday morning and again when closing out the day's receipts. Her tardiness had allowed only a quick inspection of her desk, and in the evening the overhead light had cast a deep shadow under the Louis XIV chair.

Now, her position beside the desk with natural light pouring through the window, allowed her to see the back legs of the antique were out of alignment with the indentations made in the carpet. Someone had moved the chair.

She last opened the safe Thursday night when she'd taken the previous day's proceeds out to combine with Thursday's take. Rod had run to the bank before returning for dinner. He'd also deposited Friday's money before he left for Detroit while she was in Downer's Grove. She used the night deposit on Saturday.

Alex glanced at the chair again. She was careful about setting everything back where it belonged. Why have two sets of indentations? It might call attention to that particular corner of the room.

With a sense of impending doom, Alex moved the chair, pulled up the carpet, and opened the safe. The map was gone.

Quinn Rafferty—that bastard! When had he done it? It had to be Sunday. She'd been gone all day. He'd watched the place, seen her leave, and taken the chance.

And in broad daylight, too. The nerve of that cheeky son of a bitch!

Alex stood and aimed her foot at the chair, then stopped. No, too fragile. She kicked the wall instead. Pain shot through her toes, past her ankle, and into her calf, but she was angry and didn't care.

He'd picked the lock on the back door before. Not seeing the office door in the dark on Friday night made sense, but he'd have noticed when he came back later. Getting into the office? A piece of cake for a thief like him. With all that time to search he'd discovered the floor safe.

Never underestimate a sneaky bastard.

But how did he get the combination? The dial appeared undamaged.

Maybe he had one of those electronic gizmos she'd seen on TV—the kind that beeped whenever the correct number was struck. Of course, he had one. Didn't they all?

Alex closed the safe, replacing the carpet and chair.

Now I have him.

She'd call the police, report the theft, and have his ass arrested! Hell, she'd even confess to lying on Friday night. She gave herself a mental self-congratulatory pat on the back.

Her hand grasped the phone ready to dial when a voice from behind said, "Have you thought about it?"

She let out a startled squeak and jumped, whirling about to face her nemesis, Quinn Rafferty.

I really need to put a bell over the door. "Why is it that every time we meet, you manage to scare the crap out of me?" she asked in a mixture of exasperation and irritation. "What are you doing here?"

"I said I'd give you the weekend to think things over. Have you?"

His presence made no sense. By all rights, he should have been halfway to Central America, the map in his pocket, and hot on the trail of the treasure.

She moved the Louis XIV chair in front of the desk. He didn't appear nervous, nor did he stare guiltily at the corner, further confusing her. But then, he was a thief, wasn't he, and the good ones didn't give anything away.

Quinn sat and said, "Have you thought about my offer?"

She leaned against the edge of the desk, arms folded across her chest. "I can't see where you come off thinking this map is yours. Okay, so it was stolen from your grandfather, but I bought it at an estate sale in Kenosha about a year ago."

He fished a small notepad from his pocket. "You bought it from the estate of the late Joseph Cowen who purchased it from a gambler named Johnny Baker. He won it in a poker game from a less that honest antique dealer—the kind who knowingly sells fake for real."

"The antique dealer bought it cheap from the widow of a secondhand store owner. According to the widow, her husband found it hidden behind a cheap print of another map he bought at a yard sale. Now, here's where it gets interesting."

"About time."

Quinn went on. "The aunt of Grandpa's secretary held the yard sale. She's also been on the map's trail ever since the inadvertent sale, and always one step ahead of me."

"She who? The aunt?" Alex interrupted, confused.

"No, silly, the secretary. Now, can you doubt my claim?"

"How do I know any of this is true?"

"I swear it's the truth."

"Yeah, right. Is this the part where I hand the map over and wave bye-bye? I don't think so. How do you know about this line of ownership?" she snapped. Did she really look that gullible?

"I used to be a private investigator."

"How did your grandfather get the map?"

"I'm not sure. He never said. He was always wheeling and dealing. Perhaps that's how it came to him."

He raked his hand through his hair and stared off into space for a moment, his expression softening.

"About four years ago, he suffered a heart attack and my grandmother insisted his wild adventures end. After three months of him underfoot, Gran suggested a new endeavor. Why not write his memoirs?"

"Does this story have a point?"

"Of course, it does."

"Then could we please get to it?"

"Unfortunately, what Grandpa couldn't do was type, and his organizational skills didn't exist. Enter the secretary. Eight months into the project, he got a hold of this map and dropped everything to pursue researching it—naturally using his secretary to help."

"Naturally," she drawled.

"One evening my grandmother and mother came home and found him dead in his study. It was obvious a fight had occurred. His wall safe stood wide open, and the secretary had disappeared. The map also vanished. He must have caught her in the act."

"What do you know about the secretary?" She didn't want to be interested, but couldn't help herself.

"I knew her as Victoria Sedgwick. She was a tall blonde with blue eyes and a hell of a figure. My grandfather considered her the perfect secretary and trusted her." Bitterness laced his voice.

"It sounds like you rather liked her, yourself."

"I showed up to spend a weekend and found myself coming back a lot more often than usual," he admitted, squirming in his seat.

"Were you in love with her?" For some reason, Alex found herself hoping the answer was no.

"Neither one of us was interested in anything permanent."

"You said you knew her as Victoria Sedgwick. I take it that was an alias."

"When she filled out her application at the employment agency Victoria used the name and Social Security number of eighty-six year old Mary Sedgwick. Mary Sedgwick once employed a secretary named Victoria Grayson. Miss Grayson left, along with one of the old lady's finer diamond bracelets." He gave her a hard stare. "Now do you understand? The map is mine. If you won't give it to me, I'll buy it. I'm prepared to offer two thousand dollars."

"How quickly inflation rises. The other night it was only worth five hundred."

"Come on, two grand is nothing to sneeze at."

"No."

"How about thirty-five hundred? That's a tidy profit, but my funds are not unlimited."

"No. You could offer me a million for it, and the answer would still be the same," she replied.

"Lady, don't piss me off. This is the closest I've been to that map in three years. I'm losing patience. Don't make me get nasty. You won't like me if I get nasty."

She thrust her chin out, pushed away from the desk, and stood with arms akimbo. "I don't like you now, and I'm not scared. If you planned to kill or knock me over the head for it, you'd have done so Friday night."

He leaned his head back and sighed. "Why are you being so stubborn? Can't you see how much this means to me? Besides, you don't look like the type to go off chasing after buried treasure. It's not your style. Okay, five thousand. That's my final offer. Just let me have the map."

Alex walked behind the desk and sat slumped, biting her lip. If he didn't have the map, that left only one other person who could have taken it, because only one other person knew of the map's existence *and* had the combination to the safe—Rod.

Rod! Shit, in the excitement over the missing map, I forgot all about him.

She straightened as a horrible thought raced through her mind. Oh, God! Could this Victoria person have come into the shop on Friday and forced Rod to open the safe? And where was Rod now? Hurt—or dead? She needed to check his apartment. If he wasn't there, she'd call the cops regardless of how much Quinn Rafferty objected.

Why, oh, why, hadn't she looked in the safe earlier? It would have been the logical and sensible thing to do after Friday night. It should also have been the first thing done.

Coulda, woulda, shoulda. Where did my common sense go?

The only explanation was that the craziness of the evening had addled her brains. She'd wasted an entire weekend, and it may have cost Rod his life.

"Look, Mr. Rafferty..." she began.

"Quinn, my friends call me Quinn," he interrupted.

"Mr. Rafferty, I have some disturbing news. I can't give you the map even if I wanted. It was stolen from my safe over the weekend."

Quinn stared at her for a moment, and then jumped up so suddenly the antique chair flew backward, falling over. A panorama of emotions flitted across his face from disbelief to frustration to just plain anger.

"God damn it! Son of a bitch!" he yelled, stomping around the small room like a thwarted child. The swearing continued for a full minute until he got himself under control, righted the chair, and sat down again. "How was it stolen out of your safe?"

"My first thought was that you'd come back yesterday while I was out. I can see now it wasn't you. I mean, you wouldn't be here if it had been would you?"

"Of course not! What's your other theory?"

"I haven't actually seen the map in two or three weeks. I didn't need to have it with me for my research. This is what I think happened."

Alex told him about Rod being alone in the shop on Friday and why she hadn't been in communication with him all weekend. She then explained her theory on the theft.

"Come on!" he ordered. He stood and grabbed her wrist, pulling her out of her chair and around the desk.

"Where are we going?"

"To your boyfriend's, although I'm sure we're three days too late."

"Do you think he's dead?"

"I'm sure Roderick Halston is very much alive."

She barely had time to snag her purse and lock the door. "Do you know Rod?"

"Indirectly."

"How?"

"I'll tell you later. Let's go."

The drive to Rod's apartment took seventeen minutes and during every one of them Alex's mind churned along in high gear.

It didn't take a genius to figure out Quinn thought Rod was involved, but she refused to believe that. He was in deadly danger—she knew it. And she had every intention of rescuing him and recovering the map.

As for Mr. Quinn Rafferty, well, too freaking bad. The map belonged to her and it would stay hers. End of discussion.

They approached Rod's door and Quinn asked, "You have the key?"

"No, can't say that I do."

"What kind of a relationship is this anyway?"

She was about to snap a pithy reply when he

sighed, looked up and down the corridor, and then removed a small black case from his hip pocket. Flipping it open, he selected a slender metal wand and inserted it into the keyhole.

"Is that a lock pick?"

"No. It's a pencil. I'm writing him a note."

"You needn't be so nasty. I've never seen one before and...oh!"

He turned the knob, and the door swung inward.

The drapes stood wide open, flooding the living room with light. Empty glasses and coffee cups along with several days' worth of newspapers cluttered the coffee table. Travel brochures on Central America and magazines lay scattered on the sofa. Thick dust decorated the tabletops.

A quick glance in the kitchen showed dirty dishes piled to the rim of the sink and half a pot of cold coffee with a light scum of mold on the surface. Garbage overflowed a trash receptacle in the corner. Flies buzzed around the smelly mess. A cockroach scurried under the stove.

"Your boyfriend isn't big on housekeeping, is he?"

Alex didn't answer and made her way toward the bedroom where they found even more confusion. The unmade bed with its rumpled sheets, the spread and blanket trailing onto the carpet looked cold. The closet door yawned wide revealing its emptiness, and hangers lay strewn on the floor. Dresser drawers stood half-closed, indicating that whoever lived here had packed in a hurry. Damp towels littering the tile added to the musty smell emanating from the bathroom.

Back out in the living room, Alex tried to get a grip on what she saw, her mind numb.

"She—Victoria—kidnapped him. She forced him to open the safe, and then made him drive here where she coerced him into packing and helping her get away." Even as she spoke, she knew the explanation sounded ridiculous.

"Wake up and come out of the fairy tale, honey. Rod Halston is gone and so is my map—again. Looks pretty straightforward and simple to me," Quinn jeered.

Before she could reply another voice spoke from behind them, "What are you doing here?"

Quinn whirled while Alex jumped in fright.

He smiled at the newcomer and said, "We're friends of Mr. Halston's. We haven't heard from him in a couple of days and thought we'd check to make sure he's okay."

"Yeah? How'd you get in?" the man asked.

"The door was unlocked," Alex said. She really was getting better at this spur of the moment thing. "Are you the superintendent?"

"Yeah. Man, I never figured Mr. Halston to be such a pig." The super eyed the kitchen and living room with a disgusted look. "He was a smart dresser, too. You'd think a clothes horse like him would be a mite neater."

"Yeah, you'd think," Quinn agreed. "Tell me Mr.—"

"Schneider. John Schneider."

They trailed after him as he inspected the bedroom and the bath, shaking his head. "Damn it. The place smells like a men's room."

"Mr. Schneider, do you have any idea where Mr. Halston could be?" Quinn asked.

"Naw. I knew he'd gone somewhere. I saw him humpin' three or four suitcases out to his car. When I asked where he was goin' he kinda laughed and said on vacation."

"When was this?" Alex asked.

"Friday afternoon about two or two-thirty, I guess. He didn't say how long he'd be gone, but from the looks of things here, I'd have to guess, he ain't comin' back."

She'd left for Downer's Grove at noon. Rod had promised to lock up and make the deposit before leaving for Detroit. She made a mental note to check her bank account.

"I think that's probably a good bet," Quinn replied.

"The son of a bitch left owing a month's rent, too."

"That doesn't surprise me, either. Are you ready to go, Miss Montgomery?"

"Was Mr. Halston alone or with a lady?" she inquired.

"He was alone when I saw him."

"Ever see him with a good looking blonde?" Quinn asked.

"Nope, never saw him with anybody in the four months he lived here. Anything else you need? I gotta lock this place up," Schneider said.

"I guess we're finished. Thanks for your help." Quinn steered Alex toward the door.

The drive home proved quiet. This time Alex's thoughts took a much different direction.

Well, dummy, you've done it again.

She'd thought she'd found the perfect man and once again, been wrong. Sexy blond hair, bright blue eyes, and charm oozing from every pore sucked her in like a bug to the zapper.

How many times had this happened? How many times had she let herself hope? How many times had she let her heart become involved and ended up getting bit in the ass?

When will I learn? Why the hell don't my relationships ever work? I'm sick of always being on the wrong end of the wishbone. Just once, I'd like a man to live up to my expectations.

Alex had never been one to show her deepest emotions. On the outside, she knew her expression appeared blank and undisturbed, but on the inside, she seethed. Self-disgust for allowing a man to make an idiot out of her—again—and anger at being used choked her. Well, no more. He would *not* get away with this. She'd find Roderick Halston if it took the rest of her life!

Count on it, baby. That's a promise.

****

Quinn wanted to ram his fist through the windshield in frustration. He had been so close he could almost see the map in his hands. He couldn't decide if he wanted to strangle Alexandria, Halston, Vicky, or all three of them. For the first time in nearly three years, he questioned his determination to finish this quest.

What's the use? Every time I think I have it, the damned thing slips away. Why should this setback surprise me?

At least his suspicions that Alexandria worked with Halston had vanished. She hadn't said a word since leaving and while her expression didn't give away much, her clenched jaw did. The lady appeared calm, but he bet on the inside a volcano was ready to blow.

"Come on," he said when she parked. "We need to talk."

Quinn followed her up the outside stairs. He needed to plan his next move. If she'd been authenticating the map, then maybe she could tell him something about it to make his journey easier. He sucked in a deep breath. His resolve returned. He *would* find that treasure.

"Why did you give that weasel the combination to your safe? Or are you one of those silly people who can never remember the numbers so they keep them written on a piece of paper marked safe combination?" he exclaimed in the living room.

The look she shot him clearly showed she had

violence on her mind. "I have no such problem, and Rod had the combination because he was in charge of the shop when I went on buying trips. The day's receipts could not be left in a desk drawer."

"There's such a thing as night deposits."

"Yeah, well, live and learn. I trusted him."

"Your mistake. Mine, too, I guess." He rubbed a hand over his chin. "A three-day head start? Not insurmountable. They can't just show up in Central America. They'll have to make plane and hotel reservations, and once they arrive, obtain equipment," he muttered to himself.

"They?"

He sat on one end of the sofa. She occupied the other. "Victoria had a whole string of aliases, but when I researched her, one social security number and one name kept popping up from time to time, especially in her younger years—Victoria Denton."

"When Victoria was four her mother married a devil-may-care con man named Handsome Harry Halston. He charmed little old ladies out of their life savings and anything else he could get his hands on."

"Halston?"

"Halston," he affirmed. "Her mother died when Victoria was ten, and Harry quickly put his step-daughter and his five year old son, Roderick, to work. Rod was a chip off the old block. Victoria was no slouch either."

"Are you telling me Rod was in on this from the beginning?"

"Of course, he was."

"Go on."

"Now, we have the poor, grieving widower with his beautiful, innocent children, talking soft-hearted women into letting him do odd jobs, and then ripping them off. Can you picture it?"

"Yeah, I can picture it."

"Victoria took enough business courses to support them during the dry spells. Rod learned a little about the good life and faked the rest. The three of them conned their way all across the country. Rod did it with great panache and reasonable success."

"Just because he's good-looking and charming, doesn't mean he's a crook."

The set of her lips and the angle of her jaw testified the words didn't match her feelings. This must be damned hard for her to swallow.

"Victoria was a bit more calculating, preferring a plan to set up her marks before pouncing. The people told me she'd flirt with the man. That would get her in the door, but her innocent look and sweet manner brought her over the threshold. People didn't realize it was an act."

"Including your grandfather?"

"She was hired for a legitimate job, but he bought the act, too. After Harry Halston died, Victoria and Rod occasionally teamed up. One time, they worked a double con. Rod charmed and wooed the wife, while Victoria bamboozled the husband. But, as a rule, they did their own things."

"That's the set up. I've been chasing Victoria for close to three years," he finished. "The minute I saw Rod Halston with you, I knew I had 'em."

"How did you find me?"

"I told the auctioneers who handled Cowan's estate that some of the things they'd sold might have been stolen. They let me go through the one hundred and fifty-seven pages of inventory until I found five possibilities. It took a while to track down and eliminate the other four."

"I guess it's your bad luck I was number five."

Alexandria got up and walked stiffly to the window, her hands in the pockets of her slacks balled into fists. Her body language told him she was madder than hell.

"How did you ever hook up with Rod Halston?"

"He wandered into the shop one day and kept coming back. At first, I was amused by his shy manner. He was a stranger, but I felt at ease with him."

"That doesn't surprise me. It's his job. He's good at it. He's charmed and conned tougher women than you."

"I fell under his spell. He was knowledgeable about antiques and said he'd traveled to places I hadn't. His words took me on a virtual tour of Europe. I didn't want to let this guy get away, so I offered him a job."

"Which I'm sure he eagerly accepted."

"No, he was very hesitant. I had to talk him into it."

"This guy is good," Quinn said in a disgusted tone.

"On Friday nights we'd go to dinner, and then a movie or an intimate little bar. Sometimes, we'd go dancing."

"So, how come you stayed home last Friday?"

She told him of Rod's sudden announcement on Thursday night of a family reunion in Detroit.

"Yeah, a family reunion with Victoria."

"Hey, smart ass, he was there for me when my grandfather died three months ago. He encouraged me to check out the map," she snapped.

"Of course he did! You found what he and his sister were looking for! I can't believe you gave him free rein."

"Rod had a way with the customers. I lack the gift of gab and can't spout witty repartee. Rod had no trouble in that department." She paused a moment, and then whirled to stare at him, her green eyes bright with anger. "I want my map back!"

"I want my map back, too."

"Did you ever see the map?" she asked.

"Once. As close as I can tell it was centered in present day Guatemala. Grandpa's notes confirmed it."

"That's about the size of it."

"I hoped you could shed some light on the details."

"I suggest we cooperate on this recovery."

"Miss Montgomery...Alexandria...that's a mouthful. Don't you have a nickname?"

She waved a hand. "Alex will do."

"Okay. Alex. I plan on catching the first plane to Guatemala. If I'm lucky, I'll get there first and be waiting for them. What do you remember about the map?"

She ignored his question. "Where will you go?"

"Guatemala City. It has a greater selection of places to buy equipment. Plus, I have a few cards up my sleeve."

"Quinn, suppose I tell you there's a way to know where Rod and Victoria are heading, and that you could possibly beat her to the pot of gold?"

"What are you talking about?"

"Well, I never bothered to tell Rod that for convenience and safety's sakes, I made a copy of the map."

Chapter Three

Quinn stared at Alex in stunned disbelief. For a moment he experienced that lightheaded weightlessness of a rapidly descending elevator, and the floor seemed to drop from under his feet.

A copy? There's a copy?

His mind fast forwarded, the images hard to grasp—his mother, his grandmother, and security. He could still attain everything and come out on top.

The elevator finally stopped, and Quinn recovered his equilibrium. Hope, tinged with a surge of excitement, pulsed through his nerves. He always felt this way before a big adventure.

"You have a copy?" His voice croaked.

She nodded. "Yes. I found the map stuck in a book on the Maya. I took it to a friend of my grandfather to date the paper. Then I took it to another of his colleagues to see if the wording corresponded to the correct era. After that, carting it around was a pain, not to mention dangerous. All of the opening and refolding could cause it to tear, so I made a copy and put the original in the safe."

"And, of course, you told your boyfriend where you stashed it."

"That's irrelevant. He could have seen it any time in the last two and a half weeks when he put away the day's receipts."

"Okay—no blame placed on you. Show me this copy."

Alex paused for a second before walking into the kitchen. She riffled through a drawer until finding what she wanted, and handed it to him.

"I'll take a number six, extra spicy, with an order of crab rangoons."

Quinn stared at her, and then down at the menu in his hand.

"It's Lee Chen's. He's located three blocks down Main Street on the left. If you call now and leave right away, it should be ready when you get there."

"I want to see that map." He had the feeling if he left, she would pack up and flee.

"You will. I know it's early for dinner, but I skipped lunch. I'm hungry." She thrust the phone at him. "Dial!"

He ordered, hung up, and paused at the door. "You'd better be here when I get back," he said.

She rolled her eyes. "God, you're a suspicious so-and-so. Where would I go in the twenty minutes it'll take you to walk there and back? We'll talk over dinner."

****

Alex waited until he left, then changed into a pair of comfortable jeans and retrieved the copy from its hiding place in the bookcase. It was her turn to be suspicious. Why let him know she kept it in the same book where she'd found the original? She placed it on the dining room table.

Quinn obviously wanted the treasure and was determined to get it. She, on the other hand, had a whole different agenda. She had already compiled a list of museums that could be interested in obtaining the map. It was the right thing to do. Separately, neither one of them would achieve their goals, but working as a team, they just might succeed.

By the time he returned, Alex had set the table and decided drop the bombshell that she'd be accompanying him to Guatemala.

Quinn dumped the sack of food in her arms along with a cold six-pack and pounced on the copy as soon as he saw it.

"Yes, this is what I remember seeing. I recognize these mountains and this long finger bay as being near present day Belize. That puts the treasure smack in what is now Guatemala. *The Legend of the Mayan Kings' Treasure*," he read, translating the spidery Spanish writing.

"How much do you know about the Maya?" she asked as she set his plate in front of him along with an ice-cold beer

"Not a whole lot. I know their civilization was in Central America and that the Spanish wiped them out just like they did the Aztecs."

"That's close. The Maya were incredible. They built fabulous cities that are still being rediscovered today. They believed in an afterlife and buried their deceased kings in pyramids, much like the Egyptians."

He dug into his food with gusto and said between bites, "I'm looking for a pyramid?"

"Not necessarily," she countered with a shake of her head. "If available, they buried their dead in caves."

"Do you know how many caves there are in Guatemala?"

"No, but I'm sure you're going to tell me."

"Lots. Okay. Go on."

"Most people believe the Spaniards, once they finished off the Aztecs, turned their attention to the Maya, but they were already self-destructing. By 1525, the Mayan civilization was gone."

While she'd talked, Quinn continued to eat. He swallowed, took a swig of beer and asked, "What makes you such a Mayan expert?"

"I'm not, but my grandfather was. He published hundreds of articles and dozens of books on the subject. He was a professor of Ancient Civilizations at Griffith College here in Waukegan for twenty-five years and Dean of the History Department for another twenty before retiring."

"Well, thanks for the history lesson, but I can't see how it's relevant to the map," he replied as he scraped the plate and dug in for seconds. "This stuff is damned good."

"Yeah, I know. I order at least twice a week." She eyed him for a moment as he resumed eating, and then said, "You don't care about the Maya, do you?"

"Only their treasure, honey." He grinned and pointed to her plate. "Eat up. Your food's getting cold."

Alex had almost forgotten. It was now her turn to shovel in General Tso's Chicken. God, she loved this stuff. She dug in, savoring the spicy flavor on her tongue.

"What do you know about modern day Central America and Guatemala?" Quinn asked.

"It's poor and governments seem to change every week. I know next to nothing about Guatemala specifically."

"You were the history teacher. It's time for me to do current events." He smiled while she continued with her meal. "Most of Central America is poor and mountainous. The political atmosphere isn't as volatile as it was twenty or thirty years ago, but it's still not perfect."

"Show me one in that part of the world that is."

"As for Guatemala, the past fifty years has been up and down. Democracy is paper-thin. Violence reached a peak in the early eighties."

She bit into a crab rangoon and sighed. The creamy texture melted in her mouth. He stopped his narrative, staring. "I'm listening. Go on," she said with her mouth full.

He raised his eyebrows, but continued. "Guatemala is also a major transit country for cocaine, heroin—all kinds of drugs. Money laundering is a serious problem and corruption is rife."

"How do you know so much about Guatemala?" she asked between bites.

"About five or six years ago, a buddy and I were guides for an eco-tour company in Belize. One week we decided to check out a small biosphere near the Guatemalan border."

"Biosphere? What's that?"

"It's a huge protected park like an ecological reserve. At any rate, we accidentally crossed the frontier and managed to get picked up by a local militia. They held us for about six hours before letting us go, minus our cameras and cash, of course."

Alex finished her meal and removed the plates, saying, "It sounds like a rugged, scary place."

And I'm about to go there with him?

"It can be, but at the same time, the power of tourist money is not lost on the officials. They try not to hassle visitors too much if they can help it."

"What happens now?" she asked, returning to the dining room.

"I plan to catch the next flight to Guatemala City and beat Victoria and Rod to the treasure."

"All right, I'll call Julie and see if she can look after the store for a while. She used to do it before I hired Rod. When do we leave?"

"*We* don't leave at all. Just give me the map, and I'll take care of everything."

"Mr. Rafferty, do I look simple-minded? This copy does not leave my possession. If I give it to you, I'd say my chances of ever seeing you, the treasure, or the map again are nil. I'm going with you."

"Like hell you are!"

"Get this straight. Oh, yes, I am!"

"Look lady, you are totally unprepared for an adventure like this."

"Let me be the judge of that."

"Have you ever lived outside of a city?"

"No."

"Have you ever been to Central America or Guatemala?"

"No."

"Do you speak Spanish?"

"No."

"Have you ever hiked up a mountain or through a jungle?"

"Dammit! You know I haven't!" she yelled in furious frustration. "But I'm going anyway."

"Wanna bet? You are a city girl with zero experience in either a jungle or on a mountain. Your idea of life in the rough is no Lee Chen's down the street for dinner. You don't speak the language. You'd be unable to communicate with anyone outside of a large city." His eyes had turned the color of steel, and his eyebrows met in a scowl. "But most of all, you would slow me down. I need speed if I'm going to get to that treasure first."

"Mister, the only way you're going to leave me behind is to hogtie and throw me into a closet."

Quinn rose and leaned to within a few inches of her nose, his face taking on a reddish hue. "Don't tempt me. I'll do it if I have to."

Alex glared at him, then snatched the map and whirled to rummage in a sideboard drawer. When she turned back to face him, she held a small butane cigarette lighter in her hand. A quick movement of her thumb brought forth a flickering flame. She held the map in her other hand, a few inches away.

"I will burn this to ashes unless I go."

He hesitated. "No, you won't."

She moved the map closer to the flame until the barest wisp of smoke spiraled up from the edge.

"You win!" He glared at her.

She extinguished the lighter.

He won't react well to being pushed into a corner. I'll have to be careful with my words and actions from here on out.

He leaned forward, thrusting his face to within inches of hers again. "Keep this in mind. We will be traveling light. Bring only the necessities and that does not include hair dryers. I don't want to hear any bitching about sore feet, how hot it is, how tired you are, or the conditions we'll be living in. And so help me God, if you can't keep up, I'll leave you behind. Do you understand?"

She refused to give in to his intimidation. "I understand. Now, do we have a deal?"

He straightened, heaved a sigh, and gritted his teeth, but said, "Yes, we have a deal. Let's have another look at that map."

Alex laid it on the table all the while saying a silent prayer of thanks he hadn't called her bluff. She could no more have burned that copy than she could sprout wings and fly.

The last few minutes had left her not only shaking and exhausted, but strangely stimulated, too. It made no sense. Her heart pounded and her fingertips tingled. To her horror, she realized she wasn't hyperventilating. She was kind of, well, turned on.

Oh, no. No way is that happening. Take a deep cleansing breath. Take two or three.

"Some of this writing is badly faded. I can barely read it, and don't remember the map being this big."

She snapped her attention back to the table and Quinn. Yes. The map. That's what counted. *Keep your mind on the map.*

"It isn't. The original is about fifteen inches square. I enlarged it when I made the copy. I had hopes the Spanish words come out clearer. You see? They correspond to the creases where it was folded."

"I don't recognize any of these cities on here.

40

Maybe the names have been modernized over the years. I don't suppose you have a recent map of Guatemala handy, do you?"

"No, sorry."

He stared at the sheet of paper. "There aren't many landmarks for reference points, either. I can't even pronounce these names."

"That's because they're Mayan names. Have you ever heard the story about the legend of the treasure you're seeking?"

"Can't say that I have."

Sitting down, Alex rested her elbows on the table, intertwined her fingers, and set her chin on them. "The story goes that sometime in the middle of the twelfth century five Mayan kings decided to stop fighting each other and begin cooperating to repel other invading Mayan warriors."

"Five Mayan kings?"

"The Mayan Empire was never unified, but made up of city-states, each with their own royal family—kind of like ancient Greece," she explained.

"Okay, I get it. Go on." He kept his eyes glued on the map.

"They pooled all resources, including their wealth. It was resolved to hide it in a remote location guarded by a band of five warriors, one from each city."

"Doesn't sound like trust was high on their list of priorities. So, the treasure is in a remote place. That figures."

"One by one, the cities were conquered until there were only two remaining. According to the legend, one king betrayed the other and claimed the riches for himself."

"I guess treachery and betrayal *were* high on the list." His finger followed the route of a river.

"The king and most of his army were killed. Rumors cropped up around the time of the

Conquistadors about the existence of a map. No one knew for sure."

"Until now," Quinn murmured.

"Until now," she confirmed.

"And the map has been authenticated? There's no doubt?"

"The map is very real."

"Do you have any idea where the cities are located today?"

"No. The villages may have been so small that they were obliterated by war or time. Some may not have been rediscovered yet. I don't know."

"The river flowing into this lake may be the system that eventually empties into the Bay of Amatique near the southern border of Belize." Quinn traced the twisting line with his finger. "The problem with old maps is that the distances are often skewed, especially in jungle or mountainous terrains. Map making was not an exact science. Plus, rivers change course, and landmarks disappear during earthquakes. I just hope it's not in the middle of a biosphere. We could play hell getting the treasure out."

"Oh, swell. We may pillage an ecological preserve. Isn't there some kind of law against looting these places? Does Guatemala have a Department of Antiquities or something?" Visions of Central American prisons flashed through her mind.

"Damned if I know, and damned if I care."

"Oh, that makes me feel so much better." Alex had the feeling he simply stated the truth.

"Wanna change your mind about going along?"

"In your dreams."

"You know, you don't strike me as the treasure hunting sort."

"I'm not. All I want is my map back and to make sure Rod is all right."

She was lying like a rug. She didn't give a

tinker's damn about Rod Halston. Oh, she'd like to confront him and put her fist squarely in his nose, but the map was her priority. She needed to keep Quinn off balance and this seemed like the most logical way. It would also serve to remind her she had a mission. Trekking through the jungle with a man as handsome and sexy as Quinn would not be easy.

Throughout the entire evening she'd been aware of the tightening tension. Her reactions after the argument proved the situation volatile.

Quinn stared at her, disbelief written all over his face, before saying, "Are you nuts? Your boyfriend is in this up to his ears. They're brother and sister, remember?"

"Well, it wouldn't be the first time relatives had a disagreement about something."

"For crying out loud, the super said he was alone and left in high spirits."

"He could have been wrong or—or lying. That's it! He was bribed to lie if someone came asking questions."

"I don't believe this. I thought you were a reasonably intelligent woman. I was wrong."

Alex refolded the map. "I don't see any point in continuing this discussion."

"I agree. I'm going home to make plane reservations. I'll pick you up at noon and we'll go shopping for the proper clothing. Decide what's necessary, and then pack one bag and *one bag only*. I'm assuming you have a passport." His voice clearly indicated he hoped her answer would be no.

"I vacationed two years ago in Barbados and the year before that in St. Martin. Will I need shots?"

"It's a little late to be worrying about typhoid fever and the like. Once we get there, we'll drink bottled water. Anything else?"

"I guess not. I'll see you tomorrow at noon."

She walked him to the door. Alex laid her hand on his arm and said, "I'll keep pace with you. I promise."

She should have seen it coming. After all, she'd felt the tension, so why wouldn't he? He pulled her into his arms, covering her mouth with his.

Rooted to the spot, she kissed him back as a delicious gush of warmth surged through her veins and a comforting lassitude crept over her like a drug. His arms tightened to draw her closer, her body tingling where it touched his, as though the nerve endings had sensitized to the highest level.

At some point her hands encircled his neck and tangled in the hair at his nape. The texture was soft and luxurious, like stroking satin. A low moan formed in the back of her throat before finally spilling out.

She'd never felt so vibrant, so viable and animated. She didn't want it to end, and when Quinn backed away she realized a keen sense of disappointment and loss.

Vaguely aware of his hands on her shoulders, she heard him say as though from a long distance, "I'd better get out of here. I'll see you tomorrow."

Seconds later, he was out of the door leaving her alone and feeling bereft.

Alex gathered her wits, and then mentally kicked herself.

Of all the stupid things to do. What the hell is the matter with me? What's the matter with him*? So what if his kisses make me go weak in the knees and all quivering inside? I absolutely, positively, will not get involved with Quinn Rafferty.*

There were certain qualities and criteria a man had to have before she'd let him into her life. And when she let a man get that close, the end result could only mean marriage. Few men filled the requirements, and none of her relationships lasted any longer than six months.

Maybe I'm just a lousy judge of the male species.

Each time she had believed these men possessed all the qualities she'd sought, and each time disappointment had reduced her to tears.

Well, it wouldn't happen again, especially with Quinn Rafferty. She knew up front that *he* didn't possess any of those qualities.

Alex tried to shake off her mood and picked up the phone. Time to get down to business. She'd call Julie and ask her to take over the shop for a few weeks.

****

Quinn walked to his motel in a state of severe confusion. This was the second time in three days he'd given in to impulse and kissed her. Of course, his entire life revolved around impulses, but at least his previous actions had been tempered by some sense of responsibility.

Enough to avoid complications, at any rate. In that respect, Alex Montgomery constitutes a frightening league of her own.

He had made the mistake of looking into those enormous green eyes. Before he could stop, he'd found her in his arms, their lips locked, and ready to throw away the key.

Her softness pressing against his body had almost sent him over the edge. God knew he'd been aware of every curve. Her breasts crushed to his chest, and her hips rocking on his had the usual affect.

She tasted ten times better than the headiest wine or liquor he'd ever drunk and he wanted more, much more. If she hadn't moaned when she had, he might have just had his wish granted.

Her attributes were potent, but this was one woman he had to avoid. Not only were they, in a sense, partners, but Alex was still in love with that asshole Rod as evidenced by the ridiculous explanation of why Halston had left town. Somehow, that made him angrier than anything else about this whole situation.

Damn that bitch Victoria! This time she isn't going to win. I have a map now, and I will *get there first.*

This time he would be the winner, provided he could keep his hands off of Alex.

Stay focused. Don't let your libido get in the way.

He was close to the brass ring. His mother and grandmother counted on him. He had to keep these things in mind, not Alexandria Montgomery and her to-die-for body.

Chapter Four

Alex tightened her seatbelt with shaking fingers as the plane pulled away from the gate. She shot a quick glance at the man sitting next to her. By contrast, Quinn appeared relaxed and composed, reading a travel book on Guatemala. She flexed her hands around the armrests of her seat and clenched her jaw. She hated flying and only the direst of circumstances could get her into an airplane.

"Will you relax? Everything is going to be fine. Flying is safer than driving," Quinn said.

"Yeah, yeah, so I've heard. Forgive me if I don't see it your way."

She held her breath and closed her eyes. The jet picked up speed and lumbered down the runway. Visions of smoking wreckage at the end of the concrete strip flashed through her mind until the bumping smoothed out and the tilt of the plane told her they were airborne.

They gained altitude and to take her mind off her fear she turned to Quinn. "Why are we on our way to Cancun? Why not just fly directly to Guatemala City? At least I wouldn't have to go through this again."

"There are only two direct flights a week from Chicago to Guatemala. I don't want to lose time by waiting another two days." He closed the book and turned to look at her. "Booking connecting flights through Mexico and Belize saved several hundred dollars. You said you wouldn't complain."

"I'm not. I'm curious. If speed is our priority, I'd think you'd want to get there the fastest way possible."

"We are." He stared for a moment before asking, "What's with you and flying, anyhow? I thought you went to the islands."

"I did. I took a cruise." She tried not to sound defensive.

Quinn shook his head and resumed reading while Alex attempted to relax. Now aloft, she was more at ease. The takeoffs and landings got to her as much as the fear of heights. Leaning her head back, she closed her eyes willing herself to unwind, and concentrated on Rod Halston instead. She couldn't wait to catch up with the sleazy little bastard.

She'd checked her bank deposits. A big goose egg had come up for Friday, which meant he must have closed the shop grabbing whatever money he could out of the till as soon as she'd left. The superintendent said he'd seen Rod around two or two-thirty. She started a new list of how to get even with the prick.

Alex glanced out of the window at the green and brown patchwork of farmland thirty thousand feet below, and then just as quickly averted her eyes. In spite of her fear, she requested a window seat. She hated looking out, but at the same time couldn't stand not being able to see. She knew it made no sense, and the illogical reasoning irritated her.

Quinn kept his word about proper clothing. Her wardrobe now consisted of cargo pants and long sleeved shirts in drab browns and olive green. When she'd complained about the lack of color, the smart ass had tossed more clothing at her in camouflage, saying it was better to blend in than stand out in the jungle.

Big deal. It's not like I'll be carrying an M-16.

Adding insult to injury, he left her to foot the bill stating his MasterCard still smoked from the airline tickets and would do so again when it came to the gear they needed.

Alex paid grudgingly. *Her* Visa now looked charred, too.

She turned from the window and gazed down at her feet in disgust. She had no choice but to wear the ugly boots Quinn insisted she buy. The damned things wouldn't fit into her suitcase, which meant she also had to wear a pair of the multi-pocketed pants. She resembled Captain Kangaroo in clown shoes. It would be just her luck to meet someone she knew. She wore a bright green polo shirt in fashion defiance.

Alex looked at Quinn, and realized she was taking off for the jungles of Central America with a man she hadn't known four or five days ago. Although it smacked of closing the barn door after the horse had been stolen, common sense told her she needed to know more about him. Besides, she was curious as to what made him tick.

"What's your story, Quinn? You said your grandfather was an adventurer. What about your father? Is he an adventurer, too? Where did you grow up?"

Quinn closed his book and replied, "My father was the exact opposite of my maternal grandfather. He didn't approve of, or understand, the lifestyle. He thought it irresponsible. When I showed every sign of having inherited Grandpa's genes, Dad was not happy. The friction between us grew until I turned eighteen." He shifted to face her again. "Rather than go to a boring college and study boring subjects, I enlisted in the Army. The thought of all that discipline pleased my father, and the thought of seeing far away places pleased me."

"Did you get discipline or did you count the hours until you were discharged?" She tried, but failed to see him in uniform taking orders from anyone.

"Both. When my hitch was up, I struck out on my own to taste life. I climbed mountains, backpacked in the Rockies, and hiked the entire length of the Appalachian Trail. I skydived, hang-glided, bungee jumped, and parachuted off a thirteen hundred foot cliff in South America."

"Why?"

"Why not?"

That sounded like a typical Quinn answer. "I'm envious. At least you got to see far away places."

"That's true. I traveled to Europe, Canada, Mexico and the South Pacific. Every time I came home Grandpa would relive his past through me. My father never forgave me for not having a nine-to-five job."

"What about your mother? How did she feel?"

"Mom understands my needs. She wants something more settled for me, but knows I have to do what I have to do. Gran appreciated what her husband did and never begrudged him his long absences."

"They both sound like very special women." She thought of her own sheltered and isolated childhood.

"They are. My mother often took my side against Dad."

"Are your parents still alive?"

"My mother is, but Dad died in an automobile accident almost ten years ago."

"I'm sorry. Where were you raised?"

"Paradise—Southern California. In summer, I rode horses in the valleys, surfed, and roller bladed. In winter, I skied and snowboarded in the mountains. I loved every minute of it."

"Didn't you ever have a real job?"

He grinned. "Eventually, I had to do something to pay the rent. Did I tell you I was once a private investigator?"

"Yes. I suppose that job fit right in with your

exuberant lifestyle." Her mind flashed to detective shows on TV. It sounded exciting.

"P. I. work can be very inactive and downright boring. I got my license and stuck with it for two years before taking off on my next adventure." He chuckled and rubbed a hand over his chin. "My partner said I was the worst private investigator he'd ever seen. No patience."

"What else did you do—job wise, I mean?" Was there nothing he hadn't tried?

"I taught surfing. I was a lifeguard, and led mountain climbing expeditions. I've also conducted white water rafting tours. In later years, I got my pilot's license and shuttled cargo—legal cargo— between Mexico and the Southwest. I even dusted crops for a while. You already know about the eco-tours in Belize."

"A Jack-of-all-trades, but master of none, is that it?"

He shrugged. "I never found anything that kept me interested for very long."

"You've led an exciting life." Until now, excitement hadn't been a part of her lifestyle vocabulary. "How old are you?"

"Thirty-two."

"Well, you've certainly got an interesting resume."

"Those were the fun jobs. I had plenty of boring ones as well. Hell, I even sold used cars once." He laughed.

Alex laughed along with him. "I'm grateful I never walked into that dealership."

"What about you? Have you always lived in Waukegan?"

"For the most part. I was born in Denver. My father was doing field work that summer and Mom always accompanied him whenever she could."

"What did he do?"

"He was a paleontologist."

"You mean like in dinosaurs and such?"

"Yes. That's how he met my mother. He taught a seminar at Griffith College and attended a party my grandparents hosted. He and Mom got married two weeks later. I came along three years after that."

"Dinosaurs—every kid's dream. Did you go searching for dinosaurs when you were little?" He smiled.

"If I did, I don't remember it. When I was five my folks decided they needed a break and took a second honeymoon in Florida. My mother got caught in a strong rip current and panicked. When Dad went in to save her, he was swept away, too. They both drowned."

Quinn picked up her hand and kissed it. "I'm so sorry, Alex. You must have been devastated."

Alex shrugged. She didn't recall how she'd felt. At five everything seemed blurry.

"I really don't remember them. My grandmother tried, but it was a long time since she'd been around young children. She treated me like a miniature adult. She died when I was fourteen. We'd just gotten to the point where we could have intelligent conversations."

"What about your grandfather? You haven't mentioned him yet except in reference to the map."

"My grandfather was a scholar. His position gave him the freedom to write. And when he wrote, he was totally self-absorbed, sometimes not coming out of his study for days on end. I knew from an early age that if the study door was closed, I didn't disturb him."

She paused for a moment, her eyes unseeingly focused on the back of the seat in front of her. He'd been a rather cold and forbidding man, but she loved him.

"He had no idea what to do with a five-year-old

girl. Because he had no faith whatsoever in the public school system, he hired a combination nanny and tutor. After my grandmother died, he hired a housekeeper to make sure we were fed and lived in a clean house."

"Forgive me, but that seems rather selfish. Weren't you lonely?"

"Are you kidding? I had the run of the house and the freedom to read anything in it. I was on a pirate ship with Long John Silver and in that cave with Becky and Tom Sawyer. I rafted the Mississippi with Jim and Huck Finn. When I was older, I went to war with Julius Caesar and Mark Antony and mourned at the tragedy of Romeo and Juliet. I may have been solitary, but I was never alone."

She tried to keep a light tone. In truth, there had been times when she's been desperately lonely.

"But what about friends? I mean, flesh and blood friends."

"Once I started college, I had friends, of course. That's how I met Julie. I mentioned Julie, didn't I? She's looking after the store while we're gone."

"Why an antique store? With your background I see history or literature. What was your major?"

"Business Administration with a minor in Marketing," she replied, laughing at the surprise on his face. "Our house was always jammed with antiques. My grandmother loved them. When I opened my own place, I took a few items to get started. It would all be mine one day anyway. I pulled furniture out of the rooms and the attic, and emptied dozens of boxes in the basement. That was five years ago."

"Didn't your grandfather care that you raided his home?"

She shrugged. "I don't think he even noticed."

"How come you don't live in your grandfather's house?"

"I wanted to be on my own. To save money, I converted the space over the shop and lived on the premises. That way I wouldn't need an alarm system right away. I *thought* I had invested in decent locks," she said.

"If I'd been a real thief, you could have been hurt or even dead."

"You were a real thief."

"Let's not start that again."

"Well, you can be sure that when this is over an alarm system will be a top priority."

"I should hope so. It's silly not to have one."

His critical tone stoked her irritation. "Silly? What's this quest we're on? What's this childish need you have for constant adventure? Who are you? Peter Pan? Aren't you ever going to grow up?"

Quinn clenched his jaw for a moment before answering. "When my father died, he left Mom well off financially. A large chunk of their money was socked away with an investment firm. Mom never kept a close watch on the investments. As long as she received checks every few months, she was happy. Then, the company went belly up. The investors lost over three hundred million dollars."

"I've heard of that happening, especially with people who didn't diversify. Was the guy a crook?"

"No. He just fell on hard times and couldn't cover his loses. Mom was almost broke. I helped out, but she'd only accept my checks when she was desperate. It frustrates me that she won't let me help more."

"It must be hard to have her son now taking care of her, a role reversal kind of thing. I take it you're an only child, too."

"Yes. That's why the map is so important to me. Grandpa and I saw it as a way to provide. Then, he was killed. I have to find the treasure so my mother and grandmother can live comfortably for the rest of their lives. This adventure is for them."

The flight attendant stopped by at that moment to take a drink order, and when she left Quinn reopened his travel book.

Alex leaned back, staring out the window, for once unconcerned about the height, and feeling guilty as hell. Oh, God! Just when she had him pegged as a scoundrel he had to go and get noble on her.

She turned and almost said something, then decided to remain silent. No, if she told him the truth, he'd be furious and probably refuse to help her. They'd catch the first plane back from Cancun and her personal quest would be over. She didn't trust him enough to tell him why the map was so important. He'd insist on selling rather than doing things her way.

Later, when they were in Guatemala and the time was right, she'd tell him. She just hoped he could forgive her because suddenly his forgiveness and approval meant a lot to her—more than even she had realized. She was damned if she knew why.

Chapter Five

Never in her entire life had Alex been so miserable. Hot, short-tempered, and dog-tired didn't begin to describe it. They cleared Guatemalan customs and now made their way through the sweltering, crowded main terminal. The babble of voices, crying children, and shouting uniformed authorities breaking up a fistfight, deafened her. The blare of music from the loudspeakers punctuated by announcements of arrivals and departures served the dual purpose of giving her a headache and trying her patience. She even thought she heard the cackle of chickens somewhere in the background, but refused to believe it.

She struggled through the mob to keep pace with Quinn who barreled onward without so much as a glance over his shoulder to see if she needed help.

"Damn it, Quinn, slow down."

He ignored her and kept on going. Any softening she felt toward him on the plane quickly vanished.

The layover in Cancun had been less than an hour and at the moment, she wished she'd stayed there. Mariachis and a few margaritas sounded pretty damned good.

In Belize, Quinn's former partner left a message to say their gear had been ordered and was awaiting their arrival in Guatemala City. He also hired two top-notch guides.

They checked in with yet another airline, and then been crammed into a tiny commuter plane for the last leg of the trip. By this time, even the takeoffs and landings ceased to upset her. She was too damned exhausted to care.

Alex found a bit of relief from the depressing airport when she stumbled through the doors to join Quinn on the sidewalk as he flagged down a taxi. Darkness had fallen and the air was cooler than in Cancun or Belize.

"What's your damned hurry? Do you think Rod and Victoria are on the sidewalk?" she said, panting and wiping sweat from her forehead.

"I said I'd leave you behind if you couldn't keep up."

"In the jungle, stupid, not the airport."

Quinn took care of the luggage while she fell into the cab. A moment later, she wished she hadn't. The vehicle stank with smells she feared identifying. Through a hole in the floorboards, she stared at the pavement. The windshield, cracked in several places, resembled a road map. The effect made her dizzy. The idling motor shook the entire car, its rusting parts rattling like dice in a cup. The ancient taxi was ready to fall apart.

"You don't seriously expect me to ride in this, do you? It's disgusting and unsafe."

"Quit complaining and move over." He shoved her to the other side of the cab.

The driver shot away from the curb like a rocket and proceeded to blast his way around other autos. He must have had fantasies of being a racecar driver at Indianapolis. Too scared to scream, she sat and prayed. By the time they arrived at the hotel, Alex was ready to fall apart.

Finally stopped, she staggered out onto terra firma, vowing to never set foot in a Guatemalan taxi again. Now she knew what had happened to all those old World War II kamikaze pilots when they died. They'd been reincarnated as cabbies in this Central American country.

Quinn checked them in to the hotel. The roar of traffic blasted through an open window in the small lobby. No air conditioning? She'd kill him.

She dragged her suitcase up the dimly lit stairwell. He opened the door to her room and said, "Here you are. Give me fifteen minutes to make a couple of phone calls. Then we'll get some chow. I'm hungry."

He closed the door and she listened to him walk a few paces down the hall. Seconds later, another door opened and closed.

Her room resembled a broom closet. A double bed dominated the space. The overhead light fixture consisted of a bare bulb attached to a fan. She pulled the chains, gratified to see both worked, even though the light couldn't have been any stronger than forty watts. Two doors next to a beat up dresser led to a tiny closet and a miniscule bathroom, respectively.

She flipped on the light in the bath. The shower looked barely big enough to accommodate her. A basin hung from the wall, and the ancient toilet sported a plastic seat. The mirror over the basin bore a permanent fog around the perimeter allowing maybe a twelve-inch circle for clear viewing.

Out of the corner of her eye, she caught a glimpse of something scurrying across the floor of the shower, and then disappearing down the drain.

Terrific. Whatever it is, it's big.

She dashed back into the bedroom, searching for something to put over the small hole, but found only one item. She picked it up and approached the shower with caution. There, she gently placed a Bible over the opening.

"I hope lightning doesn't strike," she muttered.

Alex heaved her suitcase on a luggage rack not even bothering to open it, and then flopped down on the hard bed. It took her a second to recognize the material gathered above her as mosquito netting.

Wonderful—just wonderful. Quinn's checked us into bug central.

By United States' standards, the place was a dump, and she seriously doubted Quinn didn't realize it. It was no doubt part of his plan to discourage her from continuing. She stared at the ceiling. It wouldn't work. She planned on sticking around for the duration—right next to him.

She rose with new determination and went into the bathroom where she washed up. The towels were thin, but clean, and when Quinn knocked she was ready.

"Hi, how's the room? Everything all right?"

"Everything's fine," she said forcing a cheerful reply. "I'm hungry as a horse. Where are we eating?"

"The desk clerk told me there's a little café with decent food about three blocks from here. He also gave me a map of Guatemala. Bring your copy. We'll see if this might be easier than I think."

The café was crowded, but they found a table near the back. Weariness washed over her, and she struggled to keep her eyes open as Quinn spoke with the waitress. She had no idea what he ordered nor did she care. In less than a minute, the girl placed an ice-cold bottle of beer in front of each of them. Beer wasn't her usual tipple, but now it looked wonderful. She grabbed hers and drank.

"Ah, that hit the spot," she said with a sigh.

"It's been a long day, that's for sure," he admitted, reaching into his pocket to remove and unfold the country map. "Let's take a look at these."

Alex pulled the copy from her purse and removed it from the zip-lock baggie, making a mental note to always carry it in her pocket from now on. One purse snatching and they'd be out of luck. He compared the two, twisting and turning the papers for several minutes.

"I was right about the river and the lakes.

They're the ones I thought, but I see no landmarks that resemble each other," he said with a frown.

"Here, let me see." She stared at the maps. "If the names on the copy represent the five cities of the legend, then we need to know if they still exist under different names. If they don't, maybe the locals know where they could have been located."

"So, it's possible one or two of these places still exist, but the others are dust?"

"I imagine the jungle can cover anything in a very short time."

Quinn rubbed a hand over his face. "We may not know the exact location, but we do have a good idea of the general direction. We'll ask questions along the way and take back roads. Someone in the villages may be able to help."

She folded her map, replaced it in the baggie, and slipped it into a pocket. "I don't understand. Why take back roads and hike? This map shows Guatemala has several main highways. Doesn't this Los Arcos have an airport? Is there a regional airline or something?"

"I thought you hated flying."

"I do, but if we want to get there ahead of Rod and Victoria, why not fly to the site? It's logical."

Quinn sighed. "I'd love to take a plane, but my credit card is damned near maxed out. And we'll have to get the treasure out of here. How are your finances?"

Alex admitted defeat. "Pretty bad. I went to several estate sales last month. Counting what I withdrew for this trip, my checking account is thin, and I don't dare put too much more on my Visa, either. But why back roads?"

"Where's our final destination?"

"We're not sure."

"That's right. We know it's somewhere in this region." He pointed to the map with his finger. "But the old map could be off by miles. So, we have to hope somebody in one of these villages can remember something about the original cities on your map."

"Why hike?" She stifled a yawn. The farthest she ever walked was from one end of an estate sale to the other.

"Just because the villages are there doesn't mean the roads are. Would you rather tramp through the jungle without food or shelter?"

"We probably won't find any of those original cities."

"Finding two of them will give us reference points. Then we can head straight for the treasure." His face appeared calm, but his eyes gleamed with excitement.

Once an adventurer, always an adventurer.

"I think you need the rush of playing bwana," she told him.

He continued to peruse his map until the waitress brought their food. It looked delicious and the aroma set her mouth watering. Chunks of chicken mixed with beans, rice and vegetables. Her stomach reminded her she hadn't eaten since the layover in Belize, a cheese sandwich and a soft drink. Something that American sounded damned good.

"Quinn, would you ask the waitress to bring me a soda? I'm afraid another beer will have me asleep in my plate."

"A soft drink costs three times what the beer does, but it's up to you. By the way, neither the café nor the hotel takes credit cards. Did you get a chance to convert some of your cash?"

Alex stopped chewing. "You know perfectly well I didn't. Am I expected to shell out for our food and accommodations?"

"You insisted on this, so you can bite the bullet."

"Don't press your luck, Rafferty."

He laughed. "I changed some at the hotel desk. Has anyone ever told you you're gorgeous when you're angry?"

Unable to tell whether or not he meant it, she ignored the remark. Besides, the comment caused her heartbeat to quicken and she *really* needed to ignore that.

"Do you know where we're going?"

"Here," he said, showing her their route. "We'll take this highway out of Guatemala City as far as Santa Cruz. Then, we'll follow this smaller road and cut across country to Los Arcos. We'll spend the night in one of the villages along the way. If not, we'll just camp out." His tone warned her not to expect five star accommodations. "You can sleep in tomorrow. I'll check out the equipment and meet our guides. We'll come get you when we're finished. Stay close to the hotel."

She nodded compliance. That sounded sensible.

"This smaller road is paved for only about half of our journey, so I don't want to hear any complaints regarding the conditions."

"You won't." She stared him directly in the eyes. "I figure I can take anything you dish out and then some."

He nodded and continued. "We'll stay at an out-of-the-way hotel or inn when we get to Los Arcos. The guides can ask around town if anyone has seen Victoria and Rod. Two blond gringos shouldn't be hard to miss."

"And if they have been there—then what?"

"We follow. If they haven't put in an appearance, we ask questions regarding the five cities."

"How big is Los Arcos?" If they were ahead of Rod and Victoria maybe a night in a real hotel was in the cards.

"A city by rural Guatemalan standards. A small

town by American. The population is around ten or twelve thousand."

Scratch the Hilton. "How long do you plan to stay?"

"Not long. If we're ahead of Victoria and her brother, I'd like to keep it that way."

"They have several days' head start. What makes you think we may be ahead of them?"

"Victoria and Rod have never tramped across anything rougher than a crowded dance floor. Nor do they have contacts for ordering equipment and making guide arrangements. That could cut maybe two days off their advantage. Plus, they don't suspect we're coming. Victoria knows I've been on her trail, but will Rod expect you to follow him?"

"Not in a million years, and I'm sure he's being coerced," Alex stated. She hurried on when Quinn threw her an exasperated look. "How can you be sure Rod and Victoria haven't chartered a plane or aren't barreling down a nice paved highway?"

"Because they're working from the same map and information we are. Vicky isn't stupid. Remember, she helped Grandpa with his notes and the authentication. She had three years to do research, and I'm sure she's come to the same conclusions I have."

"What will the people think of this American invasion complete with treasure maps?"

"Foreigners put money into the local economy. Communication may be a little rough, though. Spanish is the official language, but only about half the natives speak it. The Indians speak the indigenous dialect."

Alex yawned and struggled to stay awake.

"Let's get back to the hotel," he said.

Quinn walked her to the door, placed his hands on her shoulders, and turned her to face him. For one brief instant, she thought he intended to kiss her.

But Quinn attempted no such thing. Instead, he said, "This has been a long day. I know you're exhausted, but bear this in mind—it's only going to get worse. I know what you think of these accommodations. I saw it in your eyes. They're the best we'll see in a while. Stay in Guatemala City, Alex. I'll set you up in a good hotel where you can wait while I do all the work. I won't leave you stranded—I swear it. I'll come back."

This seemed as good a time as any to playact. Setting her jaw, she said, "No way. I am going to find Rod and make sure he's all right."

He pushed her away and snapped, "You are the most stubborn, myopic woman I've ever come across. What does it take to convince you that Rod is not under duress? Face it, he used and dumped you. Get over it!"

"I'm sure he's being manipulated by his sister." She hoped she looked earnest.

"Then you're an idiot. I'm going to bed. I'll see you in the morning. Goodnight."

He turned on his heel, walked to his door and entered, slamming it behind him.

I'm doing the right thing.

Alex repeated that thought as she crawled into bed, remembering to release the mosquito netting. She'd tell him the truth later when it was too late to back out.

Tired to the bone, she didn't bother to shower or brush her teeth. She didn't even give a damn what kind of bugs landed on the mosquito net or tried to crawl out of the drain.

****

Alex slept in until nine o'clock. Battling her way out of the blessedly bug-free material, she staggered into the bathroom where she inspected for insect life before removing the Bible. Nothing crawled out of the drain to greet her. Maybe God understood.

She turned her attention to the tiny shower. Obviously, it had been designed by and for munchkins. No matter. She needed a shower and would have to make do.

She exited the bathroom a new woman. The tepid water had trickled out, but she was clean and her hair would soon dry into a mass of bouncing curls. For the next few weeks, she could deal with resembling Shirley Temple. Clean clothes also helped lift her spirits.

Hunger drove her from the room and into the dismal lobby. After exchanging a large chunk of her money at the front desk, she tucked it and the remainder of her American money along with her passport into the safety of a zippered pocket. They joined another baggie containing a cheap map similar to the one Rod had stolen.

In broken English, the clerk directed her to a small restaurant. She had no trouble finding the little café where she ate a surprisingly good breakfast and people watched while drinking a cup of fabulous coffee.

Alex would have liked to explore the surrounding area, but with Quinn's warning to stay near the hotel fresh in her mind, she retraced her steps. Perhaps, he had already arrived. She picked up her pace, not wanting to give him any ammunition to use against her. She had no idea when he left this morning.

She beat him back and returned to her room where she studied a Spanish phrase book. Quinn showed up at noon.

"Is everything all right? I was getting worried," she said letting him in.

"It took longer to check out the gear than I thought. I'll go over it with you tonight. The guides are eating lunch. They'll meet us here. I suggest we do the same. Did you get breakfast?"

"Yes, thanks. I'm still stuffed."

"Let's eat anyway. I want to get started as soon as we're done. Are you ready to go?"

"Yes. Just let me shove my purse in my suitcase and we can leave."

At the restaurant Quinn said, "I asked some questions at the supply house. Victoria and Rod are two days ahead of us. According to the supplier, they have three cars, three guides, and enough equipment to trek across Central America and back again."

"Is that good or bad?"

"They'll be prepared for whatever Mother Nature can dish out. On the other hand, all that stuff will slow them down. I also heard their guides are not the best."

The guides and two cars awaited them when they returned to the hotel.

"Alex, this is Jorge Portilla. He speaks Spanish and English. This gentleman is Miguel Cardoza. He speaks Spanish and several dialects of the areas along our way."

She greeted the men with her newly learned Spanish. Quinn disappeared inside and soon returned with their bags, piling them in the back seat of one of the cars.

"Jorge and Miguel will lead. We'll follow. This is your last chance to back out."

"Let's go." She climbed into the car.

If Guatemala City had a trendy, glitzy area, Alex didn't see it on the drive out of town. The city sprawled like a prizefighter down for the count. The thick smog made her gag, and the horrendous traffic hadn't changed from the night before. Buses that looked ready to disintegrate if they so much as ran over a seam in the pavement, belched out clouds of evil-smelling, black smoke as they crawled along trolling for passengers. Obviously, Guatemala had no EPA. She tried not to breathe the abominable odors of rotting garbage, automobile exhaust, and open sewers.

After what seemed an eternity, they left the city behind them and headed north. The highway was paved, but lack of guardrails had Alex holding her breath on more than one occasion. The twisting road plunged up and down the mountainsides. From her point of view, the bottom looked a long way down.

Quinn must have noticed her anxiety. "Don't worry. We'll move into less rugged terrain soon."

They stopped in the small town of Santa Cruz to top off with gas, and then continued, eventually turning onto another paved road with narrow shoulders. Progressing northeastward, the traffic thinned.

Alex caught glimpses of steep ravines with gushing streams tumbling over rocks and boulders. Huge bromeliads grew in the niches of trees along with enormous orchids.

Bit by bit, conversation with Quinn ceased. He had withdrawn after they left Santa Cruz. Her attempts at small talk met with short, one-syllable answers in a clipped, curt voice. Alex assumed her presence caused his irritation. It shaped up to be a long journey.

****

Quinn's mood deteriorated. The hilly, winding road bounced them around and, in the small confines of the car he and Alex made frequent contact. At every touch, his body burned hotter.

Dammit! He should have hog-tied her and thrown her into that closet back in Chicago, stolen the map, and been on his way. But, no-o-o! He had to give in to flashing green eyes, lips made for kissing, and his libido that refused to ignore any of it. He continued mentally cursing as the miles passed.

He didn't want any distractions on this trip. When he caught up with Victoria and Rod, the results might not be pretty. He needed a clear head and his passenger possessed the ability to muddy the waters of the clearest mountain lake.

He also worried. While they shaved two days off of their adversaries' lead, catching up could present a problem. Either group might misinterpret the map, spending days going in the wrong direction. He hoped to find them before anybody had to trek through the countryside, hopefully in the towns of either Los Arcos or Lago Verapaz.

Another sharp curve brought her thigh into contact with his. Heat scorched his leg from hip to knee. Quinn inhaled several deep breaths. Maybe he could find a closet here in Guatemala. He clenched his jaw as her shoulder popped against him. It was going to be a long trip.

****

It was after five o'clock when they reached a village perched in the hills of a small, narrow valley. Turning off of the road, the cars climbed a steep incline before finally stopping in front of a small, one-story house.

Alex sighed in relief. Her ass was numb and she wasn't sure her legs would ever move again.

Jorge came back to converse with Quinn in Spanish while Miguel knocked on the home's front door. As it swung open, the woman standing in the doorway immediately engulfed him in an embrace.

"We're here," Quinn said as Jorge joined Miguel. "The name of the village is Cabalo and the lady is Miguel's aunt. She's agreed to feed and put us up for the night."

Alex exited the cramped car and walked around to relieve her stiff joints, wondering where the aunt would stash four extra people in the tiny house.

Miguel and the lady conversed rapidly in a

language not Spanish. When they finished, Miguel translated for Jorge and Quinn who then turned to Alex.

"The lady's name is Maria, and says dinner will be ready soon. She's killed one of her chickens in our honor, so when you eat, be appreciative. There's a pump right outside the door where we can wash up," he said. "As the only woman in our group, you will share the bed with Maria. Now, I want you to smile and nod your head to show how pleased you are with her hospitality. She speaks no English or Spanish, only an Indian dialect."

Alex did as instructed and hoped the woman didn't snore.

After eating, Quinn took Alex outside to show her the gear picked up earlier. The enormous backpacks with lightweight fiberglass frames looked as though they would be more at home on a horse than a human. She worried about the weight.

Quinn then gave it to her with both barrels.

"If we do end up hiking, all of our clothing and toiletries will have to be carried along with our food, water, and shelter. There are three small tents, one for you, one for me, and the guides will share one." She nodded and started to speak, but he cut her off. "We each have a sleeping bag. Cooking will be done over a campfire. We also have small battery powered flashlights only to be used when necessary."

"All right." Her voice sounded quiet and serene. She was thoroughly intimidated, but refused to show it.

"The rest of the equipment is survival type stuff."

"That seems like a lot for just four people. How long will we be camping out?"

"It depends on how far ahead Victoria and Rod are and if we can find those reference points. There'll be no sleeping in from now on. Every hour of daylight counts. I want to leave at sun-up or shortly after."

Her hand reached out to grip his arm. "I promised to keep up with you and I will."

"You've already slowed me down. Alone, I would only need one guide and deal with less gear. I'd have checked it out when I arrived and left at dawn."

He glanced down at her hand, and then pulled her into his arms to kiss her hard before abruptly releasing her.

"Go to bed. Morning will be here before you know it."

He turned her around and pushed her in the direction of the doorway. She glanced over her shoulder as she re-entered the house.

Alex quickly shed her clothes and slid into bed next to her already sleeping hostess.

Damn, why does he have to keep kissing me?

It threw her off guard and sent her mind into a time warp. Perhaps he knew and that was why he did it. She would not allow him to turn her legs into jelly again, no matter how great he kissed.

Her hand reached down to the floor where she'd left her clothing and touched the pants pocket containing the map. Reassured, she settled deeper under the covers.

She awoke the next morning having no idea whether or not Maria snored.

Chapter Six

Alex rose and dressed before the sun peeked over the horizon. If it surprised Quinn, he didn't let on. After breakfast, she thanked her hostess and climbed into the car.

"How did you like your first night in a Mayan village?" he asked.

"I slept like the dead. How long will it take to get to wherever it is we're going?"

"Depends on the road conditions. Jorge says the pavement ends in a few miles and becomes little more than a dirt track."

The asphalt didn't just end—it disappeared. No warning signs or barricades prepared them. One minute they breezed along on a hard surface and the next plummeted a good twelve inches off of the edge onto a dirt and gravel road barely wide enough to accept cars. The impact jarred her bones and rattled her teeth.

Frequently, the car slowed to a crawl to negotiate huge potholes. Alex couldn't refrain from yelping when her hip and arm made contact with the door handle and window frame. At one point she banged her head on the roof.

"This is a road?" she asked, rubbing the sore spot.

"That last gully was an old washout. Be grateful it's not the rainy season."

"Doesn't this town we're heading for have any decent roads leading to it?" Alex asked after yet another hard landing.

"I thought you weren't going to complain." His

71

voice held a combination of exasperation and resignation, like he'd known she wouldn't keep her word.

She bit back a sarcastic comment, but said in a mild tone, "These cars won't have any suspensions left."

"I'm cutting off the angle between Santa Cruz and Los Arcos in the hope of beating Victoria there. There's no adventure in her soul. She'll take the easiest route."

"But isn't what we're saving in miles being lost by our speed?"

His gaze remained glued on the rutted road ahead, but his sigh indicated he humored her, like he would a five-year-old. "The road she'll be on bends west for almost a hundred miles before turning east to Los Arcos. We'll be traveling half the distance. Must you question everything I do?"

"I wouldn't if what you did had any logic to it."

Her rear end rose and slammed down into the seat one more time. She clenched her jaw and held on.

Countless bruises later, the dirt and gravel ended with one final bone-jarring lurch, and then the car once again rode on smooth pavement.

They entered the town of Los Arcos. The light traffic gave her a chance to see the architecture of this town had more charm than that of the capitol. Passing through the main square, she caught a glimpse of the local market down one of the side streets.

The cars pulled up in front of small hotel built in the colonial style. A veranda ran along three sides of the building and a balcony repeated the structure on the second floor.

The lobby looked spacious and clean. Alex saw a small bar and restaurant through an archway to the right of the main entrance. Beyond the staircase she noticed a lush courtyard garden. Upstairs, her room faced the courtyard. Quinn's room was across the hall and the guides had a room downstairs. The décor equaled any Holiday Inn.

Quinn stopped by. "How's the room? More to your liking?"

"It's wonderful. Better than I expected."

"Los Arcos is the capitol of this province. It's also a last stop for tourists before they head into various national parks. Sure you wouldn't like to stay? There's a wonderful marketplace. You can explore to your heart's content without me nagging you."

She ignored him. "I intend to take advantage of that tub and lots of hot water."

"I'm going to nose around with the guys to see if Victoria and Rod are in town. Meet us in the restaurant at seven. We'll eat and plan tomorrow's route."

Alone, Alex shed her clothes, filled the tub, and then slid in to let her aching muscles absorb the heat. Finished, she pulled on fresh apparel.

I'm human again.

Rather than wait for Quinn, she proceeded to the bar, ordered a beer, and contemplated confessing. If Victoria and Rod were far enough ahead, it would be possible he'd simply say the hell with it and head back home. She'd never see her map again.

No, wait a few more days.

Alex had come this far and refused to turn back. She needed him to guide her through this jungle. He'd be furious when he found out, of course. No matter, she'd deal with that when the time came.

The first rule of holes—when you're in one, stop digging. Unfortunately, I'm not slinging dirt, but am still holding the shovel. In this case, it can't be helped.

With his hair damp from a shower, Quinn joined

her and ordered a beer.

"Are Jorge and Miguel eating with us?" she asked.

"No. Miguel has a cousin in Los Arcos. They'll eat with him. It's just the two of us."

"Did you find out anything?"

"Thirty-six hours. Victoria and Rod left for Lago Verapaz yesterday around noon, the guides, cars, and equipment still in tow. We're gaining on them."

The waiter brought his drink and set it before him. Quinn drank half of it in one swallow.

"Where is this Lago place?"

"About two hundred miles northeast of here. The road's paved, and if our luck holds, we'll be there by early afternoon at the latest."

They ordered dinner and when the waiter left, Alex sat back, deep in thought.

"A penny for them," Quinn said. "You have a faraway look on your face."

She tilted the bottle to her mouth and let the cold brew slip down her throat before answering. "I was thinking how much my grandfather would have loved this. He could have stayed for weeks in that village last night, and this city would have fascinated him. Left to his own devices, he'd have roamed the country for months, maybe years."

"You miss him, don't you?"

"Very much. He didn't often show it, but in his own way, he loved me. Oh, I know he was selfish and self-absorbed, yet, I never felt unwanted. How about your grandfather? What would he have made of this?"

Quinn laughed, finished his beer, and signaled for another. "He loved the thrill of the hunt and the satisfaction of being the first to discover something. His body may have been failing, but his mind was keen and his spirit unflagging. God, I miss him!"

Dinner rivaled anything Alex had eaten

anywhere, including Chicago. They ate in silence preferring to concentrate on the food. Beef served in a spicy red sauce accompanied by roasted potatoes, vegetables and a fruit salad made a powerful statement to her taste buds. The intimacy of the small table and reduced lighting set a romantic mood.

Afterward, Quinn walked her to her door and advised, "I suggest an early night. After today, tomorrow will seem like a piece of cake."

"Goodnight, Quinn."

She should have moved, turned to her door, put the key in the lock, and gone in, but the mood from the dinner table lingered. Instead, she stood lost in the swirling blue-gray depths of his eyes, unable or unwilling to leave.

Slowly, he gathered her into his arms. His hand tangled in her hair, and tilting her head back he muttered, "This is crazy." Then his mouth claimed hers.

She didn't even offer token resistance, surrendering to his demanding mouth. Their tongues stroked and danced to the beat of her heart. Twining her arms around his neck, she kissed him back with all the pent up passion of the last few days.

Hot, blazing fire burst from her belly to race through her veins and along her nerves like molten metal. This was no lazy, indolent heat, but an urgent conflagration demanding immediate attention.

His hands roamed up and down her back, stopping occasionally to squeeze her derriere. He slid one hand between them and palmed her breast, his thumb rasping across the nipple until it was hard and aching. She discovered Quinn was also hard and probably aching as well when he pulled her hips close. In another ten seconds they'd be rolling around on the hallway floor with no thought of stopping.

Quinn groaned, and then pushed her away, hands clasping her shoulders while he gasped for breath, obviously trying to regain control.

Alex panted, her eyes unfocused, her mind in another dimension, and her body screaming, "Don't stop!"

Maybe, she spoke out loud for Quinn said in a hoarse voice, "We have to stop."

"Oh, my God, what am I doing? This cannot happen," she said. Thank goodness he'd had the common sense to call a halt.

"For once, I'm in total agreement with you."

He grabbed the key from her numb fingers. How on earth had she managed to hold onto it? He opened the door and pushed her through.

"Goodnight, Alex. I'll see you in the morning."

He turned and was in his room, the door closing in less than five seconds.

Alex took the key out of the lock, closed the door, and then leaned back against it. Her body trembled as though with a high fever.

Which is exactly what I have—a very dangerous fever called Quinn Rafferty.

Each time he kissed or held her, the flame burned hotter. This kind of response had never happened before and she headed down an unknown path.

Dear God, how can I control this, and what will tomorrow bring?

****

Alex's question received an answer the following morning. To Quinn's credit, he greeted her as if nothing earth shattering had occurred. After a cheerful "good morning" to the three diners at the table, he dug into his food like a starving man. Alex settled the hotel bill while the men readied the cars for the journey to Lago Verapaz.

Then, disaster struck. The right, front wheel of the lead vehicle collapsed bringing the car to a screeching halt in the middle of the parking lot. The bumper dragged on the concrete and wedged under the car.

"Damn!" Quinn swore, jamming on the brakes and rushing forward, Alex a few steps behind. A quick inspection and a short conversation with the guides confirmed the bad news. The car had sustained serious damage. Jorge entered the hotel.

"The suspension is gone, maybe the axel as well," Quinn reported, his face set in grim lines. "The road yesterday must have shaken it apart. Damn!"

"What do we do now?" She refrained from saying, I told you so.

"Jorge is checking with the desk clerk to see if there's a garage in town."

"How long will it take to fix?"

Quinn shrugged. "Who knows? And that's assuming the parts are available. If not, then we'll have to rent another car."

Jorge rejoined them and the three men consulted. "Jorge called a mechanic. He'll be here shortly," he told her.

Shortly turned out to be the Central American definition of the word. It was two hours before the man arrived. She waited on the veranda while he inspected the car. By the way the mechanic gestured and by Quinn's reactions, the news was not what he wanted to hear. He ran his fingers through his hair, and although she couldn't hear, his lip movements suggested swearing. Jorge once again trotted past her and into the hotel while Quinn strode over to give her the low-down.

"The man says he can fix the car, but will have to send to Guatemala City for the parts. Jorge is trying to find us a loaner. If none are available from a rental agent, we may have to scrounge up a private deal. There is, however, another option."

"Which is?" she asked.

"We can jam the gear from the other car into ours, but only three of us can continue."

His stare sent an unspoken suggestion she chose to ignore. "Which guide do we leave behind?"

"We don't. We leave you."

"No."

"Alex, be reasonable. Even you said this hotel is comfortable and the food good. There's an active marketplace and bus tours to various parks. You can wait here in comfort."

"Quinn, be logical. If we have to leave someone behind, it should be Jorge. He can oversee the repairs, and then meet us in Lago Verapaz. Miguel needs to come with us because he speaks the local dialects and Spanish. I, on the other hand, speak only English and know next to nothing about cars. I wouldn't know if the car is properly fixed or not. Jorge can keep this guy honest."

Quinn shook his head. "Three men will move faster, even with the extra gear, than two men and a woman. And please, don't give me any crap about women's lib. Also, there's no guarantee the end of our journey will be Lago Verapaz. What good would it do to have him meet us there?"

"Where else?"

"There's a town about thirty-five miles southeast of Lago Verapaz we need to check out."

"So, why go to Lago Verapaz in the first place? Why not go to this other town instead?"

"Because that's the route Victoria and Rod have taken. They'll go to Lago Verapaz. I'd rather try to recover the map there than in the jungle. If they don't have a map, they can't follow."

"It's my map. I don't care where I get it back as long as I do," she stated.

They glared at each other for a few seconds

before Quinn said, "You won't give an inch, will you?"

"No."

At that moment, Jorge ran out of the hotel and said in an excited voice, "*Senor* Rafferty, I have found a car. It is an American car—a Tahoe."

A grin lit Quinn's face. "A Tahoe? We'll take it."

"It is very expensive."

"Bargain with him. Tell him we'll take the car for two weeks, maybe more, and will pay in advance."

"*Si*." He ran back to the telephone.

Quinn turned to Alex. "Reprieved! I planned on tying you to a lamp post and leaving you here."

She didn't doubt him for one moment.

It took another hour and a half for Quinn and Jorge to pick up, pay for the SUV, and pack all the equipment. They finally left for Lago Verapaz a little before noon.

Alex noticed the change in altitude and terrain. The temperature rose, as did the humidity. Mist obscured the tops of the mountains.

"I believe it's going to rain," she commented.

Quinn spoke with Jorge and Miguel. "The guys say the mist is normal. It's called a cloud forest. The area where we're going is honeycombed with caves, underground rivers, and sinkholes."

They reached the outskirts of Lago Verapaz a little before six o'clock, stopping in front of a small inn similar to the one in Los Arcos. After checking in, Quinn gave her the agenda for the evening.

"The guys and I will spread out and try to find information on Victoria's and Rod's whereabouts. Meet us in the restaurant."

It was almost eight when they joined her. Jorge and Miguel ordered and ate quickly, then left.

"Where are they going in such a hurry?" Alex asked.

"They're setting up the backpacks so we don't waste time if we have to abandon the car. Victoria and Rod left about eleven-thirty this morning. One of the desk clerks at the hotel where they stayed heard them mention the town I told you about—Abaj. The road is gravel and supposedly in good repair." He looked her square in the eye. "This is your last chance at civilization."

"What time do we leave?" Like she'd quit now.

"I want to be out of here by seven o'clock," he said.

"Don't look so dejected. Even with our troubles today, Victoria and Rod are less than twelve hours ahead."

"I know, I know. I'm going to help the guys. Dinner's on me. I'll check on you before I turn in. I want to make sure your backpack isn't too heavy." Quinn threw down his napkin and pushed his empty plate away, then left.

So much for scintillating dinner conversation.

Alex finished her meal and returned to her room. She tried to concentrate on her phrase book, but was too antsy to sit still. She traced their proposed route using both the copy and the present day maps.

Quinn mentioned the area had caves. The legend, while not specific, had intimated a cave as the location of the treasure. Perhaps, out of five ancient towns, one of them still existed, although it was immaterial for her quest.

She folded the maps and thought hard. Rod, for all his charm, was not a deep thinker. He survived on his wits and silver tongue. Nor was he particularly athletic, so jungle hiking would not be his forte. Alex suspected Victoria had the majority of family brains. She'd do the planning.

But even she would be out of her element. They sought marks in cities where they could escape from their crimes quickly and blend into a crowd. This treasure hunting stuff was new to them, too. And Rod had often moaned about the early ten o'clock opening of the store. Her ex-boyfriend was *not* a morning person. She bet he was the reason they hadn't departed until almost noon today.

Good! If the two of them continued to follow this routine, then she and Quinn could catch up in a day or two.

Alex paced, lamenting the fact she couldn't make a specific plan for retrieving the map. She'd just have to wait for the right time and hope it turned out to be the right place. She hated flying by the seat of her pants, but saw no way around it.

A light tap on the door halted her aimless strides. She opened up and stared in dismay when Quinn swung the large nylon and fiberglass contraption onto her bed.

"Here, give this a try." He helped her into it and stood back to survey the results. "How does that feel? Too heavy?"

"Heavy enough, but I'll manage. What's in it?"

"Some bottled water, food, a first aid kit, coffee, things like that. Pack your clothes tonight. We'll leave our suitcases here and pick them up on the return journey. Remember to keep the first aid kit within easy access. Don't forget you'll have to carry your tent and sleeping bag. Sure you can handle it?"

"Yeah, no problem."

She shrugged out of the pack, dumping it on the floor. The damned thing weighed a ton. She hoped she didn't fall over backwards and flop around like an inverted turtle.

Alex looked up. Quinn hadn't moved from the center of the room. His intense stare riveted her feet to the floor. A humming filled her ears, and her nerves vibrated with tension.

Then a warm glow engulfed her. She labored to

breathe, and her heart thudded hard in her chest. The warmth intensified while desire pooled deep in her belly. She couldn't tear her gaze away from his.

She wasn't aware of having moved, but somehow the distance between them vanished and with a muffled groan, he pulled her into his arms to kiss her like she'd never been kissed before. They would not stop tonight.

The heat and the madness exploded into a firestorm that refused to die. Her body shook as though in the grip of a killing fever. The thumping heartbeats pounded in her ears, and she couldn't prevent desperate little moans from forming in the back of her throat.

Alex tugged, pulled, and finally succeeded in stripping his shirt off, all without breaking the mind-blowing kiss. Her fingers fumbled with the fastening of his pants. Her shirt and bra disappeared. When had Quinn done that? It didn't matter. All she wanted was the offending clothing gone.

He shoved her onto the bed and yanked off her boots, his half-lidded eyes blazing. She stared back, hypnotized. He peeled her trousers and panties down her legs, tossing them across the room. His fingertips slowly traced her body from throat to breasts and down her stomach. When his hand cupped the seething heat between her thighs, Alex emitted a strangled sob.

The next thing she knew, he shucked the rest of his clothing and fell next to her. One touch had them rolling and thrashing around in a tangle of arms and legs with their lips glued together.

When Quinn finished ravaging her mouth, he nibbled his way down her throat and across the creamy globe of her breast until he captured the hard, erect nipple in his mouth. His tongue and teeth sent raw, burning sensations along her nerves.

With a gasping cry, she arched against him silently begging for more. He obliged, sucking hard as his hands smoothed down her body until his fingers found the very heart of her heat.

Soft cries, whimpers, and gasps were the only sounds Alex articulated. His mouth turned the blood in her veins to lava. Her hips undulated. She writhed and moaned, begging for release from the continuous coil of desire building.

With a suddenness that left her gasping in disappointment, Quinn rose above her. He panted, but managed to croak out, "Too fast. Slow down."

In answer, Alex pushed him onto his back proceeding to love him as he had her. Tangling her fingers in his chest hair, she slid her mouth down his torso. She teased his navel with her tongue and slipped her hand around his erection.

He trembled from head to foot and uttered a strangled cry, clenching the bedclothes in his fists when she took him into her mouth. Somehow, Quinn pulled her up and flipped her onto her back.

Alex cried out when he plunged into her. She locked her legs around his waist meeting his pounding thrusts with frantic lunges. The fast pace and the pressure to find satisfaction skyrocketed with every movement until finally reaching that elusive pinnacle.

Biting back a shriek, Alex climaxed—the spasms long and deep. Her fingernails scored his back, and she continued moving to the rhythm of the ecstasy until he made one final lunge, shouting his release.

Her arms and legs fell back onto the bed, limp. She floated in the aftermath of fantastic sex, her breathing and heart rate somewhere in the stratosphere.

Several minutes passed before Alex regained control, opened her eyes, and realized where she was, what she had done, and who she'd done it with.

"Aw, shit!" she yelled sitting straight up and glaring at the naked man lying next to her.

"What's the matter?" he mumbled, his eyes closed, a smile on his lips.

"You! You're what's the matter!" She scrambled off the bed searching for her clothes. "How could you have done this to me?"

"How could I—to you?" He opened one eye. The second joined it, and the smile disappeared. His forehead furrowed.

"That's right! You've been trying to seduce me from the first night we met. Now you've succeeded. Are you happy?" she said, raging as she tried to dress. She knew she sounded irrational, but could do nothing about it.

Quinn's scowl deepened. He leaped out of bed, his eyes holding a combination of confusion and irritation.

"Hold it, sister. I don't recall the word 'no' passing your lips. You enjoyed it."

"Ha!" She shoved her foot through the tangled leg of her pants.

"Ha, yourself! Admit it!" His voice rose. "And those are my pants!"

She flung the offending garment at him with a snarl. "Here—take them! Did you think a heavy backpack and a hot roll in the hay would turn my brain into mush? Did you think I'd agree to stay behind like a good little girl? Or did you just hope that I'd turn the map over to you in starry-eyed trust?"

He hopped around the room swearing and trying to maintain his balance while he dressed. Alex ripped off the shirt she'd just donned inside out.

"If I was going to steal the map and dump you, I'd have done it long ago. Where the hell are my socks?"

"I don't know, and I don't care. Just find them

and get out of my room!" She buttoned the shirt with trembling fingers, and then unbuttoned it when she saw the buttons didn't match up with the holes. If she didn't throw or kick something soon, she'd explode.

"Which pisses you off more? That you wanted me or that you got me?" he snapped.

"You are so not my type. You are one hundred percent the total opposite of what I want in a man."

"Who do you want—Rod Halston?"

"I want a man who's dependable, loyal, there for me when I need him. I want a man who considers my wants and needs above his own and *our* wants and needs above mine. I want a man who thinks things through and doesn't allow impulses to rule his life."

She was too angry to recount all of the qualifications on her list. It didn't matter. Quinn didn't have any of them anyway.

Quinn finished dressing, then grabbing his socks and boots, walked to the door.

"Dependable? Loyal? You don't want a man, Alex. You want a lapdog. Get a Shih-Tzu!"

On that parting shot, he stalked out, slamming the door behind him. Seconds later an answering slam echoed from across the hall.

All the fight drained away, leaving Alex with a sense of winning the battle, but losing the war. She sat on the edge of the bed and grasped her flushed cheeks with shaking hands.

Oh, God, what was the matter with her? Why was she so angry? She never lost control. *Never*. She was too keyed up—too satiated—to think rationally at the moment.

Regardless of her motivation, she admitted Quinn was right. She'd wanted him with a fire and recklessness she'd never encountered before or understood. Tonight, she experienced the best sex

85

since creation. And it had come from a man whom she considered completely unacceptable as her soul mate. How could she face him in the morning?

She lay back amongst the tangled bedclothes and stared at the ceiling in confusion.

****

Quinn threw his boots across the room and paced back and forth. What the hell had he been thinking? Sex with Alex was the last thing he needed. He wasn't *her* type? She sure as hell wouldn't make his top ten list either. She was the prissiest, most opinionated, stubborn, gutsy, sexy woman he'd ever met, and she had just presented him with the best mind-blowing sex of his entire life.

All day, Quinn had fought incredible desire. When she shed the backpack, reason abandoned him. With her out-thrust breasts straining against her shirt, he visualized her naked torso arched, pleading for his hands and mouth. He'd been aching and hard as a rock when they'd fallen onto the bed.

Her cries and whimpers along with the restless movements of her body drove him mad. But when she touched him and took him into her mouth, the sensations damn near sent him into orbit.

"Damn," he muttered out loud. "I swore I wouldn't get involved. Now I'm up to my ass in Alex Montgomery."

Something about her had grabbed him that first night, in spite of the fact she'd shot him—or maybe because of it.

He sensed that lurking beneath her fastidious, up-tight exterior, beat the heart of a true adventuress. Her choice of childhood reading material proved it. No *Little Women* or *Jane Eyre* for her. She chose adventure and thrills. He had woven more fantasies about her than any other woman in his life.

For what seemed like the millionth time in the

86

last few days, he cursed himself for not having left her behind in Chicago. He should have figured out a way to have stolen the stinking map.

Damn Alex and her sexy green eyes. Damn his overactive libido, and damn his inability to ignore any of it.

Quinn didn't have a clue where all this would lead. He only knew the train roared down the tracks, and there was no getting off at the next stop.

Chapter Seven

Alex dreaded walking into the hotel lobby the next morning. She'd spent the night lying awake formulating her apology. Her stomach tensed, and she wiped her clammy palms down the legs of her pants.

Jorge greeted her. "*Buenos dias.* I will take your backpack to the car. *Senor* Rafferty says to eat breakfast. We leave soon."

Alex nibbled on a tasteless tortilla and drank a cup of coffee. Until recently, procrastination and postponing the inevitable hadn't been part of her philosophy. She squared her shoulders.

Face him and get it over with.

She exited and looked around the parking lot. The guides stood near the Tahoe checking gear before packing it into the car. Quinn sat under a tree, studying the map. Taking a deep breath, she marched over.

With her bottom lip caught between her teeth, she looked at the ground, the map, and the tree—anywhere except his face.

"Quinn, I need to talk to you."

"What about?" He didn't raise his eyes.

"I want to apologize for what I said last night. I was furious with myself and took it out on you. I never meant for it to happen, but once it started, was powerless to stop. I'll be more careful in the future." She finished, still staring at the ground in front of her.

Quinn refolded the map before speaking. "It wasn't all your fault, Alex. We both lost control, and

I can't swear it won't happen again."

"How do we avoid each other?"

"There'll be four of us camping out. I see no reason to visit each other's tents." He stood and shoved the map in his pocket. "Alex, look at me."

She reluctantly raised her head. His eyes held no anger. A lopsided smile curled his lips. Even in the light of day, he looked sexy as hell.

"Alex, I'm not sorry for what we did last night."

"I'm not either," she finally admitted, shifting from foot to foot.

A look she could not identify crossed his face, causing her to wonder if he was also nervous about this morning after meeting.

"Are you packed and ready to go? Did you have breakfast?" he asked.

She heaved a sigh of relief. The dreaded apology was over and she lived through it, her dignity still intact.

"Yes, although I didn't eat much."

"We'll have an early lunch in Abaj."

Alex climbed into the passenger seat, not surprised when Miguel got behind the wheel. Having the guide drive was not a bad idea. The less physical contact between her and Quinn, the better. She knew if the opportunity presented itself and the circumstances right, they would take advantage of the situation again. A part of her hoped they would not resist temptation.

Quinn might not possess one single quality she looked for in a man, but she wanted him anyway. She had started to visualize him in her life after this adventure ended. And *that* confused her.

The picturesque town of Abaj nestled on a plateau between three hills, the view breathtaking. Below, the green jungle spread out like a multihued carpet. In the distance, a river cut a blue swath through the verdant hills. The sun sparkled off the water in dazzling pinpoints of light. Miguel pulled up in front of a cantina.

"I suggest you go in and eat while we park. I'll stay with the car. The guys can mingle with the locals to see if Victoria and Rod showed up. We'll meet you back here in an hour," Quinn said.

She hurried to obey, ravenous after her abbreviated breakfast. Alex was sipping her second cup of coffee when Quinn walked through the door and sat across from her.

"Are you done?"

"Yes. Aren't you going to eat?"

"We had breakfast in Lago Verapaz. Finish your coffee and I'll tell you what we learned about Victoria and Rod."

"Are they here?"

"They got here yesterday afternoon and left a few hours later. They've abandoned the cars and are hiking. They traipsed off with the three guides and all their equipment piled on five donkeys. They were last seen heading east."

Alex laughed. "You're not serious? My God, substitute the donkeys for elephants and they must look like Hannibal crossing the Alps."

"They'll be easy to follow. Donkeys will leave a well-defined trail." A thoughtful look crossed his face. "If they're hiking east, we could drive northeast, circle around, and come out ahead of them. They're walking and even though the road we'll use is primitive, we'd still make better time. Those donkeys will slow them down."

"Then what?"

"We keep heading east, only this time, we'll be leading."

Alex didn't like this. She ran the risk of out-running her map. "What's east?"

"My gut instinct tells me one of those ancient cities is in that direction."

"Why assume that?"

"Let's assume the original map is fairly accurate and the treasure is southeast of here. That would put the village called Pop a bit to the east or northeast of us. Get your map out and take a look."

She complied and saw the possibilities. "Gut instinct?"

He shrugged. "Why not? It's the same as women's intuition. Vicky and Rod are barging along in a straight line and probably assuming the treasure is where the map says. If we find reference points, we can allow for any discrepancies."

Alex refolded her map and gave in. Sooner or later she and Quinn, and Rod and Victoria were bound to meet like trains on converging tracks.

"All right. I guess we do it your way."

"Come on, let's get out of here."

He reached across the table and grabbed her hand to pull her up. When she regained her feet, he dropped it as if burned.

They stared at each other. His eyes turned a smoky gray. Her heart thumped as the silence lengthened.

"I guess Jorge and Miguel must be wondering where we are," she finally said, her voice barely above a whisper.

He cleared his throat. "Yeah. I guess."

They left the cantina and walked across the street. She climbed into the passenger seat, slamming the door. Quinn spoke with the guides, then got behind the wheel and turned down a side street. The houses thinned until only the jungle was visible. The road ended in a cul-de-sac.

"So, where's the road?" Alex asked.

"Dead ahead."

"What? All I see are bushes."

Quinn didn't answer, but popped the Tahoe into four-wheel drive, then inched over the edge of the pavement and through the dense foliage. Less than fifty feet into the vegetation, he drove onto a wide path.

"Are you kidding? The car's wider than the trail," she said, staring in disbelief. Branches bent and pressed against her window.

"Miguel assures me the road widens out further on."

"No wonder Rod and Victoria have donkeys."

"They had to switch. Their cars couldn't handle this. The trail is supposed to bring us out near a small village. It could be the one on the map."

He stepped on the accelerator and they bounced over the rutted dirt. After a few miles, the track widened as promised, and her claustrophobia lessened.

This cart path was a hundred times worse than the road the other day. Alex clutched at anything to keep from being flung across the seat and into Quinn's lap.

When she thought it could get no worse, it did. The light dimmed, throwing the forest into an eerie gloom. In the distance, thunder rumpled.

"It's going to rain," Quinn said, resignation in his voice.

"*Si, Senor* Rafferty. I am afraid so," Jorge answered.

"What's so bad about rain?" she asked. Jorge's voice sounded as glum as Quinn looked.

"Give it ten minutes," Quinn said.

The thunder pealed closer. A few minutes later, the heavens opened. Her jaw unhinged in astonishment. Gripping the edge of the seat, Alex peered ahead trying to see something—anything—beyond the hood besides a gray curtain of water. Rain pounded on the roof, blotting out all other sounds. Their speed slowed to almost a standstill.

"Good God, will it last long?"

"Long enough," Quinn snapped. "Don't talk to me now. I'm concentrating."

The car no longer bounced, but slid and skidded down the road, now a river of mud. A twinge of fear spiraled in Alex's chest. On the driver's side, water and debris cascaded down the hillside. On her side, the torrent passed on as the terrain dropped off sharply. She tightened her seat belt. Quinn did the same. Her heart slammed in her chest, and she bit her lip. She'd never seen anything like this.

"Shit!" he yelled.

Alex knew instantly they'd bought trouble. A boulder, eroded from its foundation by the storm, careened downhill and struck them behind the driver's door. The right side tires slid off the edge of the track. The Tahoe skidded broadside down the hill, plowing through and over the vegetation, pitching and swaying wildly until crashing into a large tree.

She fumbled for the door handle with trembling hands.

Quinn reached across her body and stilled the movement. "Wait a minute. Don't move. The tree has you blocked."

She gathered her wits and noticed the trunk pressing against the cracked glass of her window.

"Stay put. We don't know how stable the ground is. We'll check when the rain stops. Thank God, we didn't flip over."

Alex sat still as a statue trying to calm her pounding heart and trembling body. She was trapped and that scared the hell out of her more than the slide. An eternity seemed to pass before the rain finally stopped. Quinn carefully slid out of the car and inspected the ground.

"Looks okay. Slide over easy, and I'll get you out."

Alex unbuckled her seat belt and inched her way

uphill across the seat. Quinn reached in, grasped her arm, pulling her from the car. The guides exited with little trouble.

"Are you all right?"

"Yeah, I'm fine. Just a little scared," she answered in a shaky voice.

Up the hill, the flattened foliage testified to the wild ride. She thought the slide had taken forever, but they had stopped about sixty feet off the road. Beyond the tree that had halted their fall, the hillside descended in a sharp angle with rocky outcroppings. They'd been lucky—damned lucky. She clutched a small tree trying to catch her breath, and then looked at the Tahoe.

"Oh, my God."

The boulder lay wedged under the frame, lifting the driver's side wheels off the ground. She shot a glance at Quinn.

"How do we get out of here?"

"We walk."

He and the men opened the tailgate and removed the gear. Jorge helped Alex don her backpack, securing the sleeping bag and tent to it.

"Where's your hat?"

"In my backpack," she answered, unzipping the opening and removing it.

"Wear it," Quinn ordered, putting his on. "It'll keep the sun and moisture out of your eyes. Here's a bottle of water. Slide it into that narrow elastic-topped opening on your hip. Okay?"

At her nod, he continued, "This changes things. The path Vicky and Rod took isn't far away. We'll cut through and take it, too. Jorge, take the lead. I'll go second, Alex third, and Miguel brings up the rear. We hike for two hours, then take a fifteen minute rest. We'll make camp late in the afternoon and turn in early. I want to leave at sun-up. Any questions?"

Alex adjusted her hat and pack. "Not from me. I

guess I'm as ready as I'll ever be."

For the first hour, Alex spent the time getting accustomed to fifty pounds strapped on her back. The vegetation was thinner than expected and it didn't take long to find the easterly track Rod and Victoria chose. The rough trail had a downhill slant, and she now appreciated the boots Quinn insisted she buy.

She thankfully shucked her pack when Quinn called a halt to rest. Farther down the path, Alex saw the droppings of what must have been a donkey.

"Quinn, look."

"I know. I saw more a ways back. I'd say it's only about a day old. How are you holding up?"

"Fine. The pack's awkward, but I'll get used to it."

"Good, because the next two hours will be all uphill."

At first, she had no problem with the gentle rise, but then the path narrowed turning rougher and steeper. Alex leaned forward in order not to overbalance and crash into Miguel behind her. Her shoulders burned and her back ached.

Since meeting Rod, she let visits to her spa slide. Muscles once accustomed to regular workouts, now protested. The boots, while providing excellent footing, were heavy and lifting her feet developed into a chore. Her legs trembled and burned like hell. She plodded on like a robot, panting and sweating, consoled by the thought Rod and Victoria experienced the same discomfort.

"Let's rest," Quinn said, breathing heavily.

Alex looked up. They had stopped at a literal wide spot in the road. She let the backpack slide from her shoulders, and then sank beside it, lying on the ground.

"Are you all right?" Quinn asked.

"I'm fine," she lied, breathless.

"Drink your water. That was quite a climb, but Miguel says the next couple of hours are easier. There's a good place to camp near some ruins. Can you hang in there?"

"Sure, no problem," she mumbled draining her water bottle. He nodded and walked away.

She closed her eyes. *Rest. That's all I need—just a few minutes of* r*est.*

The next thing she knew, a hand shook her shoulder and Quinn's said, "Wake up, Alex. It's time to go."

Her eyes snapped open and for a few seconds she stared in confusion. Then everything fell into place.

"How long was I out?"

"Less than thirty minutes," Quinn assured her.

"Thirty minutes! You should have nudged me sooner. I don't want to hold us up," she protested, keenly aware she'd done just that.

"It gave us a chance to repack Miguel's load. We made good time. Let me help you with your pack."

She stood and almost groaned when the heavy weight once again descended onto her shoulders. The brief catnap had helped, but the change in the terrain gave her a much-needed respite.

"According to the map, the geography is a series of plateaus, and then hills. We're in that area now. I'll compare the two maps later tonight," he said.

This trek through the jungle had opened her eyes to why Quinn had wanted her to stay behind. She trudged on, determined to keep up, yet grateful when they broke out of the forest and into a small circular clearing, maybe twenty yards in diameter. Quinn and Jorge inspected the ashes of a cook fire in a blackened, stone-ringed enclosure.

"It was used within the last twenty-four hours. The donkeys were tethered by the tree line," he said, pointing out the obvious clues. "Let's set up the tents, eat, and call it a day."

Alex let the pack down and asked, "Where do I pitch my tent?"

"Between the fire and the forest," Quinn replied. "The instructions are in the tent bag. Can you follow them?"

"I guess I can put pole A into hole B," she answered, then recognized the symbolism of what she said.

Quinn, shot her an amused glance, but said nothing. He left to join Miguel and Jorge who had unpacked some of the gear. Alex unbagged her tent and read the instructions. She painstakingly followed them, then pulled back to review the results. *Hey! I have a tent.*

Turning to retrieve her gear, she looked up. Quinn stood in front of her holding cooking utensils.

"Uh, Quinn, I hope you aren't planning on me being the chief cook and bottle washer, because I can't cook. If I can't nuke it or order in, I go out."

"I figured as much. I remember your close relationship with Lee Chen. We'll cook if you'll clean up. Deal?"

"Deal."

She crawled into the tent, dragging her backpack with her. The floor measured about six feet square and the dome was high enough to allow her to sit comfortably. The front flap zipped shut in case of rain and a smaller rectangular cover in the back opened for ventilation. Both openings possessed screens.

Kinda cozy, but not bad at all.

She spread her sleeping bag out to the left, and pushed the remaining gear to the right, then rooted around in her pack until she found a T-shirt for sleeping and fresh clothing for tomorrow.

Alex poked her head out. Jorge had built a fire while Miguel mixed something in a pot. Quinn had disappeared.

She approached the men, and asked in halting Spanish, "*Donde es Senor* Rafferty?" She had no idea if she'd said it correctly.

Jorge grinned, replying in English, "Very good, *senorita. Senor* Rafferty go to wash. He will be back in a minute."

Quinn appeared from a small path through the foliage wiping his face with his shirt tail.

"Where do I find the lavatory?"

"Go that way and you'll come to a stream. Be quick and don't leave the path."

"I won't." *Honestly, does he think I'm stupid? Men!*

She dived back into her tent, and rummaged through her ditty bag until finding a tiny bar of soap.

She headed down a path so narrow the foliage brushed her arms. The stream, two feet wide and maybe six inches deep, looked as welcoming as a Jacuzzi.

Alex stripped off her shirt and bra and washed. She redressed minus the bra, shoving it into a pants pocket. Increasing heat and humidity made the garment impractical.

Back in camp, Alex sat cross-legged on the ground and ate. This camping thing didn't seem too bad. Her tent was cozy, the food filling, and as darkness descended, the cooling air promised decent sleeping conditions. She finished eating and cleaned up.

Now what? She sat back on her heels in front of the slowly dying fire. A hearty yawn gave her a clue.

Quinn smiled with an understanding expression. "Why don't you turn in? It's been a tiring day for all of us. We need our rest. Morning will be here before you know it."

"You're right," Alex answered, grateful nobody

expected her to participate in campfire stories.

She crawled into her tent and zipped the flap shut while she changed clothes. When done, she unzipped the openings for maximum ventilation. Sliding into her sleeping bag, she wiggled until comfortable. At least no sticks or rocks jabbed her in unlikely places.

The expiring embers of the fire gave off a faint glow and the sounds of the forest sprang to life. Chirping, buzzing, frogs croaking, and flapping wings all blended together in a cacophonous symphony punctuated by the dry rustling of leaves stirring in the occasional breeze.

To city-bred Alex, the noise was deafening and a bit creepy. Give her the sounds of the city any day. The swish of automobile tires on wet pavement, sirens, and even sanitation trucks on early morning rounds were sounds of a Waukegan night she could ignore, but this forest babble kept her awake and alert.

A sudden, choked off cry from the trees behind her sent her jackknifing upright and clutching the covers under her chin in startled alarm.

What the hell was that?

It sounded like someone getting mugged in a dark alley. Then, she realized that's exactly what it was. Some creature had fallen victim to a predator. The night sounds, silenced by the sudden, violent death, resumed.

Prone again, Alex let out the deep breath she'd held.

The climb today damn near killed me. I was unprepared, but I'll get tougher. Tomorrow's journey will be easier.

****

Alex adjusted the backpack on her shoulders the next morning. Stiff and sore, her legs told her the Stairmaster at the gym had not prepped them enough for mountain climbing. Her back and shoulders complained loudly at the extra weight.

Suck it up. Get used to it.

"Are you all right?" Quinn asked.

"I'm fine. The stiffness will wear off in a while."

He hadn't said much this morning and Alex assumed he had concerns about her ability to keep up. But then, maybe he understood. Maybe *he* hurt, too.

They trekked over level ground, and then descended into a valley before once again climbing uphill. The pattern repeated all the morning, and when they stopped for a break, she welcomed the chance to rest.

"How are the legs holding out?" Quinn asked, concern in his eyes.

"Not bad. That last hill wasn't too hard."

"According to Miguel, the terrain evens out, but the heat and the humidity rise. I guess it's a push."

Within a few minutes, the group continued on its way. The path, once wide and accommodating, narrowed. So far, none of the men had been forced to hack their way through the vegetation with machetes. The constant brush of leaves against her arms made Alex glad for the long sleeves.

The foliage grew thick and tall. She knew if she wandered two feet off the trail, her companions would disappear from view. The dense surrounding greenery sent shivers up and down her spine. She'd never considered herself claustrophobic, but all this herbaceous growth hemming her in gave her the creeps. She absently swatted at the pesky insects buzzing around her ears while forcing her thoughts onto more pleasant subjects.

Quinn's voice brought her out of her favorite Waukegan restaurant and back to the jungle.

"We're picking up mosquitoes. It's time to put on repellent. Cover every bit of exposed skin including down the neck of your shirt. Don't forget the insides of your ears. The little beggars are tenacious. They'll go anywhere to feast."

Alex found her repellent and sprayed it everywhere. The stuff smelled of kerosene and something organic, but she didn't care as long as it kept Mother Nature's little vampires at bay.

Now, the terrain ran sharply downhill. For over two hours they descended. The enervating humidity sucked the moisture from her body, further sapping energy she could not afford to lose. By the time they reached the bottom of the plateau, she needed a break.

Shedding the cumbersome burden, Alex collapsed onto the ground beside it. She drank and some of her energy surged back. Too tired to waste breath on conversation, Alex sat in silence until Quinn rose and donned his pack.

She remained seated stalling for just a few more minutes of rest while Miguel said something to Quinn. All three of them looked drained and beat.

"Miguel says there is an area very much like the place we camped last night about an hour and a half away. I know we'll still have some daylight left, but an early evening won't kill us," he told her. "Are you ready to go or do you need a few more minutes?"

"I'm ready." She put her hand down to rise and promptly screamed. "A—a snake! It slithered not two feet away from me."

Quinn jerked her up and flung her behind him. "Are you all right? Did it bite you?" He probed the area near her backpack with a stick.

"No. I put my hand down and saw it moving into the bushes out of the corner of my eye. Was it poisonous?"

"Probably. What did it look like?"

Alex felt lightheaded. Snakes were not on her list of favorite anythings, and a poisonous one so close made her heart pound.

"I have no idea. It may have been brown. I don't know," she replied in a shaky voice.

"Jorge?"

"There are many snakes, including the fer-de-lance and the cascabel, a rattlesnake, in the area."

Quinn nudged her pack again with his foot. "It's gone now. Make sure you put some distance between you and the high grass or bushes when we rest or make camp. Snakes like cover." He settled the pack on her shoulders. "Ready?"

She nodded. With each step, Alex scanned the trail's edges on the lookout for anything that slithered or coiled. The middle of the path looked like the safest place to walk.

They stopped to camp in a clearing similar to the one of the previous night, minus the stream.

After dinner, Quinn took out his map. "Let's see where we are and how we compare." Jorge and Miguel joined them.

"It looks as though we're about here." Quinn pointed on his map. "Do any of the places on your map correspond with this region?" His finger traced toward the east.

Alex wondered if now was a good time to come clean. She'd have to ease into the truth carefully. "I don't think so. You know, we're assuming that one of these villages still remains. Maybe they're all dust and have been for centuries."

"I'm an optimist. What's this writing near the middle? It's in Spanish, but I can't read it."

"I know. I tried, but it's in the crease and so faded I couldn't figure it out."

"What do you make of this?"

He ran his finger over a tiny, faint marking near the blurred words where the folds intersected.

"I thought it was an ink spot."

Quinn rose, entered his tent, and returned with

a magnifying glass. "Let's see if this helps."

Their heads nearly touched as they gazed at the enlarged area. The slightest move by either would bring a pair of lips in contact with the other's cheek. Alex ignored his nearness preferring to concentrate on the map.

"It's an X," she murmured.

"No. It's a small t," he replied.

"No, a cross. Like with a church."

Jorge spoke with Miguel. "Miguel says there was once a village in the area that had a very old church. The village was abandoned and he thinks destroyed many years ago during the troubles. He says the name may have been Santa Maria. He is not sure."

Quinn stared intently through the glass. "This part right here. Could it be an S-A followed by C-A or O-S at the end?"

Alex peered closer. "It's possible. But it's not Santa. There's not enough room for that many letters. It's San something CAS or COS."

"San Marcos!" Miguel said.

"Very possible." Quinn grinned. "Where is it located?"

Jorge asked Miguel who pointed on the modern map to an area northeast of their camp.

"That's about a day to a day and a half from here." He folded the maps and stood. "Let's call it a night. I have a feeling Victoria and Rod won't make the connection."

Miguel spoke once again to Quinn, who relayed to Alex. "He says there is a Mayan village called Sabau about ten miles northwest. He remembers from an old map that it once had a Spanish name— El Popa. It could be the one on your map marked Pop."

"Amazing," Alex remarked.

Tell him now! Her mouth refused to open.

"Is that all the enthusiasm you can muster?"

"Sorry. I'll dance a jig if and when we find this San Marcos or El Popa. I'm going to bed. See you in the morning."

Alex crawled into her sleeping bag. Was one of those ancient villages still around? Certainly none of the experts she consulted believed so. Lord knows, *she'd* never thought they were still inhabited. Could her grandfather have been wrong? Did the treasure exist after all?

If they turned north, she might never catch up to Rod and her map. On the other hand, with their entourage, every village in a fifty-mile radius would know about the crazy Americans and the donkeys. Picking up the trail again might not prove hard.

Alex rolled onto her side, heaving a sigh. She'd meant to tell Quinn the truth, but had chickened out. They were deep in the jungle now. He wouldn't leave her, but why take a chance? Wait until she recovered her property. Maybe that would be best. Tell him the truth *after* she had the map back.

What had sounded so simple in Chicago had now turned complicated.

"Damn," Alex muttered.

****

In his tent, Quinn put the map away, snapped off his flashlight, and settled in for the night. If they could find these villages and talk to the people, they might gain enough ground to get to the treasure first. By swinging north they ran the risk of losing contact with Vicky and her brother. Would it be worth it? Would those two make the San Marcos connection? He hoped not.

"Mom, Gran," he whispered. "We're almost there."

Chapter Eight

The snakes slithered into Alex's tent, their bodies whispering over the nylon floor until the tiny area resembled a squirming sea.

The reptiles encased her like a mummy. Nearing her neck with open mouths, they lowered dripping fangs to her face. A loud, raucous cry from outside halted their progress. They hissed and rattled.

Alex jerked awake, struggling with the folds of her sleeping bag before extricating her arms from the confinement. The angry cry echoed again. It took a moment for her to realize two birds engaged in a territorial dispute overhead.

She sat up, pushed the sleeping bag off, and held her head in her hands, waiting for her heart to quit beating like a jackhammer.

Only a nightmare. Thank God.

It had seemed so real. She'd heard the slithering and felt the drip of venom on her face. She put a hand to her cheek. Sweat—she was drenched in sweat.

Air—I need air.

She crawled to the front flap, unzipped it, and stuck her head out. Alex gulped deep, breaths of refreshing coolness. She had no idea of the time, but the eastern sky showed a faint light.

She flopped back onto her sleeping bag, flung an arm across her eyes, and waited for her nerves to settle.

Whew! That was a bad one.

She rarely had nightmares. Even as a kid, her dreams hadn't taken on scary proportions. Of course, after her encounter with the snake, the subject matter couldn't be called surprising.

Alex drifted off, and next awoke to the sound of someone whistling off-key along with the banging of cooking utensils.

She peeked through the door flap. Dawn had broken and Miguel had the fire lit. Her nose detected the aroma of coffee. Jorge collapsed their tent and packed up. To her left, Quinn did the same.

Time to hit the road.

Alex packed her gear, and then wolfed down breakfast while Quinn studied his map, a scowl marring his handsome face.

"What's wrong? Having second thoughts?"

"Neither of the places we discussed last night is on this modern map. If we detour to investigate, we run the risk of losing contact with Hannibal and company."

"I know. X marks the spot," she offered.

"You've read *Treasure Island* too many times. X never marks the spot. That's pure fiction."

"So, what do we do?"

"Our contact with Rod and Victoria is shaky at best. They're not moving fast and will probably be off course. We have two choices—follow the donkey trail or take a little side trip that could give us an advantage."

"It's your decision," Alex said with a shrug.

"We may lose time initially, but we'll gain it back if we find the villages. Grandpa wouldn't have hesitated. Let's go. We head north."

They hiked east before finding a northward leading trail. A mere two feet wide, the encroaching vegetation frequently blotted out the path. Jorge and Quinn chopped the more persistent foliage with machetes.

Alex welcomed the first rest period. Mindful of her nightmare and yesterday's close encounter, she set her backpack down in the middle of the track and sat on it. Quinn and Jorge did the same, heads down and arms dangling. Sweat dripped from their bodies.

"You guys look beat. Why not let Miguel and I go first? I don't know how to cut this stuff, but it doesn't look like brain surgery. I can handle it."

"A machete is sharp and, even in experienced hands, dangerous. I'm not sure that's a good idea given your track record with weapons."

"Very funny."

"However, since I'll be behind you, I'm willing to take the chance."

Ten minutes later, they set off with Miguel in the lead. Awkward at first, Alex made tentative swipes at the leaves until she gained confidence. She stayed a good ten feet behind the guide guaranteeing she wouldn't accidentally slice off something he needed—like a hand.

Alex quickly realized this had been a bad idea. Her shoulders burned, and her arms felt like lead. To help stay focused on the job, she counted in rhythm to her strokes—slash left, slash right, one, two, and cha-cha-cha. Her feet and body moved unconsciously to the beat in her mind.

"Let me take over. You look like you've had enough," Quinn said.

"I'm all right," she answered, swinging at a leaf.

"You've been at it for a while and gotta be tired. You're not in shape for this."

"I'll do my share, Quinn. I told you I would." Her voice rose, hating the thought he was giving her special privileges from work.

"I'm not suggesting you're a wimp. So, we rest a little early. Who cares?"

"And have you throw this back in my face at a later date? No, thanks. I will *not* slow us down." She swung viciously at a branch and missed.

"Dammit, Alex, be reasonable. I know you're hurting. Your shoulders are on fire and your arms feel numb. It's the perfect setting for an accident and a machete cut will be serious. I'm calling a rest period."

"Quit treating me like an inept, helpless—"

A shout from Miguel cut off her retort. Now that she and Quinn had stopped squabbling, Alex heard the sound of rushing water. She dashed forward.

The trail ended on the bank of a swiftly moving river perhaps fifty yards in width. The boiling torrent tumbled over rocks and boulders creating huge, rolling whitewater. The ground, scoured clean twenty feet in front of them, dropped sharply to the rock-strewn shoreline. She saw no way across, and the wild current made swimming impossible.

Alex stumbled forward, dropping the machete and her backpack, and then slid down the drop-off to kneel by a small eddy pool. Without thinking, she held her breath and plunged her head underwater for a couple of seconds. She repeated the process soaking her shirt. She didn't care. The cool, refreshing water offered an immediate solution to her overheated body and temper. The others had joined her, doing the same.

After a few minutes, Quinn rose, helped her to her feet, and back up the bank where the guides soon joined them.

"So, how do we cross this thing?" she asked.

"There's not likely to be a bridge downstream. The terrain's too flat."

She followed his gaze up and down the river. "What difference would that make? How do you figure there's no bridge?"

"This area's been scrubbed clean by floodwaters. A bridge downstream would wash out on a regular basis. We'll have to go upstream. We should find a bridge up there." He pointed over her shoulder.

Alex turned to locate "up there." Several intimidating hills rose in the distance. Her shoulders slumped in discouragement.

"How far away are they?"

"Three, maybe four miles. Look on the bright side. We'll follow the riverbank until we have to climb and won't argue over the machete."

In spite of dodging rocks, boulders, and other flood debris, the walk along the river proved easy. Gradually, the ground rose. After a couple of hours she once again climbed.

A narrow, steep trail zigzagged up the large hill. Alex crawled the last twenty yards to the top grasping bushes, saplings, and rocks to aid her assent before staggering onto a much wider, but still overgrown path. She stood bent over, hands braced on her knees, panting while the sweat dripped from the tips of her nose and chin.

"You okay?" Quinn asked, also breathing heavily.

"Yeah, fine." She straightened and followed the guides who once again used machetes on the persistent foliage until the bridge appeared like an apparition.

A rope and plank affair, with a large portion of the planks missing, held her spellbound. Closer inspection showed the rope nothing more than a braided twisting of vines and small branches with the bottom and the handrails tied off to trees. Exhibiting no visible means of support, it was an elaborate rope ladder stretched horizontally over a gorge. The river raged some two hundred-fifty feet below.

Alex stared in horror. To her mind, bridges were constructed of steel or wood, but this contraption defied all logic. Then it dawned on her she was expected to *cross* the damned thing.

"You've got to be kidding! There is no way in hell

I'm crossing that!"

"What would you suggest? If you'll notice, it's the only bridge in town. I think we should use it."

"Oh, no. That thing will move or collapse. No, I can't do this!" she cried. Even Jorge and Miguel looked doubtful.

"Sure you can. Jorge will go first with you next, followed by Miguel. I'll bring up the rear."

"No. I'll fall. I won't do it."

"Alex, you are going to cross this bridge if I have to blindfold you and lead you over like a horse. It's only sixty or seventy feet." His face was a mask of determination and her heart sank.

I'll never be able to do this.

Quinn spoke to the guides who nodded and took up their positions. Jorge grasped the braided handrails giving a few experimental tugs before testing the first plank with his foot.

Turning, he said, "It seems solid, *senorita.* Follow me, and we will go slow."

He'd proceeded about fifteen or twenty feet when Alex grabbed the pliant vines. The vibration of movement ran through them, along her arms, and straight through to her feet. Her heart pounded and her stomach clenched. She swallowed.

Oh, God, I swear I'll be good from now on if you'll just help me get across this fucking bridge.

Irreverent or not, and ignoring her unsteady legs, she took one step, and then another, slowly placing one foot in front of the other until pausing at a three foot wide gap. She gripped the rails until her hands ached, stretched her foot out straddling the gulf, and pulled hard with her arms to bring her rear foot over the space.

"Good girl, Alex," Quinn called out from the rear. "You're doing great. Don't look down."

Naturally, she did. The sight of the boiling water so far below accelerated her heartbeat. Little black dots to dance in front of her eyes. Her stomach roiled. She'd have killed to be any place other than on this goddamned bridge.

"I said, don't look down!"

"Shut up!" she hollered, blinking the dots away and focusing on the next plank.

The flimsy structure not only swayed from side to side, but also bounced up and down. Nausea churned and as crazy as it sounded, she recognized seasickness. Taking deep breaths and concentrating fiercely, she staved off total humiliation by not puking her guts out.

Alex approached the end, and then noticed several missing planks. She stood frozen on the lurching monstrosity. No way in hell she could span that space—not with a fifty-pound pack on her back. And she sure as hell had no intention of letting go of the handrails, however fragile. She watched Jorge jump the final four feet onto solid ground in horrified fascination.

The bridge bucked and her hands, already sore from the death grip she had on the twisted vines, squeezed harder. She bit back a scream.

Jorge shed his pack coming to her rescue. He wrapped one arm around the trunk of a small tree growing on the edge of the precipice, and then leaned over with the other outstretched toward her.

"*Senorita*, give me your hand. I will pull as you jump. I will not let you fall. I promise." She reached out a trembling hand and closed her eyes. He clasped her wrist in a firm hold. "*Senorita*, one…two…three!"

She jumped, he pulled, and her body flew through the air. For an instant, she had the horrible sensation she had missed and was falling into the water so far below. Then she landed on solid ground. Her momentum carried her forward staggering and stumbling until she pitched face down in the dirt.

She'd made it.

Alex sat up and jettisoned her pack. Relief at being alive flooded through her, and the nausea receded.

She looked back, watching the others' progression. Miguel had just made his leap and a few seconds later Quinn's long legs easily covered the gap.

He strode over with a cocky grin, took off his pack, and crouched in front of her.

"See? That wasn't so bad, was it?"

Alex stared at him for a moment, then balled up her fist and punched him as hard as she could on the shoulder, knocking him on his ass.

"You son of a bitch!"

In a flash, she leapt on him, pushing him onto his back. With her hand gripping the front of his shirt, she brought her face almost nose to nose with his.

"Don't you ever make me do that again! Do you hear?" she snarled, her index finger poking his chest to emphasize each word. She let him go and sat down. "I have never been so scared in my entire life."

He sat up, rubbing his body where she'd punched and poked. "I'm sorry. There was no other way. You may have been scared, but you came through like a trouper. You done good, kid," he said. He squeezed her arm, stood, and walked over to Jorge and Miguel who hid smiles behind their hands.

Quinn called a lunch break, which gave Alex a chance to regain her composure.

"Do you know where we are?" she asked.

"Believe it or not, I do." He pointed to their location on the map. "We hiked up this hill and must have crossed over at this narrow spot here. The rest of the terrain is flat. Then we start downhill. We'll camp around this area near water tonight. I promise."

"Thank goodness. I need a bath."

"I need a shave. This mess itches." He scratched the growth of two full days on his face, put away the map, and left to talk with the guides.

Alex stared after him. She had been aware of his beard all day. He *looked* like an adventurer. She bet he hadn't known fear crossing that bridge, only a sense of accomplishment at another obstacle cleared. She visualized him as a boy jumping off the roof to see if he could fly like Superman. Quinn got a charge out of danger and action that would send most people running in the opposite direction.

Alex admitted the thrill of facing her greatest fear and winning felt damned good. She had a glimmer of how Quinn must feel and held her head higher.

They made excellent time and Alex appreciated the beauty of the land. Streams tumbled downhill and waterfalls burst out of nowhere to splash and create new streams.

Later in the afternoon they found a perfect campsite in a large clearing beside a river. Upstream a small waterfall cascaded from a narrow, horizontal slit in the rock to splash into a natural pool, which then spilled over to form a stream back to the river. It made a perfect bathtub.

Jorge and Miguel left to bathe and wash clothes while she and Quinn gathered fuel and built a fire pit.

"You sure you're all right? I know you were scared, but I had no choice. It was the only crossing for miles." He scraped out a hollow in the soil.

"I'm okay, but at the time, I was almost paralyzed with fright. I'm sorry I slugged you."

He winced, his hand straying to his shoulder. "I know. I called a halt so you wouldn't pummel me again. You pack quite a punch."

"I kept hoping to recreate *Romancing the Stone*."

"Recreate what?"

She wanted to laugh at his puzzled expression. "*Romancing the Stone*. You know, the movie. Michael Douglas and Kathleen Turner. Treasure maps and buried treasure in South America? You've never seen it?"

"Sorry. The title isn't likely to pull in men. What would you recreate?"

"There's this scene where the bad guys are chasing them and they come to a dilapidated bridge. Kathleen Turner starts to cross when a plank gives way. So, she makes a grab for a vine swinging across the gorge to the other side. When she makes it, Michael Douglas follows and they escape."

Quinn shook his head. "Sorry your fantasy couldn't play out. All that Tarzan stuff—swinging from vine to vine through the jungle is nonsense. Most vines couldn't hold a man's weight. They're often not even attached to anything."

"And another Hollywood fairy tale bites the dust," Alex said with a sigh.

The men returned to consult with Quinn.

"Jorge says the water is a bit cool, but not too bad. He also says the pool is about five feet deep and shelves down rather steeply, so be careful. You can go next. Don't take too long."

More than ready, Alex ran to her tent, grabbed clean clothes, her ditty bag, and then hurried upstream. The first order of business was to wash her filthy clothes. With no thought of modesty, she stripped naked, then scrubbed and rinsed the garments twice before spreading them on the bushes to dry.

She eased into the water, gasping at the chill hitting her warm flesh. The pool measured about fifty feet in diameter, and the waterfall fell from a height of twelve to fifteen feet. The sides of the pool

114

dropped off quickly. One moment she was up to her knees and the next step brought the water level to her hips. Far enough, she decided, proceeding to lather her body and her hair.

Clean at last, Alex pushed off and swam lazily to the center of the pool where she floated on her back in pure bliss. After several minutes, she rolled over and swam to the opposite side. Here, the sides shelved less abruptly. To her left she noticed a path or ledge leading behind the waterfall.

Curious, Alex climbed out and followed the slippery trail. Mist thrown up by the spouting water enveloped her. Tiny, iridescent rainbows shimmered in the sunlight. To her surprise a small gap appeared between the rock face and the torrent allowing her to pass behind the falls.

She discovered a fairyland. The water gushed in a solid, shimmering curtain with the bright sunshine refracting through it. Erosion had carved a cave of sorts behind it, a shallow, scooped out area perhaps ten feet deep. Just enough light filtered into the space permitting vegetation to flourish. Ferns—some large, some small—covered the walls and floor, while a tangle of roots supported the ceiling. A soothing, eerie glow permeated throughout and the thunder of the waterfall blotted out all other sounds.

Alex knelt in Nature's cathedral and leaning forward, spread her fingers in the lush greenery, its texture soft, but springy to the touch. Years of slow growth permitted the fronds to intermingle until the result resembled a living carpet.

She knew the instant Quinn arrived and even though he stood behind her, his mere presence overwhelmed the atmosphere.

Alex turned slowly and sat, allowing her eyes to travel from his bare feet upwards beyond his saturated pants, past his naked chest before gazing into smoldering, unrepentant eyes.

Quinn closed the distance between them in three long strides, and then knelt in front of her. He uttered not a word. His fingers tangled in her hair, and he tilted her head back. His other hand cupped her breast, the thumb circling and rubbing her nipple.

She closed her eyes and shuddered when his lips claimed hers. They sank into the cushioning mat beneath them.

The fire, suppressed for the last few days, burst into flame. Tendrils of heat wrapped around her nerve endings. Her lips parted to admit his tongue while her hands restlessly slid up and down his back, pressing him closer.

She wanted him filling her, pounding in and out until she could stand it no more before erupting in gut-wrenching delight. Her hand caressed his chest before moving on to fondle and stroke the hard bulge in his pants. With unseeing accuracy, her fingers found the fastening. In a matter of seconds, the confining clothing disappeared and he lay naked, half on top of her.

This was not the turbulent, frenzied affair of a few nights ago. This time Quinn took it slow, his lips and teeth toying, playing with her breasts until her ragged breaths turned into whimpers. His hands stroked her thighs, his fingers drawing sensual circles on her skin always advancing until he found her moist heat and plunged in.

Her whimpers escalated into uninhibited cries urging him to wait no longer. He nestled between her thighs. Alex wrapped her legs around his waist and whispered one word, "Please."

He slid into her, hot, hard, and deep. He moved, slowly at first, then faster as the passion built and the urgency changed to frantic need. Sensation after sensation radiated through her like ripples on a pond only to wash back again and again.

The pinpoint of fire grew until no longer containable. She exploded in a climax screaming, "Quinn!" in ecstasy. Seconds later, he followed her over the edge with a cry and a final lunge.

He rolled to the side and lay on his back gasping. Alex sprawled half on top of him sobbing with sweet satisfaction into his neck.

"I said...I couldn't...promise," he said panting, and stroked her damp hair.

"I know." She kissed his shoulder. The afterglow left her drowsy and lethargic. "How did you know where to find me?"

"I was worried. You'd been gone a long time. When I found your clothes, but not you, I thought you'd drowned. So, I stripped off my boots and shirt and dove in calling your name."

"I'm sorry. The waterfall makes so much noise, I didn't hear you."

"I spotted the ledge along with disturbed foliage. I followed it. When I saw you kneeling like a goddess, I couldn't help myself." His arms tightened. "I knew we'd make love again. I watched your rear end sashaying back and forth earlier whenever you swung the machete. You've got a damned cute rear end. It certainly wasn't the smartest thing to think about, but I couldn't keep my mind from wandering to other parts of your body. I didn't come back to earth until a branch smacked me in the face."

She laughed, and then shivered.

"Cold?"

"Hmm, a little."

He kissed her hair and stroked a hand down her wet back. "I guess we should be getting back. I'd like to stay, but Jorge and Miguel might miss us and come looking.

She reluctantly separated from his warmth.

Quinn followed her out of the green grotto, through the pool to the other side where she donned fresh clothing and gathered her washed items from the bushes while he shaved and bathed. Back on the bank and dressed again, he pulled her close, kissing her long and hard. When finished, he smiled, turned, and strode down the path.

Quiet and thoughtful, Alex followed him. This time she experienced no anger.

The rich, earthy smell of the ferns; the sound of the thundering waterfall; the sight of Quinn's naked body silhouetted against the shimmering water; the taste of his skin, and the erotic, unsurpassable feel of him inside her were memories that signaled the beginning and the end, and would linger until her dying day.

Of all the nametags ever applied to her, Alex accepted "realist" as the closest. Oh, she had her moments—look at Rod—but Quinn sent her to heights like no other man on earth, shattering her illusions about what she wanted in life. She had allowed her world to turn upside down and didn't care.

She faced the truth quietly with no bells or whistles, no blinding flashes. She was irrevocably and hopelessly in love with Quinn Rafferty.

Chapter Nine

The northward journey continued the following morning. Alex knew she and Quinn looked normal on the surface, but beneath the external demeanor moved a constant, swift current of awareness. Even when not in her direct line of sight, she detected his presence, as though developing another sense just for him. The air crackled with the electricity thrown off, and only received, by lovers. It prickled along her skin and nerves.

For the first time in her life, Alex abandoned the reins of control along with her rigid standards regarding men. She loved Quinn, which brought a dilemma. How would she tell him the truth now? Had she'd waited too long?

When they stopped to rest, Quinn sent Miguel on ahead to scout for villages. He returned with good news. He found one a few miles away off the main trail.

"He says it's just a few houses, but the people are friendly and excited to see new faces. They may be able to tell us something. We'll see if they can pinpoint any of the ancient places on the map."

The village lay down a narrow, overgrown path. The people apparently eked out an existence by growing maize on two or three acre plots hacked out of the jungle behind their homes. Chickens and the occasional pig roamed the area. Twenty-two people came out to greet and stare, most of them elderly or middle-aged. In thirty years, the jungle would swallow this tiny hamlet.

A village elder welcomed them and invited the

travelers into his home where the rest of the male population joined them. Alex didn't like, but understood the rules and sat on her backpack out of the way, allowing the men to conduct business. Tired and drowsy in the heat, Alex leaned back against the wall where she slipped into a light doze. Quinn shook her awake.

"Sorry. I must have dropped off. Did you learn anything?" she asked, yawning.

"A little." He helped her to her feet and settled the backpack on her shoulders. "I'll tell you in a few minutes. Let's return to the main trail and study the maps. This place is isolated, but I'd rather not advertise our copy."

"Have they seen Rod and Victoria?"

"Not a blond hair. Still, I'd rather error on the side of caution."

After thanking the elders, they returned to the main path where she and Quinn brought out their maps.

"The head man said there are lots of abandoned villages in this area. The men told us their grandfathers spoke of such towns. The grandfathers had been told by their fathers and so on."

"So, information is anecdotal," Alex said.

"One of the men remembered hearing of great riches hidden in a cave near a river. He referred to it as the King's Cave and said it was protected by the sacred hills. Look at your copy. See these three inverted V's? Those could represent mountains. This squiggly Y could be a couple of rivers converging." He showed her with his finger. "The tail of the Y flows into a larger river. The theoretical X is east of that."

"I thought you said X doesn't mark the spot." She loved tweaking his logic. Someday she'd tell him about her year on the Griffith College debate team.

"Don't be so literal."

"Where are these hills and rivers on today's map?"

Quinn frowned. "I'm not sure. There are lots of mountains with rivers south and east of here."

"Which way do we go?"

"One man claimed to have heard a tale about his great-something grandfather who found an ancient city with a guarded cave nearby. What that means, I don't know. The story probably changed throughout the years. Apparently, this great-great was frightened by what he saw and called it a sacred place."

"Caves, mountains, and rivers are all sacred to the Maya. Any idea where this sacred place is located?"

"East of here. The elder said to look for a large boulder to the right of the trail. Behind it are several smaller rocks marking a path that is lined with cut stones—like building blocks. The village is supposed to be down that path. He didn't know how far. He'd never been there."

"It's not the treasure you're seeking, is it?"

"No, the location is too far north. I'm sure of that."

"Then why bother to go?"

"It could be one of the ancient villages and a reference point. We have to check it out."

Folding her map and putting it in her pocket, Alex said, "I guess we'll find out when we get there. What do Jorge and Miguel think?"

"Jorge is skeptical and Miguel says there could be some truth to it."

They stepped off down the trail, all eyes searching for a large boulder. Alex's mind shifted into high gear.

It would be just my luck to find out the treasure is real. I'd be happy for Quinn, of course, but unless Rod and Victoria show up at the same time in the same place, my chances of recovering the map take a serious nosedive.

But if her grandfather was correct and the treasure didn't exist, could she tell Quinn everything and still have his help finding Rod? It was a thought to ponder.

Then, she realized something she should have considered long ago. Quinn believed Victoria a killer. Surely, he wanted to pursue and bring her to justice. For that matter, why weren't the police involved? He'd never mentioned an official investigation. If the dynamic duo were murderers, wouldn't the authorities have kept Quinn updated on their progress? Wouldn't Victoria's name be on a list for border patrol or customs at the airport in Chicago? Why hadn't TSA nabbed them when they left the States?

She'd been so concerned with her agenda and convincing him to take her along she never thought to ask these questions.

Swell time to figure it out. We're in the middle of the damned jungle. I hate it when my logic falls apart.

A sudden shout from Jorge brought her back to the immediate surroundings. He pointed excitedly to the right.

"*Senor* Rafferty, look!"

There, half-embedded in the earth and vegetation, sat a rock no more than two feet high. Behind it, she saw nothing except bushes, trees, and more foliage.

"But that's just one rock and not a very big one at that," Alex commented.

"Keep in mind the story is generations old," Quinn replied. "That's a lot of rain and mud to be washed down even a small hillside. It could be buried."

Miguel apparently thought so, too. While they

talked, he dropped his pack and dug with a small shovel. Fifteen minutes and ten inches of soil later, he struck something solid—another rock. Ten minutes after that, they discovered the third.

"Well, I'll be damned," Alex muttered.

"We found the rocks. Now I wonder where the path is located," Quinn said, scanning the forest.

He and the guides conversed. "Miguel thinks it may lead off this way." He pointed to the east. "The lined path is gone, but we should be able to hack our way through this stuff."

"We could also be hacking our way to Belize," she put forth in an irritated tone.

No more hacking, please.

The guides slashed through the underbrush while she and Quinn followed until coming to an area of less dense vegetation. Jorge and Miguel spoke.

"Miguel thinks this may be the place. It's odd to have an area this large be so open."

"This is open?"

Alex examined the large circular patch and the waist-to-shoulder high bushes covering most of the ground. Trees, twenty to thirty feet high dotted the landscape. She supposed the plot could be manmade and wondered how much more of the area the jungle had obliterated.

"Everybody fan out. Walk slowly. Keep your eyes on the ground. Look for anything that doesn't belong in a jungle," Quinn ordered. "We'll work in a grid pattern."

A line formed with each of them twenty to twenty-five feet apart. Alex had no idea what to look for and concentrated on the ground in front of her, pushing her way through the bushes and tall grass.

"Hey, Quinn. What was the name of the village we just left?" she called.

"The people called it Popasinto, possibly the Pop

123

of your map, maybe the El Popa of the Spanish."

"I thought Sabau was Pop."

"Sabau and that village could be one and the same. Names change, and the village looked to be on its last legs. Maybe Popasinto is a variation of El Popa or Pop."

"So, this could be San Marcos?"

"Miguel said San Marcos was abandoned during the civil war, which would make it only twenty-five or thirty years ago. This area looks much older."

Assuming we find anything to indicate this space was ever inhabited.

So far, all she saw were bushes and thousands of insects, most of which decided to congregate around her head and neck. None landed, but the constant buzzing irritated her. She kept her hands busy waving them away.

Heat and humidity added to her misery quotient. With fewer trees, the sun blazed and sweat rolled down her face and body.

Alex quickened her pace, taking less care where she stepped. The toe of her boot struck something solid and before she could prevent it, she sprawled face down in the tall grass, the fifty-pound backpack pinning her to the ground. The force of the fall drove the air from her lungs. The others shouted and ran toward her while she struggled to breathe.

"Alex, are you all right?" Quinn asked, helping her to sit up.

"Yeah, I think so," she said when finally catching her breath.

"What happened?"

"I tripped over something."

"*Senor* Rafferty, *Senorita* Montgomery, come look at this," Jorge called.

Quinn assisted her to her feet, and they looked where the guide pointed. She gazed at a strip of stone perhaps eighteen inches long, four inches high, and ten inches wide overgrown with grass.

"What is that?" she asked. "A foundation?"

"Maybe," Quinn replied.

The men probed through the grass, pulling and tearing vegetation away. Soon a line of stones six feet long emerged. Miguel dug deeper until coming to the remains of rotting wood. He spoke to Quinn.

"He says he thinks he may have found either a doorway or a window. This isn't a foundation. It's the top of a building. The roof must have caved in years ago."

God, how grandfather would have loved this!

For the first time in days, she felt excited about the expedition. They had discovered the ruins of a village—perhaps the first to see it in centuries.

Quinn already had his map out studying it when she handed hers to him. Quiet for several minutes, he made comparisons. "This must be the village of the old man's story."

"Discovering ancient Mayan ruins is quite an accomplishment."

"*Senorita*, these are not Mayan, but Spanish. Even though the stones are very old, they are not old enough," Jorge informed her. "The Spanish may have built on top of the Maya."

"If the old man was right about the village, he may also have been right about a cave. Let's look over there."

Quinn pointed to a hilly region toward the south. It took them less than thirty minutes to reach their goal and twenty more to discover a tiny ledge leading uphill. It ended at the foot of a rock wall. Quinn scraped the vines and vegetation away to reveal the entrance to a cave.

Shaped like an inverted V, the bottom of the opening was about four feet wide. The fissure narrowed, but still allowed a man to pass through without bending. Eventually, the gap closed to a crack in the rock face. Quinn tore down more of the growth, flicked on his flashlight, and entered. She and the guides followed.

Several things assaulted Alex's senses at the same time. She heard what sounded like the soft fluttering of leaves in a light breeze. In the light of the probing torch, the walls gleamed slick, streaked with damp. Underfoot, the floor of the cave alternately crunched, and then squished as though she walked on eggs. But a horrible smell proved the most prominent perception.

Gagging, she placed her hand over her nose, coughing and gasping. "What the hell is that stench?"

Quinn angled the flashlight down to reveal the cave floor covered in a blotchy brown and white substance. He slowly moved the light upward to the roof and a sea of writhing, furry little bodies.

Alex's scalp prickled and her skin crawled. The hair on her arms rose. A shiver of pure horror washed over her.

This is ten times worse than the snake dream. I'm freaking awake.

"Bats," Quinn said. "We're probably walking on hundreds of years of guano."

"Bats? Oh, shit! We're all going to get rabies or become vampires. Let's get out of here," she pleaded.

She envisioned hundreds of the creatures covering her, much as the snakes of her nightmare, intensifying a spreading sense of panic. The claustrophobic feeling she experienced earlier in the journey returned.

I can't stand this. I can't breathe. I'll suffocate. I have to get out—now!

"It's daylight and bats are nocturnal. Ignore them and they won't bother you."

Quinn continued on, leaving her with no choice except to follow. Alex silently cursed, and glanced overhead, watching for any sudden activity.

They wound their way deeper into the cavern leaving the bats, the mess they created, and most of the smell behind. The odor now consisted of damp earth. Logic told her the cave had been here for hundreds of years and the prospect of it suddenly collapsing on her head slim, but she continued to cast frequent nervous glances at the ceiling anyway.

Rounding a curve, Quinn abruptly stopped. Alex and the guides came abreast of him.

"Dear God Almighty," Alex said in a hushed voice. "It's a burial chamber. An ancient one."

She gaped at the scene. Jorge and Miguel made the sign of the cross while muttering in Spanish. The body was laid out along the back wall of a little cul-de-sac. Dozens of earthen plates and pots surrounded the deceased along with several pieces of jewelry, including a gold and jade necklace, ear ornaments, and a carved ceremonial mask. Mayan glyphs decorated the back wall. All that remained of the physical being were a portion of the pelvis and part of the skull.

"What's the green stone? Jade?" Quinn asked, lowering his voice.

"Yes. The Maya prized jade above all other riches, even gold."

"How long do you suppose he's been here?"

"Long enough for his bones to disintegrate. He was probably king of the village."

"Not a very big send-off," Quinn commented.

"Not a very big village," she countered. "The map doesn't show anything like this, so I have to assume this is not one of the kings of the legend."

"Or else, looters have been here."

"Neither the body nor the artifacts have been disturbed. I'll bet we're the first to view him since he was buried."

"Come on. I feel like an intruder," Quinn said,

turning away, retracing their steps.

Stunned, Alex followed barely noticing the bats. Outside the cave she said, "The old man said the cave was guarded. His ancestor probably meant the bats. No wonder he got scared and took to his heels. God knows I wanted to."

"The Ministry of Culture will want to know of this," a still shaking Jorge said. "Even a small, unimportant village and king is part of our heritage and should be preserved."

"Let's get out of here. Mark the spot on the map so we can report it. We have close to four hours of daylight left. I suggest we head south-southeast. We might find San Marcos," Quinn said.

Alex agreed. The buried village and the cave with its grisly contents—both dead and alive—gave her the shivers. For once she welcomed the heat and humidity.

Jorge set off at a brisk pace, and soon found an established trail. Miguel once again jogged ahead to scout. He returned during a rest break to say a path showing signs of recent travel led off to the east. Quinn made the decision to follow it for a short time to see where it led. After ten minutes, they entered another village. In a scene reminiscent of that morning, the men talked, this time keeping the conversation brief.

"The head man says what's left of San Marcos is less than two hours away. The trail we're on leads right to it," Quinn reported.

Thanking the villagers, the foursome retraced their steps to the main path. Ninety minutes later they stumbled into the ruins of San Marcos.

Most of the buildings of the little town were reduced to rubble with the landscape making steady reclamation progress. Signs of fire showed on many of the stones. The remains of the tiny town depressed her and Alex did not feel compelled to linger. Quinn agreed, and they pushed on.

She had no idea how much time had passed, when Jorge said, "*Senor* Rafferty, do you hear?"

"Yeah, water. Moving water. Like a river."

"My map shows no river," Alex said.

"Neither the river nor San Marcos has anything to do with the legend. Someone used the town as a checkpoint. There are so many streams and rivers in the region they didn't bother to show it. My map shows a river in this general area," Quinn replied. "Doesn't sound too far away. It might make a good place to camp."

They followed the water sounds to the wide, swiftly flowing river. The skeleton of an old iron and wood bridge stood upstream. The spacious, grassy banks proved the perfect place for an overnight stop. While the current was too rapid for actual bathing, Alex knelt by the riverside to wash the grime and repellent off her face. They set up camp halfway between the water and the tree line.

Quinn had dug the fire pit and the fuel in it awaited a match. He looked up and grinned.

"Feel better?"

"I'll say. Where are Jorge and Miguel?"

He pointed downstream with his chin. "Fishing."

"Fishing? You're kidding."

"Nope. Miguel guarantees a much-needed change in diet. He and Jorge have a bet on who catches the most."

Quinn lit the fire when the sun set. The guides returned with grins on their faces and fish on their lines. After so many days of monotonous beans, rice, and tortillas, it tasted delicious.

"So, where do we go from here?" she asked.

"We cross the river and continue on our way south-southeast. Let's see your map."

Alex handed it to him. "Has it escaped your notice that the only bridge in sight is missing about eighty feet of its structure? I don't see any hills to find another."

"We can ford here or near the old span. It's tricky, but not impossible."

"Are you serious? Look at that current. We'll all be killed."

"Have a little faith, would you? I've done this before and lived to tell the tale. Trust me, okay?"

"Do I have a choice?"

"Not really," he said with a grin, and then turned his attention to the map. "I was right. Suppose the village we visited this morning is either Sabau, or Pop on your map. Here is San Marcos. That puts the hills, streams and X definitely down in this region." He pointed with his finger. "Another couple of days of hard hiking and we'll be there. Let's turn in. I want to get across this river and be on our way first thing in the morning."

His eyes blazed with excitement and anticipation. Alex tried to look enthusiastic. She knew he felt the treasure in his hands already, and wondered what his reaction would be when they arrived at their destination.

Do I really need to ask? There'll be hell to pay. And all of it coming down on my head.

Chapter Ten

"Quinn, this looks dangerous," Alex said, concerned as he tied a rope around his chest under his arms. The early morning sunlight danced off the turbulent waters of the river. She worried her lower lip. "The river is narrower by the bridge."

"It's also deeper and the current faster," he replied, wrapping the rope around his body a second time. "I checked it out earlier."

"But wouldn't it be easier to tie off the rope on the bridge pilings?"

"The pilings are close to shore, and the edge shelves off almost immediately into deep water. We'd be swimming most of the way. This is the best place. We can use the trees on both sides as anchors. We'll only have to swim a short distance."

The explanation didn't reassure her, but she had no alternative suggestions.

He pulled the knot tight. "When I'm across, I'll secure the line, come back, and start transporting. The packs are too heavy to take over in one fording. We'll do it in bits and pieces. Don't worry, honey. I'll be fine." He leaned down and gave her a hard kiss. "This is mountain climbing rope. Very strong. We've got two hundred feet of it. That's plenty. Jorge, Miguel, you ready?"

The guides had unloaded the backpacks and now tied the other end of the rope around a tree not far from the river's edge. Nervously, Alex took her place between the two men, slinging the half-inch diameter cord across her back and gripping the rope firmly. Special or not, how could something this

131

small hold Quinn without snapping?

Quinn waded into the river while the three of them inched out the rope. She kept her eyes glued on him as the water covered his ankles, and then his knees. A third of the way over the current increased, the water tumbling faster. At the waist high level, Quinn lost the battle to stay on his feet and swam.

The force of the swiftly moving water carried him downstream, and the rope twanged taut. Maintaining their footing and balance, the guides and Alex let out as much slack as possible. But while the river had Quinn in its grip, he made headway toward the opposite shore.

The rope played out faster. She glanced at the remaining coils, hoping they wouldn't end before he made it across. A shout from Miguel snapped her head around. Quinn had regained a foothold. He staggered like a drunk through the knee-high water. She breathed a sigh of relief.

He waved at them and tied off his end of the rope. The line stretched from shore to shore about three feet above the water.

Miguel rearranged the load in a backpack. He hoisted this along with one tent and sleeping bag onto his shoulders and stepped into the river. He removed his belt, tossed it over the line, then slid the leather strap through a belt loop and refastened it. At knee depth, he grasped the rope, but soon lost his footing. He kicked and pulled himself hand over hand across until he stood on solid ground. On the other side, he and Quinn emptied the pack. Quinn placed it on his shoulders and made his way back to her and Jorge.

"See? Nothing to it. A piece of cake." He grinned while Jorge prepared to cross.

"Yeah, sure." Uncertainty made her stomach churn.

"You'll do fine. Remember the bridge?"

She remembered the bridge all too vividly.

He hauled her into his arms to kiss her. "For luck."

Turning, she watched Jorge's progress as he kicked and pulled. He would soon be onshore.

"All right. How do I do this?" she asked.

"Don't worry about a pack. Take off your belt and use it as a safety line. If you lose your grip, you'll still be attached. Hang onto the rope with both hands and anchor your feet. When you swim, remember to kick hard. Hand over hand, one at a time. Move at your own pace. Okay?"

Alex nodded, took a deep breath, and waded into the water where she looped her belt over the line as Miguel had done before slipping it through her belt loop.

At least this doesn't involve heights. Instead of knocking my brains out in a fall, I'll just drown.

On that cheerful note, she grasped the rope in a death grip and tried to slow her pounding heart by concentrating on the task at hand. The strong current pulled and sucked the mud and gravel of the riverbed from around her feet. Alex securely anchored one foot into the river bottom before moving the other and kept her hands clenched around the rope. She edged sideways, like a crab.

The suddenness with which she lost her footing caused her to cry out. She expected it, but the reality alarmed her. She hung by her hands, the current trailing her body downstream, tugging and pulling on her arms. The safety belt jerked tight. She kicked for all she was worth. It worked. She moved her hands cautiously along the line.

Her arms and shoulders screamed with the strain. Scared, but determined, she made progress. And then her right foot touched bottom followed by her left a second later. The strain lessened, and soon the current subsided to a reasonable flow. Jorge and

Miguel came out to help her. She finally let go of the rope, unfastened her belt, and toppled onto the riverbank, rolling over on her back to drag in huge gulps of air. She hadn't been aware of holding her breath.

Alex rested for a moment, and then got to her feet, shivering. The water, while not cold, wasn't warm either. Reaction set in. She'd crossed a raging river without using a bridge. By focusing on swimming and keeping her hands moving, fear didn't have time to rear its ugly head.

I guess that's how it's done. Another accomplishment. Who'd have thought I could do any of this?

She rubbed her arms vigorously to restore some warmth and looked across the river.

Jorge had just exited the water on his return trip. He donned a backpack and in less than a minute once again clutched the rope and swam. When he reached shore, Miguel took his turn. The routine played out several times reminding her of a tag team wrestling match.

"How much is left?" she asked Jorge.

"Almost a full pack. *Senor* Rafferty will bring it over. He says we are too tired."

"Fully loaded? Why not make two trips?"

"*Senor* Rafferty says we are taking too long. He says he can do it."

"He's always saying that. I don't like it. It's too dangerous."

Jorge shrugged. "He says he is more rested."

Her attention slid back to the far side of the river. Quinn adjusted the backpack. He untied the rope from the tree, and then walked to the river's edge where he hesitated.

Alex understood the problem at a glance. He had more rope on his side than they did on theirs, which meant he would be carried further downstream by the current. Before she voiced her concerns to the guides, Quinn tied it off around his waist and waded in.

"Jorge, there's too much rope. We're going to have to take up the slack," she called out.

The men looked up from the backpacks and ran to help. She threw the line around her shoulders and gripped it tightly. They took up positions in front of her just as the current swept Quinn off his feet. Why on earth hadn't he waited until they were ready?

The rope tightened. Alex dug her heels in and pulled hard. Too late, she realized she anchored this tug of war with nature. It should have been one of the men. If something happened, she'd never have the strength the position demanded.

Quinn swam hard, and while they made progress reeling him in, the current had swept him further downstream. Fully loaded, only his head and the hump of the backpack remained visible above the water.

Jorge, the first man in line, had dug his heels in about a foot away from the drop off into the water. Without warning the ground gave way, pitching him head first down the short embankment onto the gravel at the edge of the river. It happened so fast Alex barely had time to react.

Miguel also fell. Alex was yanked forward to fall on top of Miguel, while the gathered rope ripped back into the water.

Jorge scrambled to his feet, grabbed the line, and screamed in Spanish. Disentangling her body from Miguel's, Alex saw Jorge holding a limp rope and whipped her head around to peer downstream. Quinn had vanished.

Fear and panic lent her feet wings. She pounded down the riverbank dodging rocks and splashing through puddles along the way. Between the heavy boots and the obstacles, she lived that old nightmare of running, but going nowhere. This happened because *she* hadn't carried a backpack across the river. *Quinn* had to do it.

Rounding a bend, she saw him struggling to keep his head above water, tumbling in the current only twenty-five feet from shore and even less from a safe foothold.

Aware of the guides running behind her, she knew that as fast as they moved, the river moved faster. Quinn once again swept around a bend and disappeared from view. A minute later, the three pursuers dashed around the curve. He was nowhere to be seen.

"God, no!" Alex sobbed. Her breath rasped in and out of her lungs.

Her legs tired and slowed. She knew she couldn't go much further. Jorge and Miguel passed her laboring figure. She had almost run out of gas when a shout from up ahead spurred her on.

Jorge waded into the shallows of the river. Bobbing gently, Quinn floated face down in the water.

****

Quinn knew he had a potential problem the instant he saw the extra rope. If he used the excess, the current would pull him further downstream once he started swimming. Tying it off short meant he'd have loose rope trailing behind him to possibly tangle in his legs. He didn't like either option, but he'd rather swim than run the risk of entanglement. He should have tied off more rope on the other side.

Something else I didn't think about.

If worst came to worst, he'd stop swimming and pull himself across hand over hand. The others would take up the slack.

He stepped into the water and waded out. The current pulled him off his feet and within a few seconds the rope snapped tight. On shore Jorge,

Miguel, and Alex appeared ready to drag. Quinn swam.

It took only a few strokes to realize he had a huge problem. He should have secured the lifeline under his arms, but the presence of the large pack made that impossible. He had fastened it around his waist where it now tugged painfully. With over fifty pounds of dead weight on his back he didn't make much headway. He struggled to keep his head above water.

This was a big mistake. I'd better pull.

He reached for the rope. At the same time a sudden jerk on the line damn near cut him in half. He fumbled at his waist trying to relieve the pressure when the constriction abruptly disappeared. He tumbled downstream.

With the rope gone, he shot down the river like a cork. Corks floated. He didn't. The bulky backpack acted like an anchor.

The current swept him on. Quinn swam hard, but knew he was losing the battle. Time after time, he plunged underwater to resurface sputtering and gasping. His legs weighed a ton, and his burning arms flailed. The shore flashed past between dunkings .

He went under again. This time it took longer to come up and when he did, he barely had time to draw in a breath before submerging once more.

He struggled to free himself of the pack, but his arms refused to cooperate. He kicked hard with leaden legs. Opening his eyes, he saw light just above. His lungs screamed for oxygen. He broke the surface and gulped in a combination of air and water. Coughing, he sank again. He had little fight left.

I'm going to drown.

He couldn't believe it. He'd been caught in rip currents and survived. A huge wave had pounded him over and over in Hawaii. He was surprised not to feel fear. Instead, disbelief and an odd sense of anger overwhelmed him.

This can't be happening, dammit! I'm a strong swimmer.

He refused to give up. He *would not* breathe the water. His lungs squeezed, ready to burst, and his vision blurred. Darkness danced in front of his eyes.

I'm not going to make it.

His strength disappeared, and he floundered just inches below the surface of the water.

He always told himself that if death knocked, he'd go quickly with little suffering. But now, faced with that decision, Quinn discovered he couldn't take that last deadly breath.

The light from above dimmed. He thought of Alex. Beautiful, sexy Alex.

Alex, I lov…

His body's desire for oxygen conquered his determination. He breathed water and felt no pain when the blackness overwhelmed him.

****

Alex caught up with the men. They dragged Quinn on shore and fumbled the heavy pack off, then rolled him on his back.

"Oh, God, please tell me he's alive," she begged, panting, her breath rasping in and out.

Jorge laid his head on Quinn's chest and said, "*Si*. His heart beats!"

Alex sank to her knees, her trembling arms clutched across her stomach. The men flipped their boss onto his face and pumped vigorously on his back. Nothing happened. They increased the pressure and the speed. Alex tightened her arms and sobbed.

Come on. Breathe, dammit! Breathe, Quinn!

Time stood suspended during the life and death drama. Not even the usual twittering and cries of the jungle penetrated the aura of timelessness. She closed her eyes and prayed silently, tears rolling down her face.

This is a million times worse than anything I ever imagined. This unknown river in the middle of nowhere is breaking my heart.

A gurgling noise brought her eyes open. Quinn's body convulsed, then convulsed again as he vomited. He struggled to his hands and knees and drew in a deep breath, succumbing to a spasm of hard coughing. That in turn triggered another bout of sickness, and he spewed more water back into the river. Gasping and coughing, he flopped onto his back, sucking in air.

He was alive! Relief rolled through Alex turning her muscles limp and useless. She collapsed on her side.

"Thank you, God," she mumbled. "I owe you one." The retching sounds coming from Quinn were the sweetest she'd ever heard.

Jorge and Miguel helped Quinn sit up. He continued to cough, emptying his lungs of the river water. It took several minutes for his breathing to return to a more normal pace.

"Thanks guys. I thought I was done for," he wheezed.

Alex pushed herself to her feet. "God, I have never been so scared. What happened?"

"Not sure," he said, his voice hoarse. "I had too much rope and tied it in the wrong place. Suddenly the line went tight and came undone. Bad knot, I guess." Using the guides for leverage, he staggered upright. "At least, we're across the river. What happened?"

Alex told him. "Before we could do anything, we lost all the line we'd reeled in. I'm sorry."

"Not your fault." He walked slowly over to his discarded backpack, picked it up and fumbled to place his arms through the straps.

"What are you doing?"

"What's it look like? I'm putting on my backpack."

"Are you nuts? You damned near drowned!"

"I'm all right. We'll rest a few minutes, and then be on our way."

She didn't believe it. Was he serious? He couldn't even breathe normally, and the man wanted to continue the hike?

"Quinn, use your head. You need to rest today."

"We can't waste time just because I had a close call."

"Jorge, talk to him," she implored.

"*Senor,* perhaps it would be better if—"

"No. Fifteen minutes and we're gone. Go get the rest of the gear."

Jorge and Miguel headed upstream to retrieve the remainder of the equipment.

"Be reasonable," she argued. "God only knows what's lurking in that water and you not only swallowed it, you inhaled it, too. It's not safe."

He rounded on her, his jaw clenched in anger and his eyes shooting sparks.

"So what if the water *might* not be safe? If I get sick, what difference does it make if I'm on a riverbank or a trail? I'd still be sick."

His face was set in grim lines of determination to push on, so Alex switched tactics.

"All right, since you refuse to act logically or with any sense, I have a suggestion. We can travel until noon, and then make camp. That way we'll only lose half a day."

She could be stubborn, too. If necessary, she'd nag with every step she took.

"*Only* half a day? Do you think Victoria and Rod are lounging around? Hell, no! They may have an entourage that would turn Elvis green with envy, but they're pressing on. So are we." A cough racked his body.

"Quinn, I know this expedition is important to you, but what happens to your mother and grandmother if you die in this jungle? Rod and Victoria don't know squat about what they're doing. They don't have the guides we do. Please, let's have a short day."

Please say yes. If not, you may not live.

Quinn made the mistake of looking into those soft, pleading emerald eyes.

Hell!

In spite of his desire to continue, he admitted she had a point. His lungs burned like fire and his stomach churned. He knew he'd seriously depleted his energy. By noon, he would feel as though he'd hiked twenty-four hours.

Damn! Dammit all!

He capitulated. "You win. But tomorrow we are up and off before dawn. Is that understood?"

"Yes, I understand. Thank you, Quinn."

Jorge and Miguel returned. He explained the deal to them. The guides nodded, and Quinn listened to Miguel.

"Miguel says there is a village five or six hours from here. It's a little out of our way, but we'll stay there. Okay?" At her nod, he hefted his pack onto his back and said, "Everybody ready? Let's go."

It took an hour for Quinn to realize he should have been less stubborn and given in to Alex. His legs shook with weakness. The backpack dug into his weary shoulders. He couldn't stifle the intermittent coughing. It seized him every few minutes and when the spasms ceased, his lungs burned. Breathing deeply exasperated the problem. He took shallow breaths.

"Are you sure you're up to this?" Alex asked after yet another episode.

"I'm fine. Just a little residual river water. Will you stop worrying? You're hovering and I hate hovering."

Guilt plucked at his conscience.

She's just worried. It's been a long time since anyone other than Mom has voiced concern. Why am I fighting her so hard? Because I'm embarrassed? Me, the adventurer, who damn near died because I got in a hurry and didn't stop to think? I never thought I'd need rescuing.

"I'm sorry, Alex. I didn't mean to snap. I know you were scared. So was I. We'll take breaks every hour. Okay?"

"That sounds like a sensible idea. Just until you're one hundred percent again."

He called a halt and when they resumed hiking, he had to admit he felt stronger. It didn't last long. The coughing concerned him. He hoped it wasn't a symptom of something worse than river water.

His waist where he'd tied the rope, hurt. At the next rest stop, he sneaked behind the bushes to inspect the damage. The skin wasn't broken, but his sides showed signs of bruising. By tomorrow, he'd be multicolored. He bent gingerly from side to side. Pain stabbed, but not enough to slow him down. Still it was a distraction he didn't need.

After lunch Quinn confessed to himself things had deteriorated. His first clue was a lack of appetite. Breakfast had come up with the river water. He should have been starving. He forced himself to eat. Plus, his step had slowed. His muscles ached. That damned cough still plagued him, but at least his lungs no longer burned as badly allowing him to breathe deeper.

He shivered with cold. In the Guatemalan jungle where the heat and humidity numbered the same, he felt cold.

Maybe it's just a delayed reaction.

He hoped that village turned up soon. He also had a headache.

"How much farther is the village?" he asked Jorge.

"Less than an hour, *Senor* Rafferty. There is an open area just south of the church on the outskirts of town. We can camp there."

"Good."

"Are you feeling all right? You look peaked," Alex said.

"I'm fine," Quinn replied. "Just a little tired. You were right. I need to rest. My little swim this morning took a lot out of me."

Keep it light, buddy. Grin and try to keep it in place for the next hour.

He suppressed yet another shiver. Alex shot him a look over her shoulder that showed she didn't believe a word he said.

"You don't feel well. I can tell. Do you have a fever? Your eyes are too bright and your cheeks are flushed."

"I thought you just said I looked peaked. Which is it? Flushed or peaked?"

"Don't make fun of me."

"I have a headache, and as soon as we make camp, I'll take a couple of aspirin. Satisfied?"

A couple? Try half the bottle. Alex is right, dammit. I probably am running a low-grade fever.

He clenched his jaw as another chill swept over him. "That village had better show up soon," he muttered under his breath, and forced himself to keep pace.

Chapter Eleven

Alex was neither fooled nor reassured by Quinn's comments. He didn't look much better than when they pulled him out of the river. She also noticed he ate only a fraction of what he usually wolfed down at lunch. His coughing worried her. It had eased, but the river couldn't have helped.

Lord only knows what kind of organisms live in that water. The possible consequences scared her.

Even though Quinn walked behind her, she was aware of his footsteps slowing. For several days, she'd been listening to firm, confident strides. Now, they plodded and occasionally, stumbled.

He's sick. I know it and what's worse, so does he.

Alex bit her lips. She knew as much about sickness and nursing as she did about hiking and camping. And Quinn didn't look the type to be a model patient.

They entered the village from the west, found the church with a large open field just beyond, and set up camp. Rummaging through her backpack, she found the first aid kit and without hesitation, marched over to Quinn who was arranging his tent.

Opening the kit, Alex extracted a small strip and said, "Sit down before you fall down."

"What's that?"

"I'm going to take your temperature. Now, sit down."

A stubborn expression crossed his face. "How many times do I have to tell you I'm fine? Just tired. I'll take a nap. By dinnertime I'll be normal."

"We can do this my way, or I can have Jorge and

Miguel hold you down. Your call."

"Oh, for Pete's sake," he muttered, complying. "This isn't fair. Of course I'm a little warm. We've been tramping through the jungle. Give me an hour to cool off."

"All right. I'll take that collapsible bucket to the village fountain, fill it, and return. You can wash your hands and face. Then I will take your temperature. I'll be back."

She stomped away, certain his eyes bored into the middle of her back. She didn't care. She grabbed the bucket and headed for the village square.

Technically, this was a small town consisting of more than just mud houses. Besides the church, Alex counted a tavern, a small inn, and shops displaying pottery and colorful weavings.

Quite a few people strolled about. Approaching the fountain, Alex nodded, murmuring, *"Buenos tardes."*

The people replied in kind and smiled. For the first time in a while she saw children playing in the streets. This town didn't appear isolated, and the dirt roads looked in good repair.

Back in camp, someone had pitched her home-away-from-home nearby. She set the bucket in front of Quinn who now lay in his tent. He glared at her, but washed up anyway. When he stripped off his shirt, she noticed the bruises and his shivering. Alex held her tongue. To say anything would cause a ruckus.

When he finished, Quinn flopped back onto his sleeping bag and crossed his arms over his chest looking like a petulant child. She was right—he'd make a lousy patient.

Alex slapped the strip on his forehead and watched the color turn from blue to yellow and finally, to red.

"Congratulations. You have a temperature of a

hundred and two. You also have chills. Cover up and I'll get you some aspirin. Then try to sleep."

He swallowed the pills with almost half a bottle of water. Lying back, he pulled the cover over his chest and said, "You were right. I should have rested."

She lightly brushed her hand over his heated brow. His admission surprised her. Maybe he wouldn't be such a bad patient after all.

Or maybe he's delirious and doesn't know what he's saying.

"Go to sleep. I'll be back in a couple of hours to take your temperature again."

Quinn turned on his side and coughed.

Alex left the tent and sought out Jorge.

"*Senor* Rafferty, he is sick?"

"I'm afraid so."

"*Senor* Rafferty is *muy* strong. Perhaps his sickness will go away after he sleeps."

"Perhaps. His body may be having a reaction to this morning's trouble. In the meantime, is there anything I can do to help you or Miguel?"

"We were going to the village and talk to the people. If you do not mind, we would like to visit the cantina."

"I have no objection. Just please be back in time for dinner. I can't cook, remember?"

After the guides left, Alex tried to keep busy, fiddling with the contents of her backpack and rearranging them. She attempted resting in her tent, but the heat and humidity drove her out. Even though pitched in the shade of the tree line, it would be several hours before the shelters cooled enough for habitation.

Worried about Quinn, she crept into his stifling tent. He slept on his side and continued to shiver. His shallow, rapid breathing concerned her. She resisted the urge to take his temperature. It had only been an hour.

She found Quinn's map and sat under a tree studying it. Alex discovered the name of the town where they camped was Santa Rita. She compared her map to his.

By tracing the route with her finger, she saw a moderately sized town located across the river from X. No more than four or five miles separated them. According to the modern map, a decent road ran through the town, San Luis, from northeast to southwest with a bridge clearly indicated over the larger river to the south. She raked a hand through her hair.

Had Quinn recognized the significance? It wasn't an isolated area. Well, if he didn't now, he certainly would when they got there. Then she'd have a whole butt load of explaining to do, especially with what they'd find at X.

At the end of her two-hour wait she crawled into his tent armed with the temperature strip, aspirin, and water. Quinn now lay on his back, the covers thrown off; his skin hot and dry to the touch.

She placed the strip on his forehead. The colors rapidly progressed through to red stopping at the indicator marked a hundred and two point six. Biting her lip in distress, she couldn't decide what to do. Waking a patient to take medication sounded silly, yet he needed more of it. Would it be safe to take more pills before the allotted time? Could a person OD on aspirin? Maybe the two taken earlier needed more time to work.

The problem solved itself when Quinn opened his eyes. "Will I make it, Nurse Montgomery?" he asked in a weak voice.

"Probably. How do you feel?"

Why do people always ask that? It's a stupid question. He's sick—of course he feels like crap!

"Hot, then cold. At least the coughing has

147

stopped. What's my temperature?"

"About the same. It's too soon for another aspirin, but would you like some water?"

He drank a full bottle and lay down, shivering. "Where are Jorge and Miguel?"

"In town. They deserve a little R and R." She tucked the cover over his quivering body. "Go back to sleep."

His eyes drifted shut and she backed out of the tent. Two more hours, and then more medication. Even if the fever broke in the next hour, he'd be too weak to travel tomorrow.

And no more macho bullshit, either. We stay here until I say we leave.

The guides returned a short time later. "How is *Senor* Rafferty?" Jorge asked.

"About the same. Did you enjoy your time in town?"

"*Si,* we talked to the people and had our beer at the cantina."

"The people seemed very friendly."

"They are, although some of them do not like or trust *norte americanos*, especially the women."

"Why?"

Jorge looked embarrassed. "There have been stories—false stories about foreign women kidnapping Mayan babies to raise as their own. Some of these stories also say the children are killed to provide the...the insides...for others."

"You mean organ donors?" Alex asked, horrified.

"*Si,* but these are...how do you say...not true?"

"Rumors? These are rumors?"

"*Si.* Rumors. Do not worry. We told the people that you and *Senor* Rafferty are married and have many children."

"Goodness. Well, thank you. I think. I was going to get some more water from the town square. Do you think that's okay? I don't want to cause trouble."

"No, *senorita,* it will be fine. This town is not as suspicious as some."

Alex grabbed the bucket and headed for the fountain. The shadows had lengthened and several women were present filling various vessels.

Mindful of this new information, Alex approached cautiously. It would be just her luck to be mistaken for a kidnapper and get stoned to death. To show her non-threatening nature, she nodded and tried to look meek. The women stared back, curiosity in their eyes.

One woman smiled at her tentatively and said, "*Ninos?*"

"Ah...no...no *comprendo,*" she stammered, not sure of the phrase.

The woman made a cradling gesture with her arms rocking them from side to side. "*Ninos?*"

The lady was asking about children. Jorge and Miguel's information traveled fast. Well, if she and Quinn had been designated the parents of non-existent children, she might as well make it good.

Lifting her chin and holding up two fingers, she replied in a proud voice, "*Si, dos ninas.*" She'd even remembered to use the right gender. The women smiled and nodded politely. She now displayed five fingers and said, "*Y cinco ninos!*"

The smiles turned into grins and the nods into applause of approval. She filled her bucket, waved goodbye, and headed back to camp.

Jorge greeted her as she set the bucket by the fire. "Dinner is ready, *senorita.*"

They were back to rice, beans and tortillas, but for once Alex didn't care. Finished, she made a beeline for Quinn's tent. Maybe he'd feel well enough to eat. Dusk had fallen, so she lit one of the flashlights and crawled in.

He still shivered. This time the temperature strip soared into the red immediately to stop at a hundred and three point six. Showing no hesitation, Alex woke him.

"Come on, Quinn. Sit up and take another two aspirins."

"I feel like shit," he mumbled.

"I know. Here," she said, placing two tablets in his hand. "Take these." When he complied, she asked, "Do you want dinner?"

He shook his head. Pouring some water into a bowl, Alex washed his face, chest, and arms.

"Feels good, honey," he murmured.

"I'm glad. Go back to sleep. I'll be nearby if you need anything."

Returning to the campfire she asked the guides, "Is there a doctor in the town? Mr. Rafferty is no better. His fever is rising. I'm worried."

Jorge spoke to Miguel for a few minutes before saying, "Yes. There may be a kind of *padre* who prays and uses local herbs," he explained.

"You mean the priest of the church is a doctor?"

"No, *senorita*. The Mayan often use the *tzahorin*—a Mayan priest."

"You mean like a shaman? He chants and uses home remedies?"

Jorge nodded and shifted his eyes to Quinn's tent and back. "*Si, senorita*. He treats sickness in many ways."

"Well, if modern medicine doesn't work, we'll see if this shaman makes house calls."

Two hours later, Alex sat back on her heels at Quinn's bedside, the first twinges of fear racing through her. The strip in her hand registered a hundred and four point two. Quinn hadn't so much as twitched when she'd pressed it to his forehead.

Coming to a decision, she edged out of the tent and strode over to Jorge and Miguel. She had to do this. She had no choice.

"I think we need help. Mr. Rafferty's fever is

worse. Will this shaman have something to break the fever?"

"*Si*. He often treats fevers." Jorge spoke with Miguel who immediately set off for town. "Miguel will find this man. I will go and get more water. I also have a bucket."

He left carrying both containers. Alone, she listened as her pounding heart drowned out the sounds of the night. Unable to sit, Alex paced in the firelight and ran her hands through her hair repeatedly.

Am I jumping the gun? Quinn is strong and in good shape. He should be able to fight this off. Maybe all he needs is a little help, that's all.

She almost had herself convinced.

Jorge returned with the extra water. "*Senorita* Montgomery, do not worry. Miguel will find the *tzahorin* and he will help."

"I sure hope so." She had no idea what to expect.

Almost an hour passed before Miguel showed up towing a wizened, little man with him. A mass of deep wrinkles lined his face and his white hair, held in place by a headband, hung to his stooped shoulders. She put his age as anywhere between fifty and death.

Several pouches of varying sizes were suspended from a sash around his waist. He carried a box covered with a small rug. More bags dangled from a long, leather thong around his neck. A machete strapped around his waist completed the picture.

Miguel lugged two bricks and a board about three feet long. He laid them down and brought his visitor forward.

The firelight cast the wrinkles in old man's face into black grooves, giving him a vaguely sinister appearance. She'd never seen a doctor like this. Her heart sank. *How on earth can he help?*

Ignoring her, the shaman spoke with Miguel

who translated for Jorge. He in turn told her, "He is asking how *Senor* Rafferty is now, and that we boil a pot of water. Miguel has already told him of the river this morning."

She gave him the pertinent facts to pass on, then filled a small cooking pot and set it on the edge of the fire.

The shaman entered Quinn's tent. He exited a few minutes later to speak with Miguel. Miguel nodded and shot her a rather doubtful glance as he placed the board on the bricks in front of the fire.

Bowing, the man knelt next to it. From one of the pouches he extracted two shallow vessels and set them on the board. Next he took what appeared to be bark chips and dropped them into one bowl. Another pouch produced a substance reminding her of Spanish moss. This went into the other bowl. Using a twig from the fire, he ignited the bark and moss. As the aromatic smoke rose, he placed his hands together and chanted, rocking back and forth.

Alex gazed at his actions with fascination. Of course. The man had assembled an altar, part of this quasi-religious-medical ritual. Whatever worked. She liked to think of herself as open-minded. Maybe a few prayers of her own wouldn't be such a bad idea, either. She knelt on the opposite side of the fire next to Jorge and sat back on her heels. They'd never believe this in Waukegan.

The water bubbled with a slight hiss. Miguel produced a tin cup for the man who filled it with a concoction of dried leaves. Pouring the water over it, he set it on the altar between the two smoking pots. The shaman repeated the chanting and swaying. He then strained the brew into a second cup and carried it into Quinn's tent. When he returned to the fire, he said something to Miguel. Jorge translated.

"He said *Senor* Rafferty drank it all and should be well by daylight."

"You're kidding. That's it? Is he done?"

"Ah, not quite," he replied, an uncomfortable look on his face.

The shaman cleaned his vessels and walked to where he'd left the covered box. Whipping off the rug, he reached inside and hauled out the contents.

Alex's jaw dropped. Turning to Jorge, she said in a rasping whisper, "What the hell is that?"

"Do not be alarmed, *senorita*. It is only a chicken."

"I know it's a chicken. What does it have to do with anything?" Realization dawned, and she inhaled sharply. "No. You've got to be kidding! Please, tell me he's not going to do what I think."

She looked back at the altar just in time to see the machete descending in a blur and strike the board with a loud whack.

Alex clapped a hand over her mouth to muffle a scream. Oh, shit! She leapt to her feet and ran for the bushes where she threw up.

When she returned Jorge apologized. "I'm sorry, but we did not want to tell you before. This ceremony is not unusual. It is part of the culture."

The shaman packed up ready to leave.

"What do we owe him?" she asked in a shaky voice, brushing her hand over her mouth and refusing to look at the scene of the death.

"Miguel gave him rice, beans and a few quetzals."

"Who gets the chicken?" She certainly didn't want it, no matter how monotonous her diet.

"Oh, it is his. He raises them."

Was he joking? Nope, he looked serious. Tomorrow night's dinner, no doubt.

"Well, thank him for the show and everything. If you don't mind, I think I'll turn in. It's been a rather eventful day."

"Of course. I understand. Miguel will see the old

man back to town."

Alex nodded, and then made her way into Quinn's tent where she once again checked his temperature. It had dropped a degree.

Well, I'll be damned.

Turning out the flashlight, she curled up next to him, resting her hand over his heart, the beat strong and steady. His breathing was quiet and normal. She relaxed.

He's going to be all right.

It had been a hell of a day—and night.

She slept soundly, not awakening until the first streaks of dawn feathered the horizon. Sitting up, she lit the flashlight to see how Quinn had fared. He had thrown off the covers and lay on his side facing her. She placed her hand on his forehead. It was cool. The fever had gone.

Chapter Twelve

"What the hell do you mean rest? I had enough rest last night!" Quinn yelled, his face red.

"You had a high fever and any doctor will tell you it's better to give your body a day to readjust," Alex reasoned.

"And which medical school did you attend?"

"It's common sense. What's one more day? We've been pushing hard. All of us could use a little time off."

They had argued like this for over fifteen minutes and Alex refused to budge. If she had to chain him to a stake in the ground, by God, she'd do it.

"May I remind you Victoria and Rod are out there and making time?"

"May I remind *you* Rod and Victoria are carrying a lot of baggage? Plus, I seriously doubt if either one of them has ever heard of the phrase sun-up."

"They're putting daylight between us."

"You said they aren't aware we're following. So, why would they be in such a rush? They're con artists. They can afford to be patient. Isn't that how they play a mark?" Rod invested six months with her to get the map.

"Yeah, and when they smell money, they go for the throat. I'm surprised we don't see their dust on the horizon." He threw things around his tent, a scowl on his face. "Where the hell are my boots?"

Alex knelt on the ground outside the doorway.

"Your boots are in a safe place. I'll return them

155

after you rest." She stared, unflinching from the glare in his eyes.

"Give me back my goddamned boots!"

"No! Not until you promise."

"Quit treating me like a five year old."

"Quit acting like one."

He glared, fists jammed against his hips, and Alex wondered if he contemplated violence. She stood her ground. He suddenly gave in and sat down.

"Did anyone ever tell you that you're a pain in the ass?" he said in a growl.

She shrugged. "Sure. You did. And not too long ago if I remember right. Look, Quinn, if I didn't care about you, I wouldn't be doing this."

He sighed, ran his hand through his hair, and then said, "Where the hell *are* my boots?"

"Don't worry. You'll get them back." She laughed. "In the meantime, why don't you study the maps, read the travel book, or take a nap? We can go into town for lunch. There must be a café. If not, then I'm sure we can get food at the cantina. A beer sounds good."

Alex retired under a tree with her Spanish phrase book and Quinn joined her with his map. They sat in a companionable silence—the kind usually reserved for married couples secure in the presence of their spouses.

What an analogy.

She darted a glance at Quinn. He unfolded the map and concentrated on the route for the next day. He still looked pale, but by tomorrow morning, he'd be back to his old self. She sat back and read.

****

Quinn traced possible trails for the rest of the journey unable to figure out why he'd given in so easily. Maybe because he realized she was right. She'd been right yesterday, showing more sense and better judgment than he. That rankled. He should

156

have known the consequences his wild ride down the river would produce.

He was the one experienced in the jungle. *He* was the one who did the dangerous things. Only this time the danger damn near killed him. For the first time, he stared death in the face, eyeball to eyeball, only winning by the slimmest of margins. The fear came later.

Before yesterday, fear had always been tempered by the thrill, the rush of whatever he'd been doing—skydiving, hang gliding or bungee jumping. There had been no thrill in tumbling down a river and nearly drowning. He recalled the disbelief and anger.

He glanced at Alex.

If I didn't care about you, I wouldn't be doing this.

Her words echoed in his mind. Did she care? Could all this gut-wrenching need, be just the tip of the iceberg? Had something deeper formed? His last thoughts before blacking out had been about Alex. He couldn't remember them exactly, but he was convinced they helped him survive.

He folded the map and stretched. Suppressing a yawn he said, "You know, I think I'll try to catch a few winks. If I'm not awake by lunchtime, roust me out."

"Sure, no problem."

He wandered back to his tent, and lay down. Yawning, Quinn put his drowsiness down to whatever it was he drank last night.

He'd awakened from a dream about water and floating to see an old man bending over him. At first, believing it part of his dream, he closed his eyes only to open them again when the metal rim of a cup pressed against his lips. The man's hypnotic eyes willed him to drink. It tasted awful, bitter and sharp, but he drank without protest, recalling nothing until morning.

Alex must have called in the local doctor. Whatever the old guy gave him sure worked. He may not be one hundred percent, but he was close. Of course, he'd probably fail all drug tests for the next six months.

He yawned again and squirmed until finding a more comfortable spot. Yeah, drugs. No doubt about it. He closed his eyes. When he awoke a few hours later, his boots were next to him.

****

They discovered a small café in town adjacent to the inn. The four of them entered and sat at a table ordering beer and the special of the day—chicken and rice. Alex forced herself to eat. She had a problem dealing with chicken at the moment.

"Tell me about last night. Was I so far gone you needed local help?" Quinn asked.

"Your temperature had risen and aspirin wasn't getting the job done. They were all I had, so I figured a folk remedy couldn't hurt," she replied.

"Whatever that vile tasting stuff was, it worked."

"Hey! I'll have you know a perfectly healthy chicken died last night on your behalf."

Quinn choked on his beer. "What?"

"It's true. Ask Jorge and Miguel."

He roared with laughter when the men finished relating the night's events. "A sacrifice! God, I wish I could have seen it."

"No, you don't. Trust me. I threw up in the bushes."

"*That* would have been worth the price of admission."

"Ha, ha." She lowered her head and pushed a piece of meat around her plate. She loved joking with him.

"Go ahead and eat, Alex. I'm sure it's not *the*

chicken."

She burst out laughing and proceeded to clean her plate, hoping there was a chicken heaven.

"What's next on the agenda?" she asked as they left the café.

"The answer to a very important question," he replied, a serious expression on his face.

"What's that?"

"Where the hell did you hide my boots?"

She laughed again. "On *my* feet. I was afraid you'd notice my size sevens suddenly resembled canoes."

He shook his head. "Ingenious."

"What do we do next?"

"Jorge, Miguel and I are going to talk to people. We might find out more about the five Mayan kings. Want to come?"

"No. I think I'll investigate that pottery shop and the textile place. If there are any more stores in town, I'll find them. When I'm finished, I'll go back to camp."

"Women and shopping. Even in the middle of a Central American jungle, you can find something to buy."

She turned away, then whipped back again as she remembered something.

"Oh, Quinn, by the way, if anybody asks, we are the parents of seven children."

His jaw dropped. "What?"

"Yep—two girls and five boys. Explain it to him Jorge." She left chuckling.

Knowing Quinn would kill her if she bought too much, she narrowed her pottery choices down to a cream pitcher and a candlestick. In the end, she did what any right thinking shopper would do—she bought both.

The pottery shop charmed her, but the textile store swept her away. She wanted everything, but settled on a long, sleeveless tunic called a *huipil*. And how could she resist the skirt with the wide, multicolored sash? Of course, she had to have the hand-embroidered blouse. To leave without it would have been a crime. The real crime turned out to be the price—less than fifty dollars. She walked back to camp telling herself she wasn't a thief.

The three men returned late in the afternoon. While Jorge and Miguel prepared dinner, she asked Quinn, "How do you feel? Are you tired?"

"A bit, but not enough to worry about. I promise we'll take it easy tomorrow. What did you do? I hope I don't have to buy a donkey just to transport your stuff." He sat on the ground beside her and opened a bottle of water.

"Smart ass. I was very restrained. Where did you go?"

"We talked to the locals and asked questions."

"About ancient Mayan villages and kings' treasures?"

"Of course. We told people I was writing a book."

"Did you find out anything?"

"The consensus seems to be that, yes, the villages on your map probably existed and could exist today under different names."

"But we'd already deduced that. I don't suppose they gave us any clues as to where these villages might be today?"

"Unfortunately, no."

"Oh, well, I guess this means we're on the right track."

"I'd say so. I went on to ask about any surviving local legends. One interested me. It had to do with a king who was betrayed by his own people. They sacrificed him in the hope a rival king would spare the village. It didn't work. The village was leveled and the people slaughtered."

"He must have been a lousy king. The Mayan

looked to their kings for guidance and protection, but then *all* legends should be taken with a grain of salt." She wanted to say, "including those about buried treasure," but remained silent, hoping he got her drift. "What made this one so special?"

He unfolded his map to show her. "This town, Santa Rita, is very close to the village on your map called Yaxha. I'm wondering if it *is* Yaxha. It's been here a long time." Excitement glowed in his eyes.

Oh, crap! Another dot connected.

"Is there any evidence of that?" she asked.

"No—just a hunch."

She brought out her map to compare and saw with a sinking heart he could be right. Not even her grandfather had believed any of these places still existed.

"Well, whaddaya know," she murmured. "Did this man have anything else to say?"

"Not much. Then I decided to chat with the town priest. I hit pay dirt. I asked him if he'd ever heard of the legend about the five Mayan kings. I almost fell out of the pew when he said yes."

"It's a well-known tale. Did he shed any light on it?"

"Yes and no. He told me he learned about the legend forty years ago when he came here as a young priest. His version is the same as yours. I asked if the five kings could have come from this area. He said it was possible. The legend is common knowledge among the people. Then he told me something else." He paused and drank from his bottle.

Her heart sped up in anticipation. Had the priest said something about the treasure?

"If you're doing this for effect, it's working. What did he tell you?"

He chuckled, grasped the back of her neck and pulled her forward for a quick kiss, leaving her slightly breathless and her heart beating faster.

"The priest said he found several boxes of ancient church diaries in a storage room in the rear of the vestry a few years ago. Some dated back centuries."

"What did they say?"

"The writing was faded, but he deciphered some of them. In the middle or near the end of the seventeenth century, a band of soldiers came to Santa Rita with a map. They questioned the locals about a vast treasure." He paused to take another drink. "One of the soldiers got drunk and talked too much. They found the map among the effects of their late commanding officer and deserted to find the treasure. The map was old and had no modern names on it."

Alex almost choked. "That's...that's interesting. Where was the treasure located?"

"Southeast of here. Just the direction we're heading. I know we're on the right track. The priest went on to say the soldier told of great riches hidden in a cave and guarded by deadly traps." He finished and sat back, a satisfied smile on his face.

"Sounds like *Raiders of the Lost Ark* to me," she replied.

"Perhaps, but remember the bats?"

She had to lead into this carefully. "You know, Quinn, there's no guarantee we'll find the cave. The entrance may have giant trees blocking it from view or an earthquake could have destroyed it. The jungle may have covered the remains centuries ago. Hell, maybe the soldiers found it."

"It's possible, but we found an old village and a burial cave, didn't we? We can find this, too."

When he gave her a quizzical look, she hastened to explain. "I'm just trying to be logical. I don't want you to get your hopes up only to be disappointed."

"I'm an incurable optimist." He laughed as Jorge

and Miguel joined them with dinner.

"No chicken tonight, *senorita*," Jorge said with a smile. "One of the market stalls had fresh vegetables. It is a feast, no?"

"A feast indeed, Jorge."

They all turned in after dinner. Tomorrow would demand an early start. Barring trouble, Quinn informed them they were only two or three days away from their destination.

****

The foursome skirted the southern edge of Santa Rita as the sun rose. Quinn led, determined to push as hard as possible today. He realized his prediction of a few days ago about finding the treasure was overly optimistic. Even without his accident and the resulting illness, they wouldn't arrive in less than three days.

He planned hiking all day, but he also promised Alex to call frequent rest stops. An hour later, he kept his word. Alex gazed at him, speculation in her eyes. He took a swig from his water bottle.

"I feel great," he answered her unvoiced question. "Almost one hundred percent. By tomorrow morning, yesterday will be a distant memory."

"You look normal, but in no way will yesterday soon be distant in my memory. You gave me a hell of a scare, not just the near-drowning, but the fever too."

"It took guts to call in a shaman, especially considering the chicken's involvement."

Alex rolled her eyes. "Of all the things I ever expected to witness, that was never on the horizon."

He welcomed the rest when they stopped for lunch. Tiredness swept over him and the thought of a short nap should have, but didn't, dismay him.

You're not as close to one hundred percent as you thought, Rafferty.

He ate slowly, hoping to stretch the usual thirty

minutes. It would give his energy a much needed boost.

****

Alex kept a quiet eye on Quinn all morning. While he may have claimed to be normal, she knew he wasn't. As the day progressed, his steps became slower and she noticed his shoulders sagging under the weight of the backpack. At least he kept his promise to rest more often.

She covertly watched him during lunch. He usually consumed his food on the trail with gusto, but now he took smaller bites and chewed longer. His hands trembled and his face had weariness stamped all over it.

He's still dog-tired, but not about to call a halt.

She knew if she requested extra rest or an early camp, he'd bristle like an angry terrier. Alex searched her mind for delaying tactics and finally decided to risk his ire.

"Quinn, do you mind if we take an extra half hour's rest? I'm tired. I know I promised not to slow us up, but I think the last couple of days are catching up to me."

He glanced at her. Did she detect relief in his eyes?

"All right. We've made good time this morning. I guess extra rest won't kill us."

"Thanks," she said stretching out and leaning against her backpack. The fact he'd not snapped at her and agreed to her request proved she was right.

When the allotted time ended, they donned the packs once again taking to the trail. The terrain gradually turned hilly and more rugged, although the climb was not as exhausting as a few days ago.

"Quinn, are we heading back into the mountains?"

"Somewhat. Take a look at the map. X is in the middle of some fair sized hills. The river cuts

164

through a deep gorge. We'll have to detour around them to the west."

"It's a shame we don't have a boat."

"It wouldn't make any difference. The river is too turbulent. X is in a small valley close to the base of the hills."

The oppressive heat and humidity sucked the energy out of her. If she experienced it, logic demanded Quinn with his energy level depleted from illness, was in worse shape. It was on the tip of her tongue to ask for an early rest stop when they suddenly broke out of the jungle, stopping dead in their tracks to stare in surprise.

"What the hell?" she exclaimed looking right, and then left. "What's this?"

She stood on the edge of a huge clearing hacked out of the forest. The level ground stretched for over half a mile from north to south, its width almost a hundred yards.

"It's an airstrip," Quinn explained.

"An airstrip? Out here? In the middle of the jungle?"

Miguel spoke, his finger pointing to the clearing. On the opposite side of the grassy runway she saw a large lump covered by a camouflage tarp.

They trotted across the open area. Jorge and Miguel pulled the covering aside to reveal stacks of tightly wrapped, plastic sheathed bricks, some of the packages marked with a big black X. The guides immediately swung around to eye the tree line.

"Oh, Jesus. We got big trouble," Quinn said.

"Is this what I think it is?" she asked, her voice shaking.

"Yeah. Drugs. And they haven't been here all that long. It's waiting for transport to Mexico or the U. S."

"What are the x's for?"

"To distinguish marijuana from cocaine."

"And they just left it here?"

"No." He helped Jorge and Miguel recover the pile of contraband. "We gotta get out of here. Now!"

"You mean drug dealers are nearby?" Her head swiveled from side to side. For the first time she'd seen fear on his face, which sent a jolt of fear rushing through her and sending her heart into overdrive.

"Hell, yes. Would you leave a stash worth millions out in the open and unprotected?"

Before she could answer they heard the faint droning of approaching aircraft.

"Run!" Quinn yelled, pointing to the tree line some fifty yards away.

They dashed for the protective cover of the jungle, Quinn grasping her hand to help her along. The backpack weighed a ton, slowing her down. In her fear-laden haste, it seemed she tripped over every rock and pebble.

Drug dealers? Smugglers? And now an airplane? She wanted to believe it was just an innocent flight from point A to point B flying overhead. Reality told her otherwise.

This has to be a bad dream.

The group made the shelter of the trees just in time. The plane's engines growled louder, and another sound added to the urgency. Four jeeps filled with men erupted out of the far side of the forest.

"Quick, hide!" Quinn hissed. They jumped into the thickest overhanging vegetation available.

Alex trembled and her heart threatened to pound clean out of her chest. Quinn lay beside her, clenching her hand in a paralyzing grip. She had no idea where Jorge and Miguel hid.

"Don't move. Don't make a sound."

Like she had any other plans. His presence helped steady her. She lifted her head to peek through the foliage. The roar of the aircraft's motors indicated an imminent landing. They hid no more than fifty feet into the trees with a good view through the leaves and brush.

The jeeps ringed the perimeter and deployed men to stand guard. To her horror one of the vehicles stopped a mere thirty yards beyond their hiding place. The drug runners, carrying automatic weapons, checked about twenty feet into the underbrush before returning to the clearing.

She felt faint and sick to her stomach with a sour taste rising to her mouth, but could not tear her eyes away from the scene in front of her.

Oh, God, please don't let me puke now.

The guards paced back and forth conversing and smoking cigarettes while the plane swooped in over the trees at the southern end of the runway. The pilot landed and taxied over the bumpy ground to the covered mound where he cut one of his engines.

It was an old-fashioned plane with two propeller motors and the third wheel, located beneath the tail section rather than under the nose, gave the plane a tail to cockpit incline. She'd seen planes like this in old movies, but had no idea they still existed.

It sported a dull gray paint job without a single marking on it, not even identification numbers. This aircraft never landed at legitimate airports.

A man on the ground pounded on the door and a few seconds later it opened. The two men talked briefly, then at a signal from the leader, several of the nearby guards, including one of the men in front of them, hurried to the pile of drugs. Ripping off the tarp, they formed a line and passed the bricks into the plane.

Come on, come on. Load the damned stuff and get the hell out of here.

She turned her head to sneak a peek at Quinn. He also watched the smugglers with an intense look.

167

He turned his head, smiled, and then put his finger to his lips indicating the need for silence. She nodded. She had no intention of saying a word. Turning her attention back to the airstrip, she drew in a deep breath to steady her nerves. It was a big mistake.

They had taken refuge in a thicket of bushes with several small trees whose low branches helped provide a canopy of safety from casual scrutiny. Their bodies lay clamped to the ground, a combination of dirt, grass, ferns and dead vegetation. It smelled of damp soil and mold.

The faint tickling in her nose gave her the first indication of what was about to happen.

No, you've got to be kidding me! This only happens in bad movies.

The tickle increased. She pinched her nose with her fingers, breathing through her mouth to stem the tide. It didn't work. The sensation built until it could no longer be contained.

She sneezed.

Quinn looked at her with a combination of disbelief and horror in his eyes. All she could do was stare back at him. Her heart lurched and pounded in her chest. Tremors rippled through her tightening muscles. Then, a twig snapping from in front of them whipped both of their heads around.

The guard, his eyes narrowed into suspicious slits, scanned the forest. He walked toward them slowly, a cigarette dangling from his lips, and his machine gun at the ready. He paced up and down in front of their position, stopping to listen. Jungle noises that had stopped, resumed.

The man hesitated and threw a glance over his shoulder toward the plane. He advanced into the trees using the barrel of his gun to poke and lift the foliage.

Alex bit her lips so hard she tasted blood and

prayed. Perhaps the noise of the engine still engaged had masked the sneeze making the guard unsure if he'd heard anything. He advanced further toward their hiding place.

Quinn's hand clenched around the hilt of his machete and his muscles tensed. She buried her face in the crook of her arm, not wanting to see death coming. She didn't want to look down the barrel of a gun. And she most definitely didn't want to watch bullets slam into Quinn's body.

She waited an eternity. The footsteps stopped, and the guard uttered a rough exclamation. A rasping sound from her right brought her head up. The man stood ten feet away. If he turned his head four inches to the right, he'd be able to see them through a gap in the leaves. She fought to stop from rising and running into the forest, screaming.

Then another sound reached her ears. He was taking a leak. She didn't know whether to laugh or cry.

A shout from the clearing swiveled his head in the opposite direction. He finished his task and retraced his steps. Relief flooded through her, and she dared a quick glance at Quinn. He also relaxed.

The engine re-firing brought her attention back to the field. The loading was complete and the door slammed shut. The entire operation took no more than fifteen minutes, but to Alex it lasted forever.

The pilot taxied to the end of the runway, revved his engines, and then lumbered down the grassy strip. The plane rose, cleared the trees, and rapidly gained altitude until it disappeared.

The man in charge shouted. The guards returned to their jeeps. The sentry in front of them paused, walking toward the tree line for one last look. Alex closed her eyes. A shudder shook her. For a moment, he had looked directly at her. When she opened them again, he was heading back to the jeep.

He jumped in, turned the key, and followed the others to the far side of the field. Within seconds the jungle had swallowed all four vehicles.

Quinn moved first and pulled her to her feet. "I don't believe you did that!"

"I don't either. I was beyond fear."

Jorge and Miguel emerged from their hiding places thirty feet behind them and spoke with Quinn.

"What do we do now?" she asked, still trembling.

"Jorge?" he asked.

"If the guard says he thought he heard something, they will come back." The guide wiped the sweat from his face with a shaking hand.

"That settles it. We get the hell out. We'll go due east for the rest of the day. Tomorrow we turn south. But right now, we double time it out of here."

Urgency mingled with fear in his face and heard it in his voice.

"Hurry!"

Chapter Thirteen

Alex and the men jogged through the wilderness, following no set trail. They forged due east, roots tripping them and bushes grabbing at their legs. Quinn refused to use machetes. If the drug dealers returned, the cuts would have the same effect as a beacon on a lighthouse. The foliage slapped at her face, stinging and scratching.

Alex shielded her face the best she could and hoped the moisture trickling down her cheek was sweat, not blood. She had no idea how much time passed since racing from the clearing. Her legs were heavy as lead, her feet hurt, and she doubted she could go much further. Quinn finally called a halt to the headlong dash. She panted like a long distance runner.

Sinking to her knees, she said, gasping, "How...how far...have we...come?"

Sweat dripped from Quinn's face. "I'd say three, maybe four miles."

"Can't...can't we slow down?"

"I don't know. Jorge, will they come after us?"

"It is hard...to say," he huffed. The guide gulped in air and straightened. "It is only a couple of hours before dark. They would not follow us in the night. Any trail we leave will be gone by morning. I also do not think the soldier will tell. They are celebrating. They will soon be drunk. We should be safe."

"Soldier?" Alex asked.

"A third of those men were dressed in fatigues and they drove jeeps. If they aren't soldiers now, they were at some time." Quinn brushed the moisture from his face and wiped his hand on his pants.

"Guatemalan soldiers are running drugs?"

"The military is not immune to corruption. Smuggling and drug dealing helps augment a pitiful salary."

Now able to breathe, she drained a water bottle and then said, "Are we far enough away?"

"Yeah, I think so. We'll rest fifteen minutes, and then continue until dark."

"How many men were there?"

"About twenty. I doubt if their camp is inhabited by that many men on a regular basis. It's there to maintain and keep an eye on the airstrip."

They shoved off at a more reasonable pace through the jungle, though Quinn still refused to use the machetes.

Alex breathed a sigh of relief. At least they no longer charged like bull elephants and this day would end soon. She had never been so tired or drained in her entire life. She wanted to lie down in the middle of the trail and not get up, but the thought of smugglers lurking in the underbrush kept her going.

When she told Quinn she was beyond fear, it had been the God's honest truth. At any moment, she expected to be discovered.

Do you hear the shot that kills you? Doesn't a bullet travel faster than the speed of sound?

She swallowed the lump in her throat. She had an inexplicable urge to sit down and bawl like a frightened child.

They staggered into the remains of a village as dusk fell. Rubble tumbled everywhere with the jungle reclaiming much of it.

"Not much left, is there?" she murmured.

"A casualty of the civil war," Quinn remarked. Jorge and Miguel left to scout the area. "What the army or the rebels didn't destroy, Mother Nature is taking back."

"Do you think the guys will find anything intact?"

"Naw, this place has been worked over pretty good."

The guides agreed with the assessment when they returned a few minutes later. "None of the buildings have a roof, *Senor,*" Jorge reported.

"What do we do now?" she asked.

"*Senor*, Miguel and I found clear space behind some of the houses. We could set up camp there."

She followed Quinn and the men to the site. Quinn's steps were heavy and exhaustion etched his face. She worried he still harbored remnants of his river tumble.

"We'll put two of the tents close to the tree line. If we have to flee in the middle of the night, we can get to cover quickly. And no fire. We eat cold food."

"Do you think we're still in danger?" she asked, looking around at the destruction and darkening forest. She broke out in goose bumps. The place gave her the creeps. It was like camping out in a graveyard.

"I don't know, but I'm taking no chances." While Jorge and Miguel set up their tent, he added, "Alex, tonight we share a tent."

"Why?" Her nerves hummed.

"If we have to run, I want to salvage one tent."

"And do you envision all four of us sleeping in it?"

"Don't be sarcastic. You'd sleep in it."

"I take it we leave the backpacks behind if that situation arises."

He shot her an irritated look. "Our lives are more important."

His glance told her he hadn't thought about the packs. He was making it up as he went along.

"I think you're freaking paranoid. I want my tent."

Her mind conjured up what could happen in the cramped confines of a tent—all of it pleasant. And all of it coming under the banner of bad timing.

"There's not enough room to pitch three tents."

"Quinn, this is *not* a good idea."

"I know, but we're too close to the trees for anyone to sleep out in the open. Too many wild things. We'll sleep in our clothes. That should help."

The humming changed into a tingle. Damn! Did he really think they would *sleep*? Even if they managed to exercise restraint, there was no way she'd drift off into dreamland. Not with all this tingling and awareness. She bowed to the inevitable, whichever way it went.

"All right," she said against her better judgment.

She knew this was not going to work. A part of her was glad.

****

Quinn breathed a sigh of relief. She was right about the tent, of course. And she wasn't likely to be happy with the sleeping arrangements either. The thought of laying that close to her sent his body into red alert. No way would he sleep.

"Look through our backpacks and get out tortillas, bean paste and some fruit. I'll set up the tent."

"We never seem to run out of tortillas. What do they do, multiply at night?"

"Miguel's aunt gave us a whole bunch of the things. She apparently made up a huge batch in honor of our stay."

While he assembled the tent, Alex gathered the food. He handed the extra tent to her. "Put this behind our tent while I arrange the inside."

She ducked around to the back. The darkness had deepened. They should be safe tonight. If he didn't know the tents were there, he'd have never seen them. His anxiety regarding their safety lifted. Other anxieties increased.

Shoving the bulky packs to the rear of the tent, he unrolled her sleeping bag, and then laughed before re-rolling it. He was calmly eating a tortilla by flashlight when Alex returned, crawled in, and stopped dead.

Staring at him, she commented, "*One* sleeping bag?"

He swallowed, took a gulp of water and replied, "There's no room. Besides, you have all that damned pottery stuffed in yours."

"Forget the pottery. This isn't going to work."

"It's the best we can do. Nothing is going to happen. When you're finished eating, we'll call it a night." He wondered if he could keep his word.

"Isn't a light dangerous?" she asked, pointing to the source of illumination. "I thought that's why you didn't want a fire."

"This can be extinguished in a second, a fire can't. Eat up. I'll be back in a few minutes. When you're done, stretch out next to the packs. I'll sleep in front in case we have trouble."

Her gaze shifted to the rear of the tent. "No way. Where would I go while you're slaying the dragons? There's no back door."

He detected the uneasiness in her voice. "I thought I'd be protecting you."

"Quinn, I don't like being closed in."

"Are you claustrophobic?"

"I never thought so until this trip. The Bat Cave had me fearing the roof would collapse at any second. I've always had a thing about heights. That's why that damned bridge almost did me in. This trapped feeling is new."

"Does it bother you to be in your tent?"

"No. I can unzip the flap and see out. The only

night I didn't open it, I had a nightmare about snakes. You don't seem to be afraid of much."

Just death.

"I guess I've been lucky." He shrugged, not meeting her gaze.

"Your heart must have gone pitty-pat when I sneezed."

"Try slamming out of my chest. Now, *that* was fear."

"Yet I noticed your hand on the machete. Would you have really used it?"

"That was the idea. I knew if he got close enough, he'd see us. I planned to kill him before he could get a shot off or yell, grab his gun, and run like hell."

"Boy, are you ever an optimist." She paused for a second, hunching her shoulders and raising an eyebrow. "I guess it could have worked. The element of surprise may have made a difference."

"Luckily, we'll never know. Okay, you sleep in front. I'm going to take a look outside." He exited the tent and walked around the clearing, returning in less than two minutes. He crawled over her, made himself comfortable, and then noticed she had unlaced her boots.

"No, leave them," he said.

"I can't sleep in these things."

"Want to be in your stocking feet if we have to make a run for it? It's safer this way." He did not necessarily refer to the drug runners.

"I still think you're paranoid," she grumbled.

He extinguished the light.

****

Alex mulled over the best way to deal with the situation. Lying on her side, her back toward him seemed the most sensible approach. She gulped, took a deep breath and attempted to settle in. He must have had the same idea for he also rolled over to face away from her.

Okay, Alex, you can do this.

She tried to ignore the heat of Quinn's body burning from her shoulders to butt.

Pretend you're in front of a fireplace and he's the fire. No! Bad analogy. Try something else.

She invited nightmares by concentrating on the events of the day. Drug runners and smugglers. She couldn't believe it. Back in Waukegan this entire trip sounded plausible, easy. Follow Rod and Victoria and get her map back. Yeah, right. Who knew?

Quinn squirmed a little, rubbing against her. Heat flared throughout her body. She eased away, putting distance between them.

Now, where was I? Oh, yeah, drug runners.

She was certain they'd all bought the farm after the sneeze. She had never been so glad to hear the call of nature answered in her life.

A blast of heat seared her back as Quinn closed the gap.

Damn! It just figures he'd be a bed hog. If I move any farther away, I'll be outside the tent.

His even breathing told her he was either asleep or the coolest customer she ever encountered. Both pissed her off. She wanted to kick him. It wasn't fair for him to drop off in a few minutes while she couldn't keep her mind off of his body heat.

Close your eyes. Close your eyes and remember Barbados. Remember the heat of the sun on the beach and laying there soaking up rays.

She *would* ignore these damned tingles and his hotter than hot body. She concentrated hard on the beach fantasy. Much to her surprise and relief, it worked.

****

The rumble of not so distant thunder brought Alex partially out of her slumber. A brilliant flash of lightning followed by another reverberating boom, jerked her into full consciousness. She still lay on her side, as did Quinn, only now he faced her, their bodies spooned while his hand spanned her stomach to keep her close. She didn't bother with humming and tingling this time. She soared straight into lust. How could she not with what pressed against her derriere?

Another flash and peal made her jump. The light show outside couldn't compete with her internal fireworks. He didn't move, but her heart thudded and a deep fire burned, turning her nerves into highways for the spreading heat. Maybe if she shifted a little the pressure of his...well, the pressure would ease. She tried to wiggle forward.

"Stop squirming," he whispered in her ear.

"Oh, you're awake—in more ways than one."

"Can't help it. I'm a man."

This time the lightning sizzled and the thunder cracked almost directly overhead. The first raindrops splattered on the tent. She jumped in reaction.

"Don't tell me you're afraid of storms, too."

"No. But I've never seen one so up close and personal before."

Why couldn't her body behave? Tremors rippled outward from within. They would soon reach the surface visible for Quinn to see and feel. The rain increased in tempo until it hurtled down in a deafening torrent.

Quinn propped himself up on his elbow, leaning across her to zip up the door covering. For reasons unknown, she twisted onto her back. He laid half on top of her.

Another flash from outside illuminated his face, showing a harsh contrast between light and shadow. His eyes glowed with the ferocity of a wild thing. Such a look should have scared her to death. Now, it added fuel to her already uncontrollable fire.

"Alex," he groaned.

"I know," she whispered, tangling her hands in his hair, and pulling his lips to hers.

Alex wasn't sure how they accomplished the feat, but somehow they flung their shirts aside. She kissed and caressed his chest. His hands stroked her breasts. When his mouth finally covered the sensitive tip, she moaned and trembled.

The storm reached its zenith. The flashes resembled strobe lights and thunder roared uninterrupted. The rain slashed down with an explosion of its own. She only heard the pounding of her heart.

Frantic fingers tugged at the fastening of his pants until it finally gave way, and she reached inside. This was what she wanted. She squeezed and stroked. He groaned deep in his chest, the sound rumbling louder than the thunder outside. He was hot, throbbing, and oh God, how she craved him. He was her drug of choice.

His hands strayed to her waist. Like a magician, he soon had her trousers undone, stripping them and her panties down her legs. Her boots stopped the garments forcing them to bunch around her ankles. The fire grew. From head to toe, she burned.

Alex parted her legs and raised her knees as he nestled between them.

"God, Alex, I want you."

His mouth covered hers. Then he slid into her steamy heat.

He moved with deep, plunging strokes. She made passionate, demanding sounds into his mouth. His tongue thrust and retrobed, mimicking his other actions.

She lifted her hips to take his lunging drives deeper.

Harder. Faster. More.

The disjointed thoughts rattled around her

mind, repeating themselves over and over. She couldn't get enough. She wanted, needed more.

Oh, God! Don't let this end.

But at the same time, she demanded a finish—a culmination of the pleasure rippling through her. Tightening her thighs on his, she abandoned all pretense of prolonging things and matched his frenzied pace.

She climaxed, her hips bucking, while he swallowed her scream of ecstasy. Quinn released with a hoarse shout into her mouth and took one final deep plunge at the same time.

Quinn collapsed on top of her and buried his face in her neck. He trembled, murmuring her name.

She hugged him, floating down from the heights of passion. The thunder was reduced to a distant rumble with only an occasional flash of lightning. The rain, however, continued to sluice down in buckets.

Propping himself up on his elbows, he kissed her forehead. "God, lady, you are something else."

"You're not so bad yourself," she replied, running her fingers through his hair.

He rolled to the side and they struggled in the close confines of the tent to dress. Finally re-attired, they lay down, snuggling in satiated bliss.

Unbidden, visions of little Quinns flashed through her mind. That silly story about the seven children didn't seem so foolish now. In fact, all those kids sounded like fun. They'd probably be organized adventurers. She wanted to laugh at the thought. Then another thought sobered her.

"Oh, God, Quinn. Do you suppose Jorge and Miguel heard us? They're only three feet away," she asked, both horrified and embarrassed.

"With the noise of that storm? No. I doubt if they heard anything over the roar of the thunder and rain." He yawned.

She rolled over and nestled back into him. He reached across to hug her closer.

"Go back to sleep, honey," he murmured drowsily. His even breathing a few seconds later told her he'd slipped into sleep.

Typical male. The words were not thought with exasperation or annoyance, but affection.

****

Movement from Quinn woke her the next morning as he fumbled in the backpacks.

"Hmm, good morning," she purred sleepily, running her hand up and down his broad back.

He turned and smiled. "Good morning. Did you sleep well?"

"Sure did. There's something about rain on the roof and a warm bed that puts me right out—not to mention great sex." She puckered her lips and blew him a kiss.

He laughed. "Shame I can't guarantee more sack time."

Fully awake now, she sat up, wondering if he meant sleep or sex. The rain had not abated from the night before. It drummed on the roof of the tent.

"It's raining."

"Brilliant observation," he said, digging deeper into his pack.

"What are you looking for?"

"Our ponchos."

"Ponchos? You mean we're going on? In this?"

"Of course. We lost a day and a half with my river adventure and illness, and more time with yesterday's close shave." He found the items and tossed one into her lap. "Here. It'll be hot, but that can't be helped."

"But, it's pouring!" She came close to wailing.

"It sure is."

"Why can't we wait until it lets up?"

"Because there's no guarantee it will. The rainy

season is about to start. This is just a prelude. I'd like to find the treasure before this becomes a daily occurrence."

He slipped the poncho over his head and crawled out of the tent. A few seconds later, she heard him talking to Jorge and Miguel.

She sat in the tiny space staring at the steady rain, despondent and dismayed. Hike in this? Breakfast shaped up to be cold tortillas and bananas—again. She wouldn't even get a cup of *hot* coffee. Sighing heavily and giving in to the situation, she pulled on the poncho, slapped her hat on her head, and crawled out.

Thirty minutes later, Quinn helped her cope with the backpack, tent, sleeping bag, and poncho. She stood in a cascading downpour. He arranged everything, and then stepped back to inspect it. She resisted the urge to salute. The rain hadn't let up one iota.

"I guess you'll do. If you want extra protection, there's a hood zipped into the poncho collar. I prefer just my hat. The hood restricts movement. It's your choice."

Like she could get to the collar. With all the gear piled on her shoulders and covered with this silly cape, she resembled a close relative of the Hunchback of Notre Dame. All she needed was the bell tower.

Call me Quasimodo.

"Be careful walking. This mud is damned slippery." He looked around. "We'll head east, and then turn south. The smugglers won't bother us now."

Quinn led them in an easterly direction for over an hour before discovering a trail heading south. Alex wrinkled her nose. With the heat and the humidity, even a dry jungle emitted an odor of decay, but in the rain those smells magnified. There was nothing clean and fresh about this rain. The jungle stank.

Quinn had been right about the footing, too. She tried to keep her balance slaloming along the path, and then pulling her feet out of the muck. The mud had a sticky, glue-like consistency. Every time she lifted her foot it was accompanied by a loud sucking noise that sounded vaguely indecent and embarrassing.

The rain continued. The poncho may have kept most of the water off of her, but underneath it she sweated like a horse. She was hot, tired, and miserable when Quinn finally called for a mid-morning break.

"How ya doin', Alex? Holding up all right?" he asked sitting on a fallen log beside the path.

"Oh, yeah. Just peachy."

He grinned. "Hey, buck up. So, you're a little wet? It's part of the adventure."

"I'm having the time of my life."

"Never let it be said I don't know how to show a lady a good time."

She recognized the line from *Raiders of the Lost Ark*. She'd bet Quinn had seen it a hundred times.

When the fifteen-minute rest ended, she flirted with the idea of refusing to move until the rain stopped, but dismissed it. Knowing Quinn, he'd just shrug and leave her behind. Mutiny would get her nowhere. She trudged on.

They ate a cold, unappetizing, short lunch. Even though the rain had ceased, moisture still hung in the air as a mist, and the trees dripped water creating their own mini-shower.

The footing remained bad and trying to avoid the morass in the center of the trail, she moved a few feet away toward the side where leaves and grass provided what she thought would be a firmer foundation.

"*Senorita*! No!" Jorge shouted from behind her.

His warning came a fraction of a second too late. The ground suddenly gave way beneath her feet. Alex uttered a startled cry. She landed with a thump on the seat of her pants, the jolt traveling up her spine to her head, and then proceeded to slide backwards down the hillside. She glanced off a small tree and yelped as pain slashed through her shoulder, then flipped onto her stomach, her face plowing through the mud. Instinct kept her mouth shut and she held her breath. Another bump rolled her back over, her hip stinging from contact with a rock. She continued to tumble and skid, not stopping until the ground leveled out.

She sat up to catch her breath and wipe the mud out of her eyes. The hill she plummeted down was not steep or long. She was less than a hundred feet from where she started. The men scrambled down the slope using trees and bushes for support.

"Are you all right?" Quinn cried when he reached the foot of the hill, his expression a mixture of fear and relief.

"I think so. What the hell happened?"

"I tried to warn you, but I was too late," Jorge said. He and Miguel helped her to her feet. "The trail is near the edge of the hill. The rain made the ground not strong. When you step there, it fall."

Quinn picked up her hat. "Are you sure you're okay?"

"Yeah, I'm fine. Just a little—"

His lips twitched. A second later, he laughed.

"What's so damned funny?"

"You are! You should see yourself."

She put a hand to her cheek and discovered she was literally covered with mud from head to toe.

"Dammit! Quit laughing!"

He ignored her. Her dignity had taken a direct hit and now he had the audacity to laugh at her? He stood fifteen feet away. Retaliation sounded like a great idea. She bent, grabbed a handful of the gooey mess, and threw it. The missile fell in front of him. She scooped up another glob taking another crack at him. This one landed on the toe of his boot. He laughed harder, further enraging her.

Okay, so she threw like a girl. She'd show him! Moving closer, she hurled more mud until the air was thick with the flying muck, some finding its target. Jorge and Miguel stayed out of the line of fire, but grinned anyway. She'd deal with them later.

Quinn called a halt to the assault when an imbedded rock bounced off his chest. Closing the distance between them, he wrapped his arms around her stifling her movements. He still chuckled. She kicked him hard in the shin. The laughter stopped.

"Ow! That hurt."

"So will this one!" She kicked again, but he moved to avoid the contact.

"Calm down. I'm sorry I laughed. You would, too, if you had a mirror."

Her anger evaporated, and she quit struggling. "It wasn't a very nice thing to do," she said in a sullen voice.

"I'm sorry, really. You're not going to hit or kick me again, are you?"

She contemplated it, and then shook her head.

"All right. Come on, let's get you up the hill."

Back on the trail she tried to scrape the mud off, all the while glaring at Quinn while he studied the map. She shot Jorge and Miguel a couple of glowering looks, too. They refused to meet her eyes.

"There's a small river about an hour or so from here. If the camping area is decent, we'll stop for the night. In spite of the rain and other things, we've made good time."

"And hot food tonight?" she asked, hopefully. Thoughts of shoving all three men down the hillside dwindled.

"If we don't get deluged again," he promised.

Two hours later they found the river and set up camp in a wide, grassy area near a bend about fifty yards downstream. With her tent secure, Alex emerged carrying fresh clothing and the ditty bag.

"I am going to take a bath," she declared.

"There's not a whole lot of privacy. Just a few rocks and some bushes."

"I don't care who sees me bare beamed and buck naked. I am going to be clean."

"We can all use a good wash. Jorge and Miguel are out gathering fuel, so you'd better hurry."

She picked her way across the rocks and through the bushes to the water's edge. The bend in the river created a shallow area near shore. It was here she stripped, washed her clothes, and then slid into the thigh deep water. Twenty minutes later, she returned to camp—mud free.

"God, that felt good," she said, spreading her wet clothing on top of her tent. They would dry by nightfall.

Quinn studied his map. "We made better time than I thought," he commented.

She joined him. The guides headed for the river.

"Where are we?"

He twisted the chart in her direction. She craned her neck for a better look.

"Tomorrow we'll bear back to the west and try to camp in or near this village." He pointed to a small dot on the map marked Montecito. "Then we'll hike to Kamachiquia. Miguel says it's a real town with a small hotel and a couple of cafes."

"I'd kill for a real bed, a real bathroom, and red meat."

He laughed, gathered his clean clothes, and turned toward the river. "So would I, honey."

He winked and patted her on the fanny. She

glared at his retreating back, but enjoyed it all the same.

****

Quinn lay in his sleeping bag, his mind alternately thinking about their final destination and of Alex. He'd meant it last night when he told her nothing would happen, and he thought he could keep his word. Then he awoke to her cuddled against him, her cute little butt rubbing against his crotch every time she moved. She moved a lot. After that, one thing led to another.

He drew in, and then expelled a deep breath. They were as combustible as fire and gasoline, and as compatible as oil and water. Her logic drove him crazy. Did she ever do anything spontaneously? Did she ever just toss an agenda out the window and wing it? All that structure and reason seemed more like chains and locks to his free spirit.

And yet, she was anything but restrained in bed. She drove him crazy in a different way there, reminding him of an incendiary device that blasted his senses into a whole new dimension. The cramped confines of last night had not slowed his libido. The storm heightened every movement, every sensation. It was one of the most memorable nights he ever spent with a woman, but then, Alex was damned memorable.

He chuckled, recalling her tumble this afternoon. She looked like a mud-caked, humpbacked rat. Her hair, saturated with the stuff, had hung in dripping, curly brown tendrils. He shouldn't have laughed, but couldn't help it. And her reaction only brought on more laughter—until the rock that is. She was certainly spontaneous then.

Maybe there's still hope for her.

He wondered what would happen when this expedition ended. She'd go back to Waukegan and he'd go...where? On another adventure? The thought wasn't as appealing as it had been even a few weeks ago. It wouldn't be nearly as much fun without her along. He realized with surprise that he'd miss her—a lot.

****

Alex wiggled around trying to get comfortable. The ground squished under her. She opened all the vents and pushed the covers off. Hot and humid, not a breath of air stirred.

In spite of the heat, she missed the warmth of Quinn's body, and his kisses, and his caresses, and his...No!

Stop thinking about it. This is not good subject matter.

She tried, but failed. *How can I be in love with the man? It's not like he's Mr. Right in my book. He's just too different from the kind of man I want—or thought I wanted. This is so illogical.*

Every time she thought she'd found Mr. Right, he turned out to be Mr. Wrong. Could Quinn—Mr. Super Wrong—actually turn out to be Mr. Right after all? She shook her head, confused. Hell, when this ended, he'd probably ditch her in Waukegan, wave bye-bye, and move on to his next thrill. She'd be dumped again. Love was obviously not logical at all.

Rolling over, she listened to the sound of rain once again pattering on the dome of her tent, a soft, gentle shower, perfect for sleeping. She closed her eyes.

Why was she so hopeless when it came to men? She loved Quinn Rafferty with a depth of passion missing with her former boyfriends. He aroused emotions she knew could never be duplicated for anyone else. She came alive and excited in his presence. Logic frequently took a dive headfirst out the window. Whatever she thought she'd felt for Rod now caused embarrassment.

Her mood changed instantly. Rod! That low-down, sneaky little rat-bastard! She couldn't wait to catch up to him. Compliant, eager-to-please Alex had disappeared. If she confronted him, he'd be surprised at the change. She hoped he was prepared. She planned to come down on him like a ton of very big, heavy bricks.

Chapter Fourteen

Bored, Rod Halston tossed his men's fashion magazine onto the floor of the tent and glared out at the slanting rain. He'd read that silly magazine so many times in the past couple of weeks he could recite it word for word. What the hell was he doing in Guatemala anyway? He should be living it up enjoying the high life in Miami or Vegas, not sweltering in this stinking jungle with its god-awful heat and offensive smells.

"A tent. I'm living like a gypsy in a tent," Rod muttered out loud, eyeing his surroundings with distaste.

What he wouldn't give to be in a swank hotel, lounging by the pool, a couple of beautiful babes beside him, and waiters bringing an endless supply of whatever drink he desired.

He deserved a king-sized bed with a soft mattress, not this...this... He couldn't even come up with a word bad enough to describe the hard, narrow camp cot.

How had he let Victoria talk him into this? For almost three years he'd been chasing that stupid treasure map, because the payoff had mammoth implications for *his* future. Now, he wondered if it was worth it. How long had he been walking—walking!—through this green Hell? He lost track of time and had no idea. Still no hoard of gold, silver or precious gems had shown up. Back in the States it had sounded so easy—follow the map, and dig up the goodies.

Rod glanced back outside at the pouring rain.

He sighed with irritation and watched his sister lean over to stir a pot on the small camp stove. If it hadn't been for the canopy extension over the front of their tent, he'd be forced to eat cold food. He gagged at the thought.

Victoria rose from the campstool and entered the tent.

"What's wrong with you?" she asked, sitting on her cot and opening a small tote bag to extract a copy of the map.

"I'm bored."

"Well, you could become un-bored by picking up your side of the tent. It's a mess." She eyed the dirty laundry and the magazines thrown around with displeasure. "You always were a slob."

He ignored her comment. "What's for dinner? I'm starved."

"You're bored. You're starved. What else?"

He shot up to sit facing her, angry at her mocking tone. "I'm hot. I'd kill for real food. I hate those goddamned donkeys. The little one bit me—twice. I want a bathroom with a Jacuzzi and thick towels. I've had it with this tent, this bed, and you giving me orders all the time!"

"Rod, you're whining. I hate it when you whine."

His petulance increased when she didn't bother to look up from the map.

"So, sister dear, show me the money. Where's this treasure I've invested so much time tracking down?"

"All right. It's taking longer than I thought, but we are making progress."

"Progress? I think those guides are leading us around in circles."

"And why would they do that?"

"Because we're paying them by the day," he snapped. "I'll bet if we tell them we only have enough money left for another four days we'll get to the treasure in double time. And why are we traveling on foot with those damned donkeys? They smell. Why couldn't we have taken the cars?"

"Because Carlos said the roads in this area often wash out or are in too bad a shape to accommodate a car."

"His family probably owns the donkey concession." Rod ran his hand through his hair. "I don't even know what I'm doing here. I want civilization."

"Rod, may I remind you that it took a whole six seconds for you to agree to this? The minute the words treasure map passed my lips you were gung ho. Besides, I needed you. I couldn't charm the auction house secretary. While you entertained her, I managed to get into the office and search their files. I found Alexandria Montgomery's name and address."

His sister accomplished the almost impossible feat of looking both smug and contemptuous at the same time. He couldn't tell if her disdain was aimed at him or the secretary. He chose to believe the latter.

"Yeah, thanks for nothing. Carol Reston was five feet tall, weighed two hundred pounds, and giggled. How could she have believed I was romantically interested in her? I closed my eyes and thought of God and country."

Victoria looked at him with an amused expression on her face, her lips curling into a smirk. "You've never thought of God or country in your life. I do, however, appreciate your flair for the dramatic. It eventually led you to Alex."

"At least boffing Alex was worth it. She's dynamite."

"I don't need to hear about your sex life."

"Why not? You were doing Quinn."

She heaved a sigh. "Is there a point to this

conversation?"

"I just don't understand why we couldn't have followed the map."

"How many times do I have to tell you? Cash Marriott did his own authenticating. I only transcribed his notes. Whenever I printed, I ran off two copies. He was very secretive about that map. He locked it in the safe as soon as he finished with the damned thing. I didn't have the combination. I didn't get that until later."

"How did you manage it?"

"I told his wife there was something I needed and she opened it. When she did I memorized the numbers."

"Why not just steal it then?" he asked, still not comprehending.

"Because he was still authenticating, so I just continued to make extra copies of his notes."

The exaggerated patience in her voice—like he was some kind of moron—pissed him off. He couldn't resist getting in a snide shot. "It's a pity he caught you at it."

"Don't start, Rod. That whole day was a fiasco. If only Cash hadn't come home from the library so early. When he saw what I was doing, he fired me on the spot, and destroyed the copies I'd just made. I had until that evening to get out. And that is why we don't have a complete map from point A to point B. Thank goodness he figured out that Santa Rita was a new name for an old city. It gave us a reference point. That's as far as his authenticating took him."

"Too bad he came back when he did that night. Another five minutes and we'd have been gone. Your timing was really screwed that day, Miss Perfect."

She narrowed her eyes and glared. "Well, I'm not the one who killed him."

"He hit me first and besides, I never touched him when he went down. It wasn't my fault," Rod said, the whiney tone returning.

"He was still just as dead. I'm sure there's a legal term for it."

"Which brings me to another problem you created. Why hide the map with your crazy Aunt Iris?"

"I always visit her after a job. She accepts any explanation I give. It's a great place to lay low until I can fence any valuables. I hid the map because this time someone died. If the authorities *did* catch up to me, I didn't want it in my possession." Victoria paused and shook her head, a looked of remembered disbelief on her face. "That stupid picture hung on that stupid wall ever since I was a kid. Who knew Aunt Iris would develop a passion for yard sales?"

"As soon as she realized all that junk could bring in a couple of bucks."

"Since we're playing the blame game here, why did it take you six months to get the map from Alex? The old charm not working? You must be losing your touch...or your appeal," she said with a malicious grin.

"Alex Montgomery is one tightly wound woman, except in one area—romance. It only took a couple of dinner dates to figure out what she wanted in a man. I also discovered her desire for order and control could be by-passed with a few sweet words and a gentle touch. At least, *I* got the map."

"You are so oily."

He took it as a compliment and shrugged. "I do what I have to do. I couldn't move until she trusted me completely. The first time she left me in charge I searched, but came up dry. The map wasn't in the shop or her apartment. I thought we'd made a mistake."

"How unfortunate for you. All that wasted time with Carol," Victoria said, the nasty grin still in place.

He pretended he hadn't heard. "Then she took me to meet her grandfather. The minute she told me he was an expert on the Aztecs and the Mayans, I knew where to find that map."

"So, why didn't you get it? He was an old man. Couldn't you have just broken in and stolen it?"

Rod hated it when his sister played inquisitor. "He had a live-in housekeeper whose husband tripled as the chauffeur, gardener, and all around handyman. They were both protective of the old boy. The house resembled a museum, stuffed full of antiques and clutter."

"No wonder Alex opened an antique store. She had an endless supply of merchandise."

He looked around the tent. "Is there anything to drink besides water? It's after five o'clock."

"One of the reasons we're traveling with five donkeys is because you insisted on bringing a case of wine and a half a case of scotch. No, we don't have anything else to drink. You drank it all, which is why we never left a hotel or campsite before noon."

He chose to ignore her jibe. The comment about his appeal still rankled and he felt the need for further justification. "As I was saying, the house was a museum, but her grandfather's study looked like a war zone. The old boy had papers and books stacked everywhere. I was forming a plan of attack when he up and died. I backed off, gave Alex a shoulder to cry on, and let her sort through the mess."

"Why put yourself out?" his sister murmured, fingering the map copy in her hand.

"Exactly. She found the map and authenticated it. I spun a tale about a family reunion to explain why I wouldn't be around for the weekend. It bought us time. When she left the shop, I rifled the safe and called you."

"Well, I guess all that matters now is we have the map and a copy of it," Victoria said.

"I copied it because I hoped all that writing would show up better on a white background, but it's too faded. Not even the guides could make it out. I just hope there's a big pot of gold at the end of it."

She pushed a wayward strand of hair behind her ear.

"Cash Marriott was convinced of it. He said the legend was well-known and no evidence of any huge treasure find in Guatemala by either the Spanish or anyone else had ever come to light."

"In that case, I'm glad you called me in. We make a good team."

Victoria blew out a breath and said, "We *can* work well together. Our styles differ, but the results are the same."

"We must be pretty good. Neither of us has ever bought jail time. To the best of my knowledge, Harry was clean, too." He forgot the verbal jabs of earlier and reminisced. "Do you remember the Murchisons?"

"I seduced the husband who paid me a lovely sum to just go away and not tell his wife, while you did the same to the little woman."

"Only my payoff was in jewelry." He laughed. "It was a perfect set up. Neither could complain to the cops. He didn't want her to know he strayed and paid, and she was in the same boat."

"I often wondered how she explained the disappearance of a diamond necklace to her husband."

He grinned at another memory. "My favorite was the one where I pretended to be twenty and you claimed to be my forty-year-old mother."

"All that make-up took hours to put on, but it was worth it in the end." She rose, stretched, and made a face. "I'd better go stir those beans again. Cheer up. Dinner is almost ready, the rain is letting up, and we're about to have the biggest pay day of our lives."

"It better be. I'd hate to think I went through all of this for nothing. I want my fair share."

Victoria left the tent. Rod lay back down and picked up the discarded magazine of earlier. Thumbing through it, he stopped to admire and visualize.

I really like that jacket. Casual, yet elegant. I'd look terrific in it. Hmm, $1200. Not bad for cashmere.

He moved on to silk shirts, worsted trousers and Italian shoes—all designer.

Gotta go first class. With a wardrobe like that, I'll look spectacular. And a car—something fast, sporty and preferably European.

With the right clothes and the perfect car he'd attract every silly, rich, middle-aged woman in Florida, all of them eager to invest their millions with him.

I'll make Palm Beach my headquarters .

He flipped a page and continued to daydream.

****

Disgruntled with her brother, Victoria leaned forward and stirred the pot of slow-cooking beans, then added rice. So, Rod hated the cuisine—what else was new? He'd been bitching about it since day one. It never occurred to him she was just as sick of it. Even as a child he'd been a greedy, selfish little brat. As much as he craved the treasure, she wanted it even more. It would be her escape.

She hated her life. She was tired of the lying, the cheating, and the stealing. Cash Marriott's death had been a wake up call. For the next few months, she ran to cover scared everyone she passed on the street was an undercover cop ready to slap the cuffs on her. Victoria wanted out of this life, the only one she'd ever known. She wanted to do things legitimately. That map was her ticket to freedom and its loss a blow. The recovery had taken a long, twisting road, and now that the end was near, she allowed herself the luxury of thinking about the future. But the trip down memory lane with Rod had her thinking of the past instead.

She sat on the campstool with her elbow on her knee and her chin in one hand, a wooden spoon dangling from the fingers of the other. Old resentment surfaced.

Damn my mother and her obsessive love for Harry Halston. She knew what he did and ignored it, exposing me to his crimes.

Harry didn't show a whole lot of grief at her mother's death. She cynically believed the only reason she and Rod weren't abandoned at the funeral home was because her stepfather saw the possibilities that a widower with two adorable, blond-haired, blue-eyed kids in tow would create sympathy. The son of a bitch conned and fleeced susceptible women for years until cute and adorable outgrew the roles.

But that didn't deter Handsome Harry. No sir, not one bit. He instructed his children in the intricacies of his craft, and then sent them out on their own to hone the skills.

Father of the year candidate.

By the time he died, both she and Rod were proficient at lying, stealing, and conning.

It hadn't been until secretarial school that Victoria realized another way of life existed. She held enough legitimate jobs over the years to know there was something to be said for the nine-to-five lifestyle. Maybe she could meet some nice man, get married, and have a couple of kids.

I still have my looks and my health.

But what would happen when she turned forty—or fifty? This treasure guaranteed a decent place to live along with a secure retirement. What a market strategy—steal a map and go dig for treasure. Well, unlike Rod, at least she had a strategy planned.

Tucking another errant strand of hair behind her ear in irritation, she whipped a bandana out of her pocket and tied it over her head, knotting it in the back of her neck. She stirred the pot again, resuming her thoughts.

Rod. Victoria had no illusions regarding her half-brother. Rod never planned anything further into the future than a few weeks. He adapted well and always landed on his feet regardless of the circumstances. His glib tongue and silky manner had worked since childhood.

He'd blow through his share of the treasure in a few months, spending it on fancy clothes, a hot car, and a big apartment.

When it's gone, he'll go right back to conning.

Other than blond hair and blue eyes, gifts from their mother, the resemblance between the two of them was superficial. Rod inherited every ounce of his father's good looks and *he* wasn't called Handsome Harry for nothing. Her brother proved the phrase "a chip off the old block." He would be conning little old ladies out of their life's savings into his forties, fifties and even sixties.

"It's just not fair," she muttered.

"What's not fair?" Rod asked, joining her under the canopy.

"That middle-aged, graying men are considered distinguished, while women are just considered old."

He threw back his head and laughed. "What's the matter, sis? Feeling your advanced age?"

"Sometimes. Rod, do you ever wish for a more permanent life? You know, a real job, a wife, and a family?"

A look of utter horror crossed his face. "Are you crazy? A job where I let someone else tell me what to do and when to do it? A wife who'll nag me to mow the lawn, fix the door, take out the trash, and then have a headache every night of the week? Can you actually see me with a bunch of whining brats around?"

She heaved a huge sigh. "No, I guess I can't."

"I'd kill them all. What brought this on?"

"I don't know. Maybe I'm hearing my biological clock ticking. Maybe I'm just ready for a change. For the past year the image of a husband, a family—the whole picket fence routine—doesn't sound as dull as it once did."

"Good God! I need to get you out of this jungle and back to Las Vegas or Miami before your brain completely turns to mush," he muttered. "Look, when we find the treasure, you'll snap out of this funk you're in."

She shrugged. "Maybe, maybe not. Who knows?"

"I thought Quinn had your attention for a while."

"Quinn was fun at first, but once I started working on that map, he became a potential problem. I had to keep him distracted. Luckily, Cash played his cards close to his vest. I don't think he told his grandson a whole lot."

"He must have said something. Quinn's been on our trail since the beginning." He looked into the pot. "Is this stuff ready?"

"Just about. I can't believe Quinn has been this tenacious. Of course, his grandfather's death probably has something to do with it."

"Do you think he's followed us here?"

She shrugged again. "Here in the jungle? I don't know. It depends on whether or not he's found Alex."

"So what if he does find Alex? We have the map," he declared, eyeing the bubbling pot again.

"I don't trust him, which is why I've had the guides checking our backs for the last few days. What about Alex? Will she come after us?"

"Alex? You've got to be kidding!"

"Do you think she called the cops when she discovered the map missing?"

Rod snorted, a contemptuous look crossing his face. "Alex? She may have declared me a missing person, but that's all."

"How can you be so sure?"

"Because Alex will be in denial for weeks. She thought I was Mr. Perfect. Alex wanted a loving man, sensitive and kind to small animals. When she finds out she's been had, she'll do what every mark does—nothing. She'll be too embarrassed to admit she's been taken in."

"But what if she does?" Victoria persisted.

"I'll say she gave me the map—that she didn't believe it was real. I'll maintain I ended things—not ready to settle down yet or something plausible like that. Alex will look like a disgruntled ex-lover. Don't worry. I've got it covered."

She spooned some of the beans and rice onto a plate and handed it to Rod before serving herself.

He curled his lip. "God, I'm sick of this food!"

He looked across the campsite into the guides' tent. She followed his gaze. The men lounged around an overturned crate, playing cards in the lantern light.

"It looks like Curly, Larry, and Moe have already eaten," he said.

"About an hour ago. And their names are Carlos, Roberto, and Juan. Lower your voice. They're only thirty feet away. They can hear you."

"So what?" he shrugged, but complied, shoveling food into his mouth. "They don't speak much English anyhow."

"I wouldn't be so sure of that. Carlos communicates pretty well, and the other two seem to understand what we're telling them."

"Come on. They're from Guatemala, for Pete's

sake. They can't be too smart or they wouldn't still be here."

"Rod, one of these days that arrogant attitude is going to get you into serious trouble."

"You know, Vicky, sometimes you can be an awful pain in the ass," he said calmly, helping himself to more food. "I assume we're pushing on tomorrow if this damned rain finally lets up. Where are we going?"

She pulled the modern day map out of her pocket and unfolded it, hoping the rain ceased. Rod had flatly refused to hike in the downpour.

"We head southwest. Carlos suggested we go to a little town in that area to re-supply. It's about a day and a half or two days away."

"A town? With a real hotel and a real restaurant?"

"Maybe, but we'll camp out. Carlos says there's a large open area about a half a mile south of town."

"Camp out? When there's a hotel with a bed and a bathroom available? Are you nuts? I'm not going to play Boy Scout when something better is down the road."

"Brother dear, may I remind you my meager savings have financed our search and this trip. We're almost broke."

He glared at her, and said, "How does Carlos know so much about this place?"

"He's a guide. He says lots of tourists stop there. He also said he and Roberto were through this area a few months ago. They know the trails. Juan was raised in a village a few miles away. According to Carlos, our final destination is two or three days further on," she answered with more patience than she felt.

"Carlos says this. Carlos says that. How do we know he's telling the truth?" The sulky look on her brother's face told her he was still steamed about camping out.

"Why would he lie?"

"So he can lead us into the middle of nowhere, then steal the map, and leave us to get out on our own."

Her shoulders slumped in sudden fatigue. She was sick and tired of this whole business. The fact Rod could be right didn't help. The thought had crossed her mind also, but the two of them couldn't have done this on their own.

Rod dumped his dirty dishes next to the stove and stood, glancing once again toward the guides' tent. The three men still played cards.

"You know, now that it's stopped raining, I think I'll just stroll over. Maybe I can find out more about this town. I might join the fun by teaching them a little poker or blackjack. Get some of our money back." He ambled over and within a few seconds the sound of laughter drifted across the campsite.

"Thanks so much for offering to help with the dishes," Victoria muttered.

Typical Rod—use, and then move on. Why not? He used *her* whenever it was convenient. She didn't remember one incident in his entire life where her brother did anything to help anyone else unless he benefited. When she got her share of this treasure, she swore she'd change her name and move to Smalltown, U. S. A., losing Rod forever.

She tried to imagine a straight life, one where she received respect and had friends, not marks. One where she earned her pay. Of course, Rod would maintain they did earn whatever they stole. And how twisted and amoral was that?

Damn it, she wanted something more. An accomplishment to make her proud, and never again having to worry if the cops were just around the corner.

After cleaning up, she sat on her bunk, lit a

lantern, and studied the modern map. Yes, two days to the town for supplies, and then another two or three days to the treasure. By this time next week, she could be independently wealthy. Her finger traced the route to the supply town with the unpronounceable name—Kamachiquia.

She shivered slightly as a sudden vision of Quinn popped into her mind. Victoria dismissed it. Why worry about him now? He was probably still in the States, and even if he was in Guatemala, how the hell would he find her? She had the map. *Unless Alex also made a copy. No, Rod would have known.*

A wave of uneasiness rolled over her, prickling her skin and scalp. She had the sensation someone walked on her grave. She shivered again, her fingers tightening on the map.

Chapter Fifteen

"We'll be there by noon and can have a decent lunch," Quinn promised. He hefted his backpack onto his shoulders, preparing to leave the campsite.

"I'm looking forward to the hotel with a hot bath and a soft bed," Alex replied, adjusting her pack into a more comfortable position.

"Me, too. Are you ready?"

Alex hoped today's journey was easy. Yesterday's march found the trail wide and well-defined. The path still wound up and downhill, but she no longer felt any pain. *Thank God for small favors.*

Quinn had bounced back to normal. With his energy restored, his firm, reassuring footsteps bolstered her confidence.

In spite of her relief and anticipation of civilized surroundings, other things crowded her mind. Things like telling Quinn the truth. She hadn't really lied, just omitted certain things. And what would she confess first?

She practiced. *Quinn, I love you.*

Not bad. Straightforward and to the point. It might also soften the blow for the rest of her admissions. But did she really want to hit him with the most important declaration of her life in the middle of a jungle? Or in a hotel room? She would prefer to be attired in a sexy little dress, strolling with him hand in hand along a moonlit beach. The only problem was she didn't have a sexy little dress or a beach available.

Deep in her fantasy, Alex ran smack into Miguel

205

as they stopped to rest.

"Sorry," she muttered in embarrassment. She'd better leave the daydreaming to bath time and concentrate on where she was going. To cover her confusion, she asked, "Tell me about this town. Is it large?"

"It is called Kamachiquia, *senorita,*" Jorge replied. "There is a nice hotel and many cafés. It is a town where people come, and then go on. I do not know the English word for it."

"You mean a stopover?"

"*Si,* that is it. There is a marketplace and many shops to buy food for the journey."

"We can re-supply, get a good meal, and a decent night's sleep," Quinn said. "Tomorrow, we start on the last leg. We'll plot the route over lunch. If we keep up this pace, we should arrive in three days, maybe less."

Three days! With a definite time frame, guilt and a hint of panic surfaced. Time to test the waters.

"Quinn, what would you do if we got there and there was no treasure?"

"What do you mean, no treasure?" He shot her a speculative look.

"Suppose we get there and the treasure just can't be found. What would you do?"

"This isn't the first time you've hinted at that possibility. I thought you said the map was authentic."

She licked her lips. "It is, but there's been a long time between the legend and the map. I wondered if maybe it hadn't been discovered years ago. Remember the priest's story about the soldiers."

"Alex, my grandfather was also in the process of authenticating the map. The last time I talked to him he told me he could find no evidence of a large treasure having been found by *anyone* in Guatemala. If those deserters had discovered it, I think someone would know. They wouldn't be able to keep quiet about what they found."

"I hadn't thought of that. But if they had the map, why didn't they find the treasure?"

"My guess is their former comrades caught up to them and executed the whole lot for desertion. It makes sense. Are you ready to go?"

"Yeah. Sure." So much for breaking it to him gently. And he hadn't answered the question of what he would do.

Besides wringing my neck, I can think of several scenarios—all unpleasant.

She couldn't procrastinate any longer. She'd tell him and face the consequences. Tonight, she decided. She'd fill him full of food and beer, and then confess. *Hope I live to see tomorrow.*

"Next stop, Kamachiquia," Quinn said, grinning.

****

They entered the town of Kamachiquia from the west shortly after eleven o'clock. Larger than Santa Rita, but smaller than Los Arcos, the sidewalks bustled with both locals and tourists passing through, taking advantage of market day. Crowds thronged the stalls set up on the main thoroughfare. Down the side streets, Alex saw shops of all descriptions.

The small hotel was located on a corner of the town square opposite a bank. A restaurant and what she later learned was the equivalent of City Hall occupied the other two corners.

After her time in the jungle, the hotel looked like a palace. Bright and airy, the overhead fans kept the air circulating. It would take her a while to get used to air-conditioning again. She spied a restaurant through an archway to her left and a large bar with a dance floor to the right.

She couldn't resist asking the desk clerk about it as she registered.

207

"*Sabado, senorita. Musica y...*" he made a dancing motion.

"Good grief! A nightclub in the middle of nowhere." She looked at Quinn. "Saturday, huh? What day of the week is this?"

"Sorry, honey. It's Wednesday, or maybe Thursday, I think, but we'll go to lunch at the best restaurant in town. My treat."

"You're on, after I get my hot bath."

"Let's meet in the lobby at one," he said in the hallway. "Bring your map and we'll compare routes."

She opened the door to her room. Light flooded through two large windows. She crossed the dark polished floor to close the blinds against the glare, stopping for a moment to gaze at the activity in the square below, then turned to inspect the room. White walls and a bedspread of brilliant Mayan colors gave the place a pleasant, cheerful look.

Alex dumped her backpack on the bed and immediately sorted her dirty laundry 'before checking out the bathroom. The tub contained a shower with a retractable clothesline running the length of it. Apparently, she would not be the first person to do laundry in this hotel.

Sighing in relief when hot water gushed out of the faucet, she shed her clothes leaving them in a heap on the floor. Sliding into the silky warm water, a groan of pure delight escaped her. Never again would she take the simple pleasures for granted.

Finished, she refilled the tub to scrub her clothes and stepped back laughing. Damned near very piece of clothing in her backpack was suspended from the clothesline, the towel bars, the shower rod, and draped over the rims of the tub and sink. The only things left were the clothes on her back and the Mayan items still in the sleeping bag.

She left the room to meet Quinn and hoped the steady plink of dripping water droplets hitting the various pieces of porcelain would cease by nightfall.

"How many layers of dirt washed off?" he greeted her in the lobby with a smile.

"All of the mud from my little tumble the other day is finally gone. Now where is the best restaurant in town?"

Quinn crooked his elbow, bowed, and said, "Allow me."

She laughed and dropped a curtsy in kind, then took his arm. "Charmed, I'm sure." She still chuckled as they exited the hotel. "Where are the guys?"

"Jorge and Miguel showered, and then headed for the nearest cantina. After that, who knows?"

They found the restaurant located down a side street. The simple rustic décor reminded her of an old country style steakhouse not far from her grandfather's home. Waukegan seemed to belong to another lifetime. She hadn't even given the shop a thought since boarding the plane, and hoped Julie wasn't having too hard a time of it.

After ordering, Quinn unfolded his map. "Let's see yours. Now that we're so close, maybe we can pinpoint a few more places."

Alex handed over her copy and scooted her chair closer to his for a better view. As her arm and shoulder brushed his, a little electric zing vibrated through her body. She inched away, and then changed her mind, sliding back. Anything to feel that zing one more time. She leaned against him again for a brief, light touch. Yep, still there. She curbed the temptation to oscillate back and forth like a pendulum. Common sense prevailed. Not only did they have to look at the maps, but they were also in a public place.

Cool it, Montgomery. Later.

"So, what do you think?" she asked.

"I think I was dead on. Look here. On your map these inverted V's must represent mountains and the squiggly Y between them is definitely a river. And here is X just to the east of this mountain." His finger jabbed at her map.

"How does that relate to your map?"

"Take a look at these mountains southeast of here." He pointed out the town of Kamachiquia, and then dragged his fingertip in that direction.

"All right, I can see that there are some mountains and a river, but unfortunately, there's no X."

He showed her the maps, comparing them. "Take your reference points and follow the lines. See Pop? Now, look at Sabau. Very close. Here is Santa Rita and the village of Yaxha on your map is a possibility."

"Yaxha looks to be west of Santa Rita," she commented.

"Remember, distances on old maps can be inaccurate. See? Pop-Sabau," his finger moved, "to Yaxha-Santa Rita. And look what lies in between— good old San Marcos!" He sat back, triumph gleaming in his eyes.

"If you really want to give your imagination a workout, try linking the buried village we found and this little village on my map marked Xahul."

"Jorge said they were Spanish ruins."

"And the Spanish often built on or near the original Mayan towns."

"How did the Spaniards miss finding the cave?"

"Who knows? Maybe they never thought to look for it. Maybe they never investigated beyond the bats. Lord knows if I hadn't been with you, I'd have run like hell." She suppressed a shiver at the memory. "Perhaps they found the area inhospitable, what with all the night creatures flying around and abandoned it."

"So, do you think they're connected?"

She hesitated. "No, not really, but speculation is

fun."

Quinn chuckled. "I suppose we could make a case for finding all of the villages." He studied his map for a moment, and then sobered. "I do have a problem with where X is located though."

"What's that?"

"Here to the west, maybe five or six miles away on the other side of the river is a town—San Luis."

She stared as though seeing it for the first time. "It doesn't look very big."

"It's big enough. I'd say about two or three thousand people." He stared intently and frowned. "Looks like there's a bridge of some sort across the little river to the east."

"A bridge?"

"There's no road, so I have to assume it's a footbridge. Our Y river doesn't have a name—at least not on this map. It flows south before emptying into the much larger, Rio Montebello."

"Isn't that the river that flows into Belize?"

"Into the bay south of Belize," he corrected. "What concerns me is this road following the no-name river. It crosses the Montebello southwest of the town, and just west of the confluence."

"Why does a road bother you?"

He shrugged and furrowed his brow. "Because it's so close to X."

They refolded the maps as the waiter brought their food. The shredded beef dish was good, but not the thick T-bone or burger of her dreams. And French fries; she could make do with a few of those, too. Oh, for a couple of golden arches. Alex ate and continued to daydream.

****

Quinn ate, but barely tasted his food. He was busy mulling over this latest revelation. Why did the road and bridge bother him? Because it indicated civilization so close to the treasure? Perhaps, but in this country it wasn't unusual to find complete wilderness a few miles outside even a fair sized city. He mentally shrugged. Maybe he had a case of high anxiety now that the objective was near.

He glanced at Alex. Now *there* sat something that should bother him. When she'd slid her chair next to his, it had taken every ounce of willpower to ignore the surge of pure lust that raced through him. He craved her like a drug. No amount of rehab would ever completely cleanse her from his system. The thought scared the hell out of him.

Alex looked up and caught him staring at her. He hoped his face didn't reveal any of what he thought. Given their volatile history together, they could easily ignite and end up doing it under the table.

"How's the food?" he asked.

"It's great. How's yours?"

"Terrific." He supposed it was true.

Quinn turned his attention back to his plate a bit perplexed.

What would you do if we got there and there was no treasure? Her question puzzled him. She'd made a couple of negative references over the last week and her enthusiasm was nowhere near what it should be for someone about to unearth a treasure.

What would you do if...? The words ricocheted through his head. He looked at her bowed head and a wave of uneasiness washed over him.

She's hiding something. But what?

She'd sworn the map was authentic and he believed her. After all, his grandfather had believed it, too. And what about Halston? God knows she gave every indication she wanted to find the slimy bastard. The thought irritated him and a dart of jealousy gnawed in his gut. Surely, she wasn't still in love with her ex-boyfriend. The waterfall flashed through his mind. No, Alex wouldn't screw his brains out if she still felt something for Rod Halston. That wouldn't be on her list of principles. He knew she had to have a list for something like that. She had lists for everything else. He gave himself a mental shake.

Stop this train of thought, Rafferty. It'll drive you nuts. No male has ever figured out the female of the species. No, there's something else she's not telling me.

True, she had never seemed overly concerned about the treasure, and he remembered her comment back in Chicago about getting her map back, but his impression had been it was a pride thing. It was hers, and in her mind Vicky and Rod had stolen it. She wanted it back.

He had a gut reaction about this and over the years had learned to trust his instincts. Suddenly, a vision of Victoria flickered before his eyes. The hair on the back of his neck bristled.

Now, why think of her? Alex might be eager to find Rod, but he had no desire to ever come in contact with Vicky again. He'd love to drag her back in chains to answer for his grandfather's death, but the authorities had made it clear there was no case. So, why would she pop into his mind? He shook his head again.

"Are you all right?" Alex asked, sipping coffee. She had finished eating and pushed her plate back. "You looked miles away."

"I was thinking about our route tomorrow. I'll consult with Jorge and Miguel later. Are you done? More coffee?"

"No, thanks. I'm fine. What do we do next?"

"I was going to take a short stroll through the market place, and then call on the local priest. Want to come?"

She grinned with a mischievous gleam in her eye. "Me? Pass up a chance to shop? Never!"

"All right, but window shopping only. Your sleeping bag won't hold any more." His uneasiness dissipated, but did not disappear.

****

Alex loved strolling through the packed marketplace with Quinn. She couldn't decide which experience was more exciting, him holding her hand, or the fabulous clothing viewed in the stalls. She restrained her consumer urges, but almost came undone at the leather goods on display at ridiculously low prices. Hand-carved wooden items fascinated her, and she drooled over the sculpted jade miniatures and beautifully set jewelry.

Here, Quinn allowed her to buy. When she chose a jade necklace with matching earrings, he bought her the bracelet.

"Quinn, I don't know what to say. Thank you. It's sensational," she said, donning the items.

"Women and jewelry," he murmured. "Are you finished here? It's almost three-thirty and I'd like to talk to the priest. The church is on the main drag about four blocks from our hotel. Want to come along?"

"No, I don't think so. I may wander around here or find a café and have a cold drink."

"All right. We'll have dinner tonight at the hotel. I'll see you later."

He went his own way, while she continued to amble through the market, fingering the bracelet and daydreaming about Quinn.

****

"Damn it, Vicky, you take this miserable beast. That's the third time he's tried to bite me in the last five minutes," Rod demanded, dodging yet another attempt by the donkey's snapping jaws.

And I always thought third time's a charm. "All right, Rod. Give him to me."

They switched animals, Rod giving the fractious

creature a wide berth. It was a good move. A hind leg lashed out narrowly missing his thigh. Victoria smothered a laugh. Charm and sweet talk were wasted on a donkey.

"So, how far away are we?" he asked.

"About an hour or so. Carlos says we'll skirt the town's east side and set up camp south of there."

"I've got a flash for you. I refuse to eat beans and rice for dinner again. If this place has a hotel, there has to be a restaurant. I want real food."

"Whatever!" she snapped. His whining and complaining drove her nuts. "Just stay focused. We're close to the treasure."

"I hope it's in a cave like you said, because I have no intention of digging like a peasant."

If you knew where a quarter was buried, you'd dig.

She kept the irritation out of her voice and replied, "According to Cash's notes, it was in a cave—one of those burial things with lots of chambers. Like a pyramid, I guess."

"Why doesn't that damned donkey try to bite you? He's gentle as a lamb now."

"Maybe he just doesn't like you, Rod. I'm sure there are lots of people out there who would just love to, if not bite, at least, kick you."

Her brother muttered something under his breath, but shut up, which was what she intended. She should have known he'd be like this. It would have been so much easier and quicker to have left him back in the States, but there was no way he trusted her. Just like she didn't trust him. Given the opportunity, he'd push her off a cliff, and then take all the treasure. Victoria decided to keep a closer watch on him.

An hour later they entered the eastern edge of Kamachiquia and swung south to their campsite where the gear was unloaded and the tents set up.

Rod lounged back against a tree trunk, watching her and the guides do the work—his usual routine.

She walked over and stood in front of him, hands on her hips. "You know, just once, you could lend a hand."

"Why? You and the Three Stooges have everything under control," he replied in a lazy voice.

"They're more useful than you'll ever be!"

"My talents lie in other directions. Physical labor is not one of them." He smirked. "Is my cot ready? I'd like to take a little nap."

"No, it is not and I don't intend to do it for you." Victoria's voice rose. "If you don't want to sleep on the ground tonight, I suggest you do it yourself." She resisted the urge to haul off and belt him.

Grinning at her, he rose and squeezed her shoulder as he sauntered past. "Sometimes it's just so much fun to watch your cool demeanor shatter."

Little twerp. Now that all the real work was done, he would agree to setting up his own bed. Maybe, she'd push *him* off a cliff. She stomped over to where the guides had tethered the donkeys. Carlos and Juan were inspecting the hooves and legs of two of the animals, their conversation rapid and brief.

Wishing she understood the language, she asked, "Is there a problem?"

Silly question. Of course there was a problem. There was always a problem. If they didn't find this treasure soon, she'd kill someone, preferably Rod.

The men jumped to their feet and nodded respectfully. "*Si, senorita*. This burro has hurt foot and him a bad knee. I go to market, get new," Carlos explained in broken English.

"Damn! Will it cost us much money?"

"A little. Rest make well again. Take time."

"How much money?" she repeated through clenched teeth.

"Ten American dollars," Carlos said with an apologetic look.

She heaved a huge, irritated sigh. Damn. Barely five hundred dollars remained in her on-ground budget. Thank goodness she had the foresight to put aside money at the hotel in Guatemala City for return airfare. She didn't need to pay for more donkeys and supplies. Unfortunately, she didn't have any other choice.

"All right. Go do what you have to do. Where's Roberto?"

"He makes our tent nice."

"Well, we need supplies. Take him and the donkeys. I'll get the list of things we need."

She walked across the campsite, taking malicious satisfaction in knowing the donkey that hated Rod was not lame.

Entering the tent, she saw her brother stretched out on his cot, hands behind his head, eyes closed. Disgust and sheer dislike rolled through her. Why should he be comfortable?

"Hey, Sleeping Beauty, wake up," she said, giving the edge of his bed a sharp nudge with her foot.

He opened one eye and murmured, "What? Do I look too relaxed for you?"

"Yes. Get up. Two of the donkeys are lame. The guides are going into town to make a trade and get more supplies. Go with them." She rummaged around in her backpack until finding the list she wrote the night before. "Here. Take this list and help them."

"Certainly not—unless one of the donkeys is that nasty little piece of work."

"Rod, you are going into town and you are finally going to do something to help. Is that clear?"

"And if I refuse?"

"I will set your bed on fire in the middle of the

night!"

She meant what she said. In her mind's eye, Victoria saw the satisfying picture of flames dancing and her brother jumping around the tent, his hands slapping at the fire burning his ass.

Rod made a rude noise and finally rose. "All right, all right. I'll go. I don't know what's put the burr up your butt, but take a chill pill." He snatched the list from her hand. "I'll need money."

She handed him a wad of bills. "Don't spend it all."

He stomped from the tent, and she sat down heavily on her cot, head in hands. God, would this journey never end?

****

Rod walked across the campground disgruntled and mildly pissed. What the hell was Vicky's problem? She'd been a nag and a shrew for the past four or five days. He was sick of it.

He joined the three men, avoiding the evil donkey, and then left. He sulked as he walked. Obviously, the quest for the treasure had taken a toll on his sister. All that searching and the effort to stay one step ahead of Quinn Rafferty must have stretched her nerves well past the breaking point. Maybe being alone for a while would help her get it together.

We'd better find this treasure soon or I swear I'll kill her.

He liked the thought of being in town, although keeping company with these three gave him a royal pain. However, a town was a town. He saw no reason not to ditch his escorts in order to have a little fun. There had to be a bar somewhere.

They entered the town and a few minutes later found the square. This was more like it. A little action. The crowded sidewalks teemed with people. Two weeks ago, he would have sneered at the village and its inhabitants. Now, his spirits lifted.

Walking behind the men and the donkeys, he kept his eyes open. It didn't take long until he spied a cantina.

"Carlos, do you need me for anything?"

"No, *senor*. We make trade. No worry. We make good deal. Roberto *muy* good trader."

"Yeah, sure. Whatever. I think I'll just wander around for a while. I'll see you back at camp," he said, ignoring the supply list in his pocket.

Turning, he walked back the way he had come. Passing a small outdoor café, Rod crossed the street and entered a lively cantina. When his eyes adjusted to the dim interior, he saw the place was about half full. Judging from the number of backpacks on the floor and tabletops, this particular establishment struck a chord with both locals and tourists.

A bar ran along one side wall while rough-hewn tables dotted the floor. Tucked into a corner stood a tiny raised platform. Several guitars propped against the wall and an instrument resembling a xylophone told him that come nighttime, this place could be fun.

Pleased with his choice, he ambled up to the bar and ordered a rum and coke. He preferred scotch, but when in Rome. The bartender set his drink in front of him where he stared at it for a few moments, then carefully took a swallow.

It might not be Bacardi or Mount Gay, but it wasn't bad. This was just what he needed—a break in the boredom and from Vicky.

He took a deep breath and swiveled around on his bar stool to survey the room, his eyes eventually making contact with a flaxen-haired beauty sitting at a table twenty feet away. He winked at her. She left her companions and strolled over.

"Is this seat taken?" she asked in accented English.

"Only by you. Have a seat," he replied, turning on the charm and doing a quick evaluation.

She stood at least five-feet-eight and had a figure that wouldn't quit. *Stacked like a brick outhouse.* Her blonde hair hung straight to her shoulders and the blue eyes held a hint of decadence. He immediately summed her up as a girl who liked to party.

"May I buy you a drink?" he asked in a smooth voice.

"Thank you. You are American?"

"Yes. My name is Paul...Paul Rogers. And you are...?"

"Inga. I am Inga from Stockholm."

Hot damn! This must be his lucky day. A Swede. He'd heard they were like rabbits, doing it anywhere, anytime. He wondered if she had a hotel room.

"What would you like?"

Inga gave her order and asked, "Why are you in Guatemala?"

"I've always been fascinated by the country and decided to visit. What about you?"

"My friends and I are at University in Uppsala. We do study on the Mayan."

"What a coincidence. I was an assistant to the Dean at a small college in Chicago. He was an expert on the Mayan."

God bless Alex and her grandfather. They're going to help me get laid.

"How thrilling. Who was Dean?"

"Maxwell...George Maxwell," he replied.

"I have read his books! He is much loved by Mayan scholars. We hear he die a while ago."

"Yes. It was very sad. He was a great man. That's why I'm here. I'm paying tribute to my friend and colleague." He hoped he looked dejected and ordered another round.

Damn I'm good.

He talked, flirted, and drank with Inga for almost two hours until her friends rose and called to her in Swedish.

"I must go now. Would you like to meet here later to listen to music?"

He made a date for eight-thirty, and then watched as the statuesque Scandinavian departed. Oh, boy! Tonight shaped up to be one satisfyingly good time.

Some booze, some sweet talk, and wham, I've got it made in the shade. With a little luck, those fabulous long legs will be wrapped around my waist by ten o'clock.

He left the cantina and walked back through the town, realizing he was a little drunk, but who cared? Maybe today would be a turning point. Maybe his uptight sister would mellow out, and he'd get a Swedish massage. Then, tomorrow they'd be on their way. By the end of the week he'd be stinking rich. All of a sudden, life seemed a hell of a lot better than a couple of hours ago.

He branched off onto the path leading him back to camp with a spring in his step and a song in his heart. Rod began to whistle a tune never thinking to look behind him.

Chapter Sixteen

Alex wandered around the marketplace, then decided to explore. She found the town easy to navigate. Resisting the urge to stop in the various shops, she strolled up and down the streets until coming to a little café with a small outdoor seating area.

Choosing a table under the awning out of the late afternoon sun, Alex ordered lemonade, sitting back to people watch and fantasize about Quinn.

How had he managed to turn her world upside down in the space of three short weeks? Her regimented life was in a shambles and she didn't care. Quinn was so different from the perfection of her former demands. Never again would she find that old comfort zone of precise placement and regulated activities. Quinn had smashed the mold.

She shook her head. As if Quinn Rafferty fit into any mold. He was his own man and would do what he wanted. Could she live with that? If he decided to explore the Outback or paddle up the Amazon, would she wave good-bye and stay at home selling antiques?

The surprising answer to that was, not completely. She'd still want to keep her store. She worked too hard to give it up. But in spite of all the intrigue and rough living conditions, she was having the time of her life. Until Quinn came along, she'd never thought of doing anything like this. Waukegan now sounded as boring as her life had been before.

Alex sipped the cold lemonade and rubbed a fingertip over the cool jade stones of the bracelet.

This journey had changed her so much. She'd seen and done things in the last few weeks that boggled the mind. She faced her fear of heights by crossing that god-awful bridge, and experienced the thrill of adventure traversing a raging river even though it had almost killed Quinn. The smugglers terrified her. Yet she knew safety in Quinn's care. It made no sense. It wasn't logical, but she didn't care.

How could I have changed so much in such a short time?

It was as though aliens had snatched the old Alexandria Montgomery and replaced her with a daring, adventuresome clone.

She picked up her glass to take another drink. A glance at her watch showed it was almost five o'clock. She'd have one more lemonade, and then return to the hotel. After dinner, she'd confess everything. *Now* was the time.

She sipped her second drink, watching the people in the street. The crowd was a mix of locals and tourists, the former dressed in traditional garb, while the latter paraded past in shorts or cargo pants.

Her eyes moved up the street to the entrance of a cantina where a group of very fair-skinned people exited. They looked Scandinavian. She wished she had the sunscreen concession. Two minutes in the sun would have that tall blonde girl looking like a lobster. She continued to watch the group until they turned the corner.

Several patrons left the bar to mingle with the crowd. Cocktail hour must be over. She chuckled. Then, all amusement died.

Rod Halston emerged from the cantina. Her jaw dropped in total astonishment. Alex watched, unable to move, her hand covering her mouth. He tossed a casual glance back into the bar before strolling away.

The paralyzing surprise lifted. She flung a few bills on the table and took off after him. Quinn! She needed to find him, but the church was in the opposite direction. She had no choice. She'd follow Rod, see where they were staying, and then come back. Rod and Victoria wouldn't go anywhere tonight. It would soon be dark.

At first, trailing him proved easy. She put people on the sidewalk between them. Crossing the square, she contemplated darting into the hotel to see if Quinn or the guides had returned, but decided against it. She might lose Rod.

Her quarry turned south at the fountain. They entered a more residential neighborhood. Now, tailing became difficult, forcing her to put more distance between herself and her ex-boyfriend.

The road gradually narrowed until the houses and pedestrians ceased to exist. Following him transformed into a challenge. If the little weasel looked back, he'd see her. Alex moved to the side of the diminishing road, ready to duck into the foliage if necessary. The area was isolated, and she wondered what would happen if Rod saw her. It was not a pleasant thought. She toyed with the idea of breaking off surveillance and finding Quinn.

Rod bore left at a fork in the road. He began to whistle a tune she recognized immediately—*It Had To Be You*. He often whistled the old song after they made love, claiming it was a tribute to her. Any thoughts Alex had about abandoning the chase evaporated.

You lying, thieving little bastard! I don't care if you hike to Timbuktu; I'm following.

The trail twisted and turned giving her more chances for concealment. She closed the gap and patted the zippered pocket of her pants. Through all the water and the mud, the plastic baggies had done their jobs. The look-alike map she secured from her grandfather's house and her copy of the stolen map remained safe and dry.

She didn't know how far into the jungle they trekked, but reasoned it wasn't too great a distance. Rod wouldn't want to be very far from the action of a town, and walking was not one of his favorite pastimes. Alex derived grim satisfaction at the thought of his unhappiness the last couple of weeks.

A bend in the path masked the entrance to the campsite and she damned near blundered in. To her right, a few feet off of the trail, stood a large tree surrounded by bushes. It would provide excellent cover and a good view. Sliding through the foliage, she crouched behind the tree, then peeked around it and surveyed the scene in front of her.

They had managed to fill most of the large area. On the far side, three tethered donkeys dozed, heads down, their packs on the ground nearby. To her left and her right, stood two large tents, each with a canopy over the entry. The tent and canopy on the left sheltered a cooking stove, a couple of lounge chairs, and provisions.

A strange contraption hung from a tree limb about ten feet in front of her. It suddenly belched forth a loud zapping noise. A battery powered bug zapper?

Alex wanted to laugh at the absurdity. No wonder they needed five beasts of burden to haul all of this junk. Heaven only knew what was in the tents.

"Vicky! Hey, Vicky," Rod called out. Silence and another sizzle from the bug zapper answered him. "Vicky, where are you?"

"I'm right here," a voice from the forest replied. A tall blonde woman emerged from a small footpath next to the tent on her left carrying a mesh laundry bag full of dripping clothing.

So, this is Victoria.

She looked Rod's sister up and down. The woman boasted an impressive figure with golden hair skimming her shoulders. At the moment, her clothing consisted of a pair of wrinkled slacks and a long-sleeved camp shirt. Sneakers adorned her feet.

Rod, ever the fashion plate, wore khaki slacks, a safari jacket and footwear that resembled a cross between hiking boots and high-topped sneakers. He looked ridiculous.

"Where have you been?" he asked.

"Doing laundry. There's a stream down that path."

"Great. I need fresh clothes. I'm going back into town for dinner."

"What makes you think I did yours?" Victoria glanced at her watch. "It's about time you got back. Where are the guides?"

Rod shrugged. "Beats me."

"I told you to go with them. Where are the supplies?"

He took a slip of paper out of his pocket. "Oops. I guess I forgot."

Victoria dumped the bag next to the canopy and strode over to him. She ripped it out of his hand and glowered.

"You forgot? How the hell could you forget? It was the only thing you had to do. Have you been drinking?"

"Ah, Vicky, get off my back," he whined.

Alex pressed her fingertips against her lips. *How could I ever have thought him attractive? This guy is a weak rung on the evolutionary ladder. What was I thinking?*

Humiliation that she'd been taken in by such a shallow piece of work and relief that she'd recovered, flooded though her. Wow, what a narrow escape.

"I ask you to do one simple task and you wind up in a bar. I suppose you also spent the money I gave you." The blonde's scowl deepened.

"Not all of it. Look here, Vicky, I needed to relax and don't see how a few rum and cokes can change the world. Besides, what use would I be staying with the guides? I don't speak the language, and I'm lousy at bartering." He turned toward the tent on the left. "I'm going to catch a short nap before dinner. I have a date with a blonde and need my energy."

"Wanna bet?" Victoria's voice rose an octave.

"Vicky, I'm warning you! I've had it up to here," he gestured with his hand to his eyebrows, "with your orders and constant nagging."

"And I'm fed up with you and your laziness. We need those supplies." Two red patches flared on her cheeks.

Rod shrugged with a bored expression. "We'll get them in the morning."

He moved toward the tent again. Victoria grabbed his arm and pulled him around, showing surprising strength.

"Like hell we will! You'll get them right now. And just to make sure, I'm going with you." The anger on her face was reflected in her tone.

Alex ducked deeper into the brush. Victoria dragged her brother down the path, past her hiding place, with Rod protesting and cursing all the way.

"Vicky, stop it! Quit being such a bitch!"

"Lazy, good-for-nothing, worthless piece of…"

"Don't you dare say it!"

Alex slowly released a pent-up breath. *No love lost in that family. I wouldn't turn my back on either of them for an instant.*

Their voices slowly faded. Standing to peer down the path, she no longer saw them although the angry exchange remained faintly audible. A new idea popped into her head.

Their leaving presented a golden opportunity. The trip to town and back would give her time to search for the map. She had no idea where the guides were, presumably in town, maybe at a bar.

Alex glanced down the path again. Rod and Victoria had disappeared. Cocking her head to one side, she listened, but detected nothing of human origin.

Before she could talk herself out of it, she whirled and ran into the camp. Victoria had dropped the bag of laundry in front of the tent on the left. She ducked into the opening, and then paused to calm her nerves. Her heart pounded in her ears while her legs shook like jelly on a plate.

Two cots were set up complete with a couple of small pillows, blankets, and a folding table separating them. Duffle bags peeked out from under the foot of each bunk.

All the comforts of home. The only thing missing is a family portrait on the wall.

It was palatial compared to what she had lived with for the past couple of weeks.

One side looked neat and tidy while the other resembled a pigsty. Remembering Rod's apartment, she had no problem guessing which cot was his. Instinct told her Victoria was the keeper of the map. After viewing the exchange between the two of them, she saw why entrusting it to Rod would not be in the cards.

Alex knelt at the foot of Victoria's bed, unzipped the first bag, and pawed through it. Underwear, bras, and socks were the only contents.

Re-zipping the bag, she crawled to the side of the cot and hauled out another duffle. Neatly packed inside were several pairs of slacks, a few shorts and blouses. Being careful not to disturb things too much she squeezed the clothing, listening for the telltale crinkle of paper hidden in a pocket. Nothing. On the bottom she found a bag containing the usual toiletries. The clear plastic of the smaller bag showed the map wasn't in this duffle either.

Alex spied a large tote bag propped against the table. It had to be in there. She opened it, quickly finding the modern day map of Guatemala and a copy of *her* map.

At least they had the sense to make a copy.

The only other items in the bag were mosquito repellent, a wallet with American dollars, a passport, and several bills in the local currency, but no map.

She searched under the pillow and blanket, and then sat on the edge of the cot holding her head in her hands. Victoria didn't have it. Damn! A horrible thought she'd not considered crossed her mind.

Oh, God, please tell me they didn't toss the map into the trash after copying it.

Alex strode to the doorway and poked her head out. The jungle emitted the usual sounds, but nothing human—yet. The clock ticked. Whirling, she squatted at the foot of Rod's bed.

Dirty laundry spilled out of an open bag. She gazed at filthy underwear and extremely smelly socks. Since no stick miraculously appeared in front of her, she had to touch the items. Gritting her teeth and holding her breath, she did it. The search yielded nothing.

She pulled a second duffle containing clean clothing from under the cot. Alex squeezed, but heard no paper sound.

The last duffle sat on top of the rumpled bed. The sudden cry of a bird in the trees reminded her time was passing. She needed to hurry.

The bag held a jumble of miscellaneous junk, a travel book, and magazines, including the last two issues of *Playboy*, but nothing else.

Alex searched the cot, and then stood to stare at the array of reading material. Tears clouded her eyes. The map wasn't here.

Disappointment, anger, and despair surged through her. All the research, the jungle, the bridge, the river, was for nothing! She had been so confident, so convinced they still had it she couldn't believe she'd failed. She thought about the things under the canopy, and then dismissed them. It wasn't likely to be stuck between the rice and bean sacks.

Damn! Damn! Damn!

Her tears spilled over, and a swell of frustration grew. Heaving a sobbing sigh, Alex grabbed the nearest magazine—a *Playboy*—and threw it as hard as she could against the wall of the tent. It bounced back landing on Rod's cot. Something fell from between the pages and dropped at her feet.

She bent over, picked it up, and then clutched it to her chest. She sucked in huge gulps of air, this time struggling with tears of joy. Her map—safe and intact. Rod used it as a bookmark. How ironic. That was the way she had first found it.

She glanced at the open pages of the magazine where it had fallen to the bed, then laughed softly, and murmured, "Thank you, Miss April."

Alex had no time to lose. She needed to make the switch and get out of here fast. Rod and Victoria or their guides could return at any moment. Her fingers trembled with excitement and anxiety. She could barely fold the map or unzip her pocket.

Forcing herself to calm down, she worked the mechanism until it opened, extracted the replacement map from the watertight baggie, slipped it between the pages, tossed the magazine at the open duffle, and slid her map into the protective plastic. She ran nervous, fumbling fingers over the locking mechanism before returning the package to her pocket.

Patting it for luck, she ran through the campsite and onto the trail, slowing to a fast walk to avoid tripping over roots. The gloom intensified as the sun sank lower in the sky. She needed to tell Quinn what she'd done and get the hell of out of town. If she found Rod and Victoria, then simple logic told her they could just as easily find her.

She'd gone a short distance when from up ahead she heard voices raised in anger. Rod and Victoria were returning and from the sound of it, still arguing. Glancing around, she saw no decent hiding place nearby. The voices drew closer. Her heart lurched in her chest.

Doing an abrupt about-face, Alex retraced her steps until she found her refuge of earlier. She'd stay there, let them get settled into the camp, and then hightail it for the hotel. Scrunching down into the covering foliage, she waited for them to pass, her heart thudding so loudly she was surprised they didn't hear it.

Rod and Victoria came around the bend, herded into camp by four gun-toting men. Victoria was furious and Rod blustering. Alex's jaw dropped in consternation as the bizarre scene unfolded.

"You can't do this to us! Do you know who you're dealing with? We're Americans, you can't treat us this way," Rod yelled, the lead bandit shoving him in the back with several hard jabs.

"Just keep walking," the man told him.

"We trusted you. You were supposed to guide us," Victoria said in a snarling voice.

"As soon as we knew what you were looking for, we guided you right to my uncle," he replied, laughing.

They entered the campsite, the men pushing their prisoners into the center of the clearing. An older man said something to the other three in Spanish. One entered the tent on the right, emerging with several lengths of rope, while another forced Rod and Victoria to sit down back-to-back.

The two were quickly trussed together like Thanksgiving turkeys.

"Juan, make ready the other burros. 'Berto, start to take down our tent and pack as many supplies as you can. I'll get the map," the first man said.

"Carlos, I will get you if it takes the rest of my life," Victoria said through clenched teeth.

"That is your privilege," Carlos replied, heading for the tent. He exited a few minutes later holding the white copy, the modern day maps, and the wallet.

"There was another map in a magazine," Juan called out, fixing a pack onto one of the donkeys. "I saw it on the ground one day as he read."

Nodding, Carlos re-entered the shelter, returning within five minutes in possession of the bogus original.

From her hiding place, Alex stared in fascination. She couldn't believe how close she'd come to being tied up with Rod and Victoria or to losing the map forever to these thieves.

Maybe I should try to slide out of here now.

The fear of discovery kept her still. If she tried to leave now, she might get captured. If she waited, she ran the risk of being caught following them down the path. Neither option was attractive, but she figured delaying made more sense. At least that way she could take her time and not have to run in the dark.

Two of the guides folded the tent while Carlos packed up the food and useful gear.

"Why did you wait so long?" Rod asked. "You could have stolen the map any time. At least then I wouldn't have had to suffer in this stinking jungle."

"My uncle lives in Lago Verapaz. When we met with him, he needed time to get closer to the treasure."

"And made sure he had plenty of time to get here by telling us we had to hike," Rod said, trying to throw a glance at his sister.

Carlos laughed. "The roads are very bad, so you would have had to walk anyway. I just made sure our journey took longer."

"How did you know where we were going?" Victoria questioned.

"At the hotel in Los Arcos, you left the maps in your room while you had dinner. It was a very easy lock to pick. You made marks on the map of today. We traced everything and gave it to Uncle Jose. He picked this town to meet."

"I notice your English is improving," she spat out.

"I spent eight years in your wonderful country, five of them in the Florida State Penitentiary. A small charge of burglary. That is where I met Juan who was serving a sentence for drug trafficking. We were deported together. Roberto is Juan's cousin," Carlos explained.

"Just one big, happy family!"

"You should know, *senorita*."

One donkey was loaded, and the men began on the second when the uncle said something. Nodding, Roberto trotted across the camp to disappear down the path. Alex crouched down as far as she could when he passed.

"Where's he going?" Rod muttered.

"Berto is making sure the path is clear and will wait for us in town. There are many tourists today," Carlos answered in a cheerful voice.

Alex breathed a sigh of relief she hadn't left her cover. The man would have easily caught up to her.

"If you take the donkeys and our money, how will we survive?" Rod asked.

"That is not my concern, *Senor* Halston."

"Are you going to kill us?"

233

Juan laughed. "If we had wanted to kill you, we would have done so in the jungle. You would already be dead. By the way, which of the Three Stooges am I?" He laughed again as Rod's mouth opened and closed like a grounded fish. "I know more English than I let on. In prison, they show many comedy movies. It is supposed to take our minds off of where we are. The Three Stooges were very popular. You and your sister are like Abbott and Costello. You, *Senor* Halston, are an idiot. You make fun of places and people whose customs you do not understand. You are lazy and your whining is not that of a man. You are nothing more than a spoiled *nino*."

"Why…why you…you…peasant," Rod said sputtering.

"Oh, Rod, shut the fuck up," Victoria snapped.

"Juan, are you ready?" Carlos called out, filling a backpack with the rest of the food. "Uncle Jose is anxious to go. We need to be out of town by nightfall."

"A few more things to load and we can leave."

Minutes later, the uncle and Juan departed with the donkeys. Carlos stood over Rod and Victoria for one last farewell.

"Eventually, you will free yourselves, but I warn you, do not try to follow us. This time we will not be concerned about your safety. For many years we have heard of this treasure and of a map. Now, we have it and will not give it up. I will also take these." He held up two passports. "They will bring a good price on the black market. I do not know if your country has a consulate in any of the towns of this region, but the American Embassy is located in Guatemala City. And now, I must go. It has been a pleasure doing business with you. *Adios*."

With that said he gave a mocking salute and hurried down the path. Alex soon lost sight of him in the dimming light of the jungle.

"Come on, help me get out of these ropes," Victoria demanded in a hard voice, struggling with her bonds.

"This is all your fault! If you hadn't lost the map in the first place, this wouldn't have happened," Rod replied.

"And I told you to stay with those three in town."

"What could I have done to prevent this?"

"I should have known better than to rely on you for anything. If you'd done as I said, you may have noticed something fishy, and returned to camp. At least, we would have been prepared—could have defended ourselves."

Victoria sported twin patches of red on her cheeks. Alex wouldn't like to be on the receiving end of that anger when it exploded.

"How? We met them at the end of the path. They had the drop on us before we knew what was happening. How do they know we won't go to the police?"

"And tell them what? That a map to a fabulous treasure we stole in the States has now been stolen from us? Like anyone would believe it. They'd probably die laughing." Victoria yanked viciously on the rope.

"Ow! Damn it, that hurt. Quit pulling so hard."

"Do you suppose you could try helping us get undone? Relax your hands so I can work this knot."

"What difference does it make if we do get loose? They have a head start and are armed."

"I have a gun," she stated.

Rod ceased struggling and turned his head, a look of astonishment on his face. "You have a what? How come you didn't tell me?"

"And have you play cowboy by strapping it on your hip to look cool? I wanted to keep its presence quiet."

"Where is it now? Did they find it?"

"I doubt it." She glanced toward the tent. "It's in with the wet laundry. The bag's still sitting where I left it."

"What's it doing in there?"

"I was in the jungle. I took it along in case I saw an animal or a snake."

"Where did you get it? You couldn't have gotten it through security in the States or customs down here."

"Don't ask," she explained.

"Hurry up with these ropes."

"I'm doing the best I can!"

Alex had heard enough. The men had moved at a brisk pace and should be far enough ahead not to be a threat. She crawled from her hiding space. Peeking through the foliage, she saw Victoria still worked at the ropes. Rod still complained. The bug zapper committed another loud insect execution. On that fitting note, Alex turned her back and proceeded toward town.

Quickening her steps in the increasing gloom, and peering around each bend in the trail to make sure the coast was clear, she stumbled out onto the path to town—alone—and hurried on, moving warily past the scattered houses. With the need for stealth behind her, she broke into a run.

Entering the town square, Alex wove her way through the diminished crowd and leaped up the steps of the hotel breathlessly asking the desk clerk, "*Senor* Rafferty, is he here?" She hoped the man understood.

He shook his head. "No, *senorita*. Come and leave..." he held up five fingers three times. Fifteen minutes. She'd missed him by fifteen lousy minutes.

"*Jorge y Miguel?*" she asked.

"*Jorge y Miguel* go *Senor* Rafferty."

Questioning the clerk further was useless. She

didn't know how to phrase "where did they go" and wouldn't understand him if he told her. She'd have to find Quinn on her own.

"*Gracias*," she muttered, then whirled and dashed back into the street.

So, the guys were together. Where? A cantina? They passed a respectable looking one a couple of blocks away this afternoon. She turned and ran for it.

Alex burst through the door to the little tavern. All conversation stopped, the patrons turning to stare. She ignored the men and gazed around the room, but saw no one she knew.

Back out on the street, she paused. Where else could they have gone? Did the priest tell Quinn something that required the presence of the other two men? She headed for the church, hoping she remembered the directions Quinn mentioned earlier.

It didn't take long to find. Entering, Alex looked around the pews. Several penitents prayed, but she saw neither Quinn nor the guides. Near the altar a door opened and a priest emerged.

Hurrying forward, she asked, still panting, "Father...do you...speak English?"

"A little, *senorita*. How may I help you?"

"Has a...*Senor* Rafferty been to...see you in the last couple of hours?"

"*Si*. He ask many questions and we talk. He leave about thirty or forty minutes ago. He say he was looking for a young lady. You?"

"Yes. I think so. Thank you, father."

Decorum forced her to use restraint and not run in a house of worship, but once outside she took off again. Maybe he had returned to the hotel—or the marketplace. That's where he'd left her. He and the guides could split up and cover more area.

She headed for the shops. All except a few stalls had closed. Slowing to a walk to catch her breath, it didn't take long to determine Quinn was not here. They must have doubled back to the hotel.

Taking a deep breath, Alex called upon her waning stamina to jog back to their lodgings. Climbing the stairs to the second floor, she stopped in front of Quinn's door, knocking and calling out his name. Silence answered. Frustrated, she rattled the doorknob. Locked. Damn it! She couldn't waste any more time.

Turning away, Alex groped for the key in her pocket, opened the door to her room, entered, and slammed it behind her, then swung into action.

Throwing her backpack on the bed, she barged into the bathroom, ripping her still damp clothing from the lines. All she wanted to do was get out of town, or at least out of this hotel. She'd sit up all night in an alley if necessary.

She tossed the clothing next to her backpack. How long would it take to get back to Guatemala City? When was the next flight out to the States? What would Quinn do when he finally heard the truth? She didn't want to think about that one, but swore to tell him as soon as they were out of here.

Alex was jamming her clothes into the backpack when a sharp knock on the door scared the hell out of her. She uttered a startled cry and whirled. The door opened and Quinn entered.

"Alex, where the hell have you been? I've been looking all over town for you."

"God, you scared the bejesus out of me. Where are Jorge and Miguel?"

"They're around town making inquiries about—" He stared at the backpack and the clothes she flung into it. "What are you doing?"

"I'm packing. Look, Quinn, I haven't got time to argue or explain, but we have to get out of here—now!"

"What? Are you nuts? Rod and Victoria are

actually in Kamachiquia. The priest told me one of his parishioners said he saw tourists with donkeys east of town. Jorge and Miguel are trying to find them. Alex, they're here."

"I know, I know. They're camped to the south."

He crossed the room, grabbed her arm, and swung her around to face him. "How do you know?"

"Because I saw Rod come out of a bar and followed him." She turned back to continue packing.

"You followed him? My God, did they see you?"

"No, they had their own problems."

He swung her around again, his expression a mixture of exasperation and puzzlement. "Stop this silly packing. What problems?"

God, didn't he understand they had to get out of here? Alex tossed the shirt onto the bed.

"They argued. That's all I have time to tell you. We have to get out of this hotel. We'll camp somewhere and head back to Guatemala City at first light."

"Why? What did you see and hear at their campsite?"

She took a deep breath. "Quinn, we don't have time for a discussion about this now. I know you don't understand, but please believe me when I say, we have to leave."

She sensed danger was close. Shivering, she broke out in goose bumps.

"Why?" he demanded.

"I'll tell you later. Trust my instincts for once."

"No, damn it. Tell me now."

"Just pack."

Her heart pounded and the urge to scream was strong. Every minute they argued wasted time.

"Alex, we aren't going anywhere until you calm down and tell me exactly—"

The door to her room burst open. They both whipped around to face it.

"Hello, darling. Miss me?" Rod said.

He walked through the door closely followed by Victoria. Quinn backed up a step. Alex did the same and stared into the business end of the revolver Victoria pointed at them.

Chapter Seventeen

Alex's first reaction was one of admiration. They had moved fast after getting free. And how did they trace her to the hotel? Had they seen her leaving? In her panic to pack and get out of town, she'd forgotten about the gun. After all that had happened in the past couple of weeks, not even being held at gunpoint scared her. Well, not too much. However, her instincts about impending danger had been correct.

"Hello, Quinn," Victoria greeted in a cool voice. The gun never wavered. She leveled it at Quinn's chest.

Rod closed the door and leaned back against it with a smirk.

Hang in there, asshole. I'm going to wipe that silly smile right off your face.

"Hello, Victoria. Fancy meeting you here. It's been a long time," Quinn replied just as coolly. The expression on his face looked calm, but anticipating. Alex could almost see the wheels turning in his mind.

"Up until two hours ago, I'd have said not long enough. How did you find us?" the blonde woman asked.

"Are you kidding? You and the caravan left a trail a five-year-old could follow. Every villager between here and Abaj is laughing about the crazy gringos with the donkeys."

"Wrong answer, Rafferty," Rod drawled. "We've been checking our backsides for the past five days. No one has followed us. Wanna try again? How did

241

you show up here?"

"And I'd like to know why you killed my grandfather. Did he catch you red-handed?"

"We didn't kill Cash. He and Rod fought, but that's all," Victoria maintained.

"Then explain how he ended up with a crushed skull," Quinn answered in a hard, anger filled voice.

Victoria wet her lips before replying, "It wasn't our fault. I swear. All we wanted was the map. We're con artists and thieves, not killers."

"I guess that makes everything all right then. Please forgive my suspicious nature. Why did you set my grandfather up as your next mark? He and my grandmother weren't rich."

"I didn't at first. I was almost broke. The proceeds from my last payoff were nearly gone, so I went back to legitimate work, this time. There was nothing else on the horizon."

"So, you just kind of stumbled into my grandfather's house?"

"The employment agency sent me to Cash Marriott. Since the job included room, board, and a good salary, I jumped at the chance. You could call it the luck of the draw."

"No, my grandfather was a damned good poker player. I'd call it playing with a stacked deck. How did he get the map?"

"I don't know. He just showed up with it one day, ordered me to put his memoirs aside, and help by typing his research notes. It only took a couple of weeks to realize he was onto something. That's when I contacted Rod."

"Why? What did you need him for?" Quinn asked. His lip curled in a contemptuous sneer.

He'd as much as called her former boyfriend worthless. Alex wanted to laugh, remembering Victoria's words to Rod not too long ago. Rod's face flushed an unbecoming red. The arrow had found its mark.

*Just wait, Rod old buddy. There's more to come,
if I can pull it off.*

She swung her attention back when Victoria
answered Quinn's question. "I needed someone to
check up on the notes and to keep an eye on Cash
when he left the house."

"Why kill him?"

"We didn't. He was supposed to be out that
night. For some reason, he came home early. Rod
and I had just opened the safe when he walked in.
Since it was obvious what we were doing, he
threatened to call the cops and headed for the
phone."

Rod continued. "I grabbed him and he took a
swing, hitting me on the side of the head. I swung
back. We fought for a few seconds, and then I pushed
him away. He dropped in front of the fireplace, got
up, and came after me again. Suddenly, he clutched
his chest and staggered a couple of steps. The
hearthrug was scrunched up during the struggle. He
tripped over it, fell, and hit his head."

"You could have called an ambulance on your
way out. Instead, you just left him there to die!"
Quinn's voice rose and his eyes spit fire.

"I think he was dead before he hit the ground. I
checked, but couldn't find a pulse. Vicky grabbed the
map, I grabbed her bags, and we got the hell out."

"Why steal the map before he was done
authenticating it?"

Rod snickered. His sister shifted from foot to
foot before answering.

"That day, Cash had gone to the library and the
librarian made a comment about all the research
being done on Mayan treasures. She said a man
claiming to be Cash's research assistant had been in
with some to notes to investigate. Naturally, it was
my brother." She threw Rod a nasty look. "Cash

came home, caught me making the extra copies, and fired me."

"I understand that. He'd put up with a lot of things, but he hated disloyalty. He also hated computers. Never could get the hang of them. If he had, he would have done his research on the Internet, and you wouldn't have had the chance to copy anything. How did you lose the map?"

Alex wasn't sure, but Quinn had a look in his eyes that told her he was formulating a plan. Unfortunately, Victoria had a gun. She had to stop him from doing something impulsive.

"My father had an older sister. My Aunt Iris is an airhead. She fusses and twitters around and can't keep her mind on anything longer than fifteen minutes. She's also gullible. The silly twit believes everything I tell her. She thinks I work for a multi-millionaire who travels a lot and gives me generous time off. I go to her after a con."

"Only this time it was a little bit more complicated, wasn't it?" Quinn said.

"We knew there would be a lot of heat in Los Angeles about your grandfather's death and the robbery, so Rod and I split up. He went to Vegas with most of my money to score a new mark, and I headed for my aunt's in Phoenix. I couldn't afford to rest too long. I needed to get a new job, so I left for Denver. I hid the map behind a print of another old map hanging on Aunt Iris's wall. When I returned the print was gone and the race was on."

"It took us over two years to trace its path to the late Joseph Cowan and his estate sale. A little charm, a little attention, and the secretary at the auction house answered all my questions. They led me straight to Alex," Rod said, the smirk back on his face

Alex had been silent, preferring to let Quinn deal with his end of the map quest in his own way.

He needed answers and closure. Now, it was her turn to get explanations—and satisfaction. She had a plan. Granted, she'd devised it on the spot, but she crossed her fingers that it would save the map and not get them killed.

"If you knew I had the map, why did you wait so long to steal it?" she asked.

Rod shrugged. "I figured it was somewhere in your shop. You were always there, and by living over the place, I couldn't risk breaking in at night to look for it."

"Some people wouldn't have been so cautious," she remarked dryly, throwing a quick glance at Quinn. He was engaged in a stare down with Victoria. She had no idea if he caught her comment. "So, you just bided your time, huh?"

"More or less. I waited until you went on your first buying trip. Nothing turned up. I was afraid you'd sold the damned thing. Then you took me to meet your grandfather."

"How thoughtful of me," she said.

"The minute you told me he was some kind of an expert on the Maya I knew the map had to be there. Then he died."

"How convenient for you. You could have stolen it anytime after I found it. Why wait a month?"

Alex hoped her face showed none of the anger building in her. She wanted the whiny bastard unsuspecting.

"Well, darling, you were doing all that work to see if it was real. Why should I put myself out?" He laughed lightly. "Besides, you knew who to contact. By the way, did that last guy you talked to give you his seal of approval?"

"Yes," she answered curtly.

She glanced at Quinn again and from the expression in his eyes, she knew he had a plan of action.

No way, babe. Not before I'm done. I've earned this.

During all the explanations, Rod had abandoned leaning against the door to come further into the room and now stood five feet to the right of his sister. The time had come. She mentally crossed her fingers that the expression on her face was earnest and hopeful, before advancing a few steps toward him.

"Don't move!" Victoria ordered in a harsh voice, her gun hand never wavering. The evil-looking weapon still aimed for Quinn's chest. She obviously considered him the greater threat.

Ignoring her, Alex said, "Rod, I don't know what kind of hold she has over you, but you don't have to do this. Come back to Chicago with me. We'll start all over, no questions asked. How about it? Just you and me, the way we were before all of this nonsense began."

"I don't believe it," Quinn muttered.

Victoria snorted back a laugh.

Alex stood in front of her ex-lover, his smirk growing into a grin.

Rod shook his head, "Alex, Alex, not even you can believe I would ever do that. I don't stay anywhere for more than a few months. Hey, kid, you were fun while it lasted. I don't need you anymore."

"But...but Rod..."

"Sweetie, the thrill is gone. The ride is over. Live with it. Have yourself a good cry and chalk it up to one of life's little experiences."

"Oh, Rod, I have no intention of crying," she said in a syrupy voice. The bubble of anger and contempt had climbed into her throat, reaching the flash point. "I think I'll sing."

"You'll what?" he asked, the smug look giving way to puzzlement.

"I said I'm going to sing."

Zero hour.

Alex doubled up her fist and drove it as hard as possible into his stomach just below the breastbone, the impact vibrating up her arm.

Oh, yes! The first tremor of satisfaction rippled through her—almost, but not quite as good as sex.

The air blasted out of Rod's lungs in a loud whoosh. Pain and astonishment replaced puzzlement. At the same time, she used her heavy hiking boot to stomp hard on his sneaker-clad foot. He emitted a sound that sounded like "ow", but it was hard to tell since he remained breathless.

Oh, baby, I'm just warming up!

She stomped again for emphasis, her foot tingling from the contact. This time the "ow" was easier to understand. He bent over to grab his abused instep.

Alex cut off his yelp of pain when her fist made contact with his nose in a vicious uppercut. She felt the jolt clear up to her shoulder. Blood spurted and his hands went to protect his face. Grasping his shoulders for support, her knee slammed into his groin like a pile driver. She repeated the action.

Oh, yes. It feels so good. Close to orgasmic. I'll have to remember to tell Quinn.

Rod dropped to the floor, writhing in agony, and able to articulate only a strange, gasping gurgle.

Leaning over him she said in a snotty voice, "Sing, Rod. Solar plexus, instep, nose, and groin. Self-Defense 101 at Griffith College when I was sixteen. Live with it. Chalk it up to one of life's little experiences...sweetie!"

"Jesus," Victoria muttered.

"Nobody uses me and gets away with it. Nobody!" Alex declared. She drew her foot back to kick him, and then thought better of it. He wasn't worth the energy.

Victoria stared, a look of respect tinged with

amusement in her eyes. Quinn simply stared. Alex turned and sat on the edge of the bed, her revenge complete.

Ignoring her groaning, sobbing brother, Victoria swung her attention back to Quinn.

"So, how did you end up here? And never mind the lies. I'm pretty sure I know. Little Miss Black Belt made a copy, too, didn't she? I have need of it now, so fork it over, and we'll be on our way."

"Why the hell do you need another map?" Quinn asked.

"Let's just say our guides were less than honest."

Quinn laughed. "You were robbed? I guess there really is no honor among thieves, huh?"

The irony of the whole ordeal struck Alex as bizarre. The ring of theft had come full circle.

"I thought that would amuse you. They also took the original. We stopped by the fountain trying to decide which way they'd gone when I saw you walk into the hotel. The desk clerk gave us your room number. The shouting led us here. Now, enough true confessions. Hand over the map."

"Vicky, this may come as a shock, but we don't have one. We knew where you'd be and followed. I guess your guides were a little short on back-watching skills."

Alex almost rolled her eyes at the serious, sincere look on his face. She damned near believed him herself.

"No, Quinn, I don't buy it. You've got one all right. I'll search your rooms and strip you both naked to find it. Make this easy. Cough it up."

Rod finally managed to make it to his knees, his hands cupping where her knee had found its mark. His face twisted in rage and what she hoped was severe pain.

"You bitch!" he said in a croaking voice.

Alex shrugged her shoulders in contempt and

disinterest. "I'd say the same if I were in your position."

"You will be. I can't wait to search you!"

"I've heard the old knee to the groin thing can cause impotence. Let me know if it's true, will you?"

"Fucking bitch!" His lip curled in a snarl.

"Shut up, Rod," his sister snapped. "The map, Quinn, now!"

"The only map I have is of modern day Guatemala. I swear it."

"I don't believe you. Move over and sit next to the Terminator. Rod, quit wheezing and grabbing your balls. Start searching. Begin with the suitcases."

Quinn took a step toward Victoria. "I said move over there." She cocked the gun.

Alex had enough. The situation had deteriorated and the last thing she wanted was any kind of a personal search. She believed Victoria *would* strip search them. Then they'd find the real map in record time. The woman's expression bordered on desperate.

The time had come to get rid of these two. Standing, Alex fumbled with the zipper on one of her pockets.

"I've had it! I'm tired of this wretched jungle, this miserable country, and of you. I got what I came for, and I hope your nuts hurt for a week. I'm going home where the only thieves I encounter are muggers and the occasional shoplifter who can be arrested by real cops. You two make me sick." She pulled the copy out and threw it on the floor in front of Rod. "There it is. Take it. I don't care."

"Alex!" Quinn roared, horrified disbelief written all over his face.

Rod grabbed the map and staggered to his feet, then still bent over stood behind his sister. Quinn made another move toward Victoria, but stopped when she raised the gun higher and aimed for his heart.

"Don't be an idiot, Quinn. I know how to use this and won't hesitate to do so. Rod, is it the map?"

"Yeah, it's real. Let's get out of here," he muttered, casting a victorious, yet vicious look at Alex.

"Where's the room key?" she asked.

"On the dresser," Alex said pointing

"Get it, Rod. Hurry up. We need to get out of here."

"You got want you wanted. Just go. The sooner you do, the sooner I can get out of this dump," Alex said in a weary tone.

She didn't feel weary. What she did feel was Quinn glaring at her. A quick glance at him verified it. His eyes burned black with fury.

Victoria didn't miss the exchange. "Come on, Rod. These two are about to fight like alley cats. Sorry, Quinn, but I always come out on top. Oh, and don't try to follow us again. This time, *I'll* be watching the back door. A body in a hotel room is awkward, but a body in the jungle will just rot."

The two of them backed toward, then through the door, closing and locking it.

There was two seconds of silence before Quinn exploded. "How could you? How could you do that to me?"

"They'd have found it anyway."

"I had a plan. I was going to rush Victoria and disarm her. With Rod incapacitated, it would have been easy."

"She'd have shot you before you'd gone two feet."

"No, she wouldn't. It was a bluff. She couldn't risk the sound of a shot. Damn it all! Why didn't you let me handle it?" he yelled. His face turned red, and he clenched his fists.

"Quinn, please, let me—"

"Is that the real reason you insisted on coming? Is that all that mattered to you? Punching Rod's lights out?"

"If you'll just calm down a—"

"I will not calm down! Alex, I trusted you. I thought we were partners in every way. You've not only betrayed me, but my mother and my grandmother as well. God, I could just strangle you."

For an instant, she wondered if he'd use those fists to deck her. The anguish in his eyes, on his face, and in his voice tore at her.

"Quinn, I understand you're angry, but I can explain everything."

"There is no explanation for something like this!"

"Just listen. Where are you going?"

He stalked to the door and rattled the knob furiously. When it refused to give, lashed at it with his foot until the wood splintered and the door swung open.

"Quinn, wait a minute. Where are you going?"

He turned to glare at her in such rage she fell back a step, silenced. His chest heaved and his eyes narrowed into slits.

"Going? First of all, I'm going to get drunk. Then I'm going to form a plan. I intend to get that map back. Don't count on coming with me. Lady, I don't care where the hell you go as long as it's in the opposite direction from me!"

He stomped through the door, his footsteps echoing down the hallway. Alex looked at the ceiling, trying not to cry.

I should have told him the truth earlier.

But she didn't and now faced the consequences. She wanted to run after him, and then rejected the idea. He was too angry and raw to listen to any explanation offered now. Later, when he had a chance to calm down, she'd tell him the whole story and why she'd given up the copy tonight.

Sighing, she pushed the desk chair in front of the shattered door and glanced at her watch. It was only a little after eight o'clock. It must have stopped. No, the second hand still swept around the dial.

Like a robot, Alex resumed packing. At least Rod and Victoria were gone. However, she'd feel a hell of a lot better when they put a few more miles between themselves and the brother-sister act.

The loss of Quinn left her cold and desolated. She sat on the edge of the bed, her eyes clouded with unshed tears and a crumpled shirt in her hand. Let him have his anger and his whiskey tonight. He was entitled. Tomorrow morning, he'd listen.

****

Quinn stormed out of the hotel. He still couldn't believe it. The betrayal was like a knife in his back and he'd never seen it coming. Alex had screwed him royally. At any other time, he'd laugh at the accuracy of his terminology, but tonight, he saw nothing funny about it.

How could he have been so stupid? She manipulated him from the beginning to find her ex-lover and seek revenge. He felt dirty and used—violated. She didn't give a tinker's damn about him, his mother and grandmother, or their futures. All that "Rod is being coerced" crap was just that—crap! She'd homed right in on his overactive hormones, using sex as the instrument to cloud his judgment. She was no better than Victoria. She was worse. He didn't love Victoria.

He slowed his step and entered a cantina. Sliding onto a stool at the bar, he ordered rum. A good, potent rum. He killed it in one swallow and ordered another. This time he sipped as his temper eased somewhat, but not his heartache.

He loved her. What a time to discover it. He relived every kiss, every caress, every fevered moment.

Damn! He bolted the rest of his drink and slammed his empty glass on the bar, signaling for a refill.

How could he have let this happen? And when had it happened? He'd realized Alex was different from day one. He groaned remembering how the light had shone through that flimsy little nightgown showing him a tantalizing view of a fantastic body. His hormones had been at warp speed ever since. And she'd known it. Known it and used it.

"Boy, Rafferty, you sure know how to pick 'em. You had to choose one with a body to die for, intelligence, a wry sense of humor, and a treacherous, black soul. A grand slam," he muttered into his glass.

He ordered another drink only this time sipped it slowly. Getting drunk sounded like a good idea, but it wouldn't help the situation.

All right, think! The map is gone. How do I get it back?

He had no idea where Rod and Victoria camped and was damned if he'd ask Alex. Besides, he didn't want to tromp through the jungle in the dark. He'd look for them at first light. Even it they took off tonight, they'd set a slow pace. Rod would walk bent over with his legs wide apart for a while. Alex packed a wallop. The old adage about a woman scorned flitted through his mind.

Get your mind off of her. Concentrate.

Taking Victoria down would be no problem, in spite of the gun. She'd be no match for three men. Rod would be easier considering his physical condition at the moment. Or maybe he'd be better off following the two. Even if they watched their backs, they'd leave a trail a mile wide.

Quinn lifted his glass, and then stopped abruptly with it halfway to his lips. Wait a minute! He didn't need the map. He'd studied and compared the copy and the modern map every day for over a week. There was no reason to follow Rod and Victoria. He *knew* where he was going and which route was the fastest. He *knew* how to get there. Could that have occurred to Alex when she tossed the map at Rod?

Leave Alex out of this. Whether she knew or not is immaterial. She still handed the map over to my archenemies without so much as an ounce of remorse.

He lowered his glass to the bar and pushed it away. No more rum. He needed to think. He just might salvage his family's future after all.

Quinn left the bar and returned to the hotel where he found Jorge and Miguel waiting for him. After informing them of the night's events, he then told the guides of his plan. They in turn gave him the news they had a general idea of where Victoria and Rod's camp was located.

In his room, Quinn made several phone calls, and then studied his modern map. He turned out the light and went to bed. By dawn, he and Miguel would be gone. Jorge would deal with Alex. Disengaging himself from her physically was easy. Emotionally would take longer, a lot longer.

****

Alex experienced one of the most miserable nights of her life. Unable to lock her door and with the safety of the map her highest priority, she removed it from her pocket. She contemplated putting it under her pillow or the mattress, but those seemed like obvious hiding places. She wanted it closer, attached to her body if possible. Using Band-Aids from the first aid kit, she secured the plastic encased map to her tummy. It was uncomfortable, but at least no casual intruder would think of looking for it there—she hoped.

Sleep was impossible, and she thought she heard Quinn return sometime around midnight. Alex wanted to wrap him in her arms telling him everything. She curbed the urge on the theory he was probably drunk and not in a forgiving mood.

She slept fitfully, arose the next morning at seven-thirty, took a quick shower, and finished packing. Was Quinn now ready to listen? She'd give him another half-hour. A hangover might be her only ally.

With the map now safely back in her pocket, she fastened the last buckle on her backpack when someone knocked on the door.

"Quinn? I'm coming, I'm coming."

Kicking the chair out of the way, she opened it. Jorge looked at her with a somber expression. Her spirits fell to the floor. Alex knew he was the bearer of bad news.

"Good morning, *senorita*," he said, awkwardly shifting his weight from foot to foot.

"Good morning, Jorge. Is Mr. Rafferty ready to leave?"

"I am sorry, *senorita*, but *Senor* Rafferty and Miguel leave at sunrise. He ask me to give you this." He handed her an envelope.

"Oh, I see. Would you like to come in while I read?"

"No, *senorita*. If you are packed, I will take your bag down to the lobby."

Nodding her assent, she waited until he left before ripping open the letter. Among the contents were a sheet of paper and several hundred American dollars worth of Guatemalan currency. Alex slowly opened the note and read.

"Miguel and I are going on as planned. Four or five hours to the southwest is a town called Mesados. It has a hotel and bus service. It will stop in Los Arcos and you can continue on to Guatemala City. I made a reservation in your name at the Hotel American. Enclosed is enough local money for anything you need. An airline ticket is waiting at the

Trans Global Airline ticket counter at the airport. Do not miss the plane. If you do, you're on your own. Jorge will guide you to Mesados and see you onto the bus or into the hotel.

I wish I could say I wasn't bitter, but I can't. I don't understand or forgive your actions. Have a safe journey."

He hadn't bothered to sign it. She sat on the bed and swallowed her tears. He'd left her. It was her worst fear—alone and abandoned. A cold emptiness nestled in the pit of her stomach. She gulped more tears.

Alex tried to push her misery aside and think logically. At least he left some money, and she had Jorge for a portion of the trip. She supposed she'd get by with her Spanish phrase book until reaching Guatemala City.

Glancing at the letter, she could no longer stop the pain ripping through her. With a gut-wrenching sob, she buried her face in the pillow and cried her heart out. She'd lost him and had no one to blame but herself.

Heartsick, she eventually rose and bathed her splotchy, swollen face with cold water, then left to join Jorge downstairs. She didn't care if he saw the ravages the tears had brought or what he thought. Nothing mattered anymore.

"If you don't mind, Jorge, I'll have a very quick breakfast, and then we can go. My door was damaged last night. Please find out how much to repair it."

"*Senor* Rafferty take care of everything this morning, *senorita*."

"I see. Well, I'll only be a few minutes. I'm sorry you're delayed in your journey with Mr. Rafferty and Miguel."

"It is no problem. I will carry your backpack and leave the tent and sleeping bag here. I will get them when I return. I have only a small pack to carry back, and I move very fast."

Alex ate, too numb to taste the food. Twenty minutes later they were on their way southwest to Mesados. The trail was wide and Jorge assured her they would make the town and her bus by two o'clock.

Following the guide, she wondered how Quinn would react when arriving at X. He'd probably do the same as she—demand answers.

I haven't seen the last of him.

Hope that maybe not all was lost lifted her spirits. It was the only thing that kept her going. She regrouped and resolved to get him back. Alex gave him two weeks tops.

Chapter Eighteen

Alex leaned her elbows on the counter cupping her chin in her hands. Depressed and forlorn, she couldn't whip up enthusiasm for anything. She was bored. That had been the state of affairs ever since she returned from Guatemala ten days ago. After the excitement and danger of the journey, Waukegan with the everyday life that had suited her before, now grated on her nerves. It was just plain dull.

She caught a glimpse of her glum reflection in a gilded mirror hanging on the wall. She made a face and turned her attention back to the notepad on the counter.

Sighing, she picked up her pen and tried to focus. She needed to go on a buying trip soon. Antique kitchen utensils had been popular lately, as had picture frames.

It might be a good idea to see if I can find a couple of Hoosier cabinets. One kitchen antique often led to another and a hutch was the perfect place to display the smaller items.

Alex jotted the idea on her 'to do' list, and then tossed her pen down. Oh, what was the use? She couldn't concentrate on anything at the moment. A quick look at one of several clocks in the store showed it was four-thirty, almost closing time. No customers in over an hour told her to call it a day. But then what would she do? Another video? Another microwave dinner? Another night alone to think and remember?

Memories of Guatemala were bittersweet. Where was Quinn now? Had he made it to San Luis?

Had Rod and Victoria shown up? What had the reactions been? Had they all given up or were they determined to continue the search, convinced they'd made a miscalculation?

The last leg of her journey home was lonely. Jorge set a fast pace along the trail. They spoke little. She had nothing to say. With every step farther away from Quinn, her heart grew heavier and, not for the first time, Alex wondered if her actions and secrecy had been worth it.

They entered Mesados in time to catch the bus. Thanking Jorge, she boarded the rickety vehicle and waved a sad goodbye. As the bus pulled away, the guide jogged down the street the way they had come to return to his comrades.

The bus bumped and jolted over potholes while stopping at every village and hamlet along the way. Night fell by the time they pulled into Los Arcos. She spent her free time in Guatemala City buying new clothes and trading in the backpack for a suitcase. For the first time in her life, she slept on an airplane.

Alex jerked out of her reverie when two of the clocks chimed the three-quarter hour simultaneously. The hell with it. It was time to close.

She bent over to slide the notepad into a cabinet when the newly installed bell over the front door tinkled, indicating a last minute customer. Rising, she tried to smother the irritation, and then stopped dead. Her breath caught in her throat, and her heart thumped with slow heavy beats.

Quinn locked the door and flipped over the 'closed' sign. Turning, he strode to the counter, leaned over, grasped her shoulders, then pulled her up and halfway over the barrier to kiss her senseless.

When he finished, he said, "We need to talk."

Shaken and trembling, Alex wet her lips looking

him square in the eye. "Yes, we do. I knew you'd want answers."

Her gaze ran over him. God, he looked good, his eyes more blue than gray today. In her last view of him, they'd been the color of a thundercloud about to spawn a tornado.

"Let's go upstairs where we won't be interrupted," he said.

"Why don't you get us some dinner while I shove today's receipts into the safe and make myself a whole lot more comfortable?"

"Lee Chen's?"

"Of course."

"A number six, extra spicy with an order of crab rangoons?"

"You remembered?" she asked in surprise.

"I've remembered a lot of things during the past week or so, especially where you're concerned. Make it two and call in the order. I'll be back in twenty minutes."

He leaned over, kissed her again and left.

Locking the door with trembling fingers, she emptied the till, and then shoved the money into the safe, replacing the chair hurriedly. Who cared how many indentations there were in the carpet? She'd come a long way.

She raced upstairs, changed into a caftan, and then stopped to catch her breath, trying to bring her sizzling nerves and pounding heart under control. Her fingers stroked the cool jade of the bracelet on her left wrist.

He came back! She feared he wouldn't, but he had. And he wasn't angry. How could he be angry and kiss her like that?

Closer to thirty minutes passed before he climbed the outside stairs to her apartment.

"You forgot to call in the order."

"Oh, so I did. I'm sorry."

He set the bag on the counter and folded his arms as he faced her.

"You knew there was no treasure from the beginning, didn't you?"

In answer, she brushed past him saying, "Have a seat."

He followed and sat at the dining table as she pulled a book out of the bookcase and handed it to him.

"*Mayan Myths, Legends, and Truths* by George Maxwell," he read. "George Maxwell?"

"My grandfather. You'll be interested in the chapter on page one hundred thirty-eight."

Alex returned to the kitchen to fill their plates, stopping to inhale the aromas of spicy, garlicky chicken and fried rice.

"It says here and I quote, 'The legend of the five Mayan kings and their purported treasure first surfaced sometime in the mid-16th century shortly after the Spanish conquest of present day Guatemala,'" he read as she set his plate and a cold bottle of beer in front of him. "When did your grandfather write this?"

"In 1980 or thereabouts. It was one of the few books he authored that had any sales outside of the academic community," she explained, digging into her food and letting the spicy flavor roll over her tongue before taking a swig of beer.

"So, the treasure never existed at all," he mused, closing the book and turning his attention to the food.

"There are several theories about that. One is that the treasure existed, but was stolen by invading Mayan from the north. The second theory is that the Spanish discovered it when they first conquered the area, but never recorded or shipped it to Spain. The first theory is probably the closest."

"Why?" He took a bite of the spicy food and

swallowed some beer. "This tastes great, especially after beans and rice for the last three weeks. Beer?"

"Hey, what can I say? I've developed a taste for it. Where was I? Oh, yes, the theory. It just seems more logical."

"How come?"

"The Spanish recorded damned near everything. They were meticulous thieves, and there's no mention in any Spanish archives regarding a treasure from that area."

"How do you know?"

"My grandfather researched his work carefully."

"So did mine, and that's what he thought, too. Could it still be undiscovered?" he asked.

"No, I doubt it. I don't think there was much of a treasure to begin with. Those five villages were small and any riches they may have had were few and far between. Remember the cave we found? It appeared undisturbed, yet contained very little. I think that over the years the size of the treasure has been magnified."

Quinn went back to the kitchen for seconds and another beer. "Yet, you swore the map was authentic. You were very emphatic about that." He sat back down.

"I didn't lie."

He stared at her. "It *was* the map, wasn't it? I thought so. From the beginning you wanted your map back."

"Everybody—you, Victoria, Rod—all assumed that when I said it was *real*, I was referring to the treasure. Even your grandfather made that assumption. I suspected otherwise the minute I took a good look at it."

"The priest at Santa Rita said the diaries mentioned the Spaniards had a map. So, it dates from the mid-to-late 16th century?"

"Try the end of the 11th or early 12th century."

"Are you to telling me it's Mayan?" he asked, his eyebrows rising.

"Yep! The Conquistadors probably found it when they ravaged some Mayan town. Over the years it's been followed and written on in Spanish. Let me start at the beginning."

They cleared away the dishes, opened more beer and settled on opposite ends of the sofa as she began her story.

"Apparently, my grandfather never bothered to look through the box I gave him. I found it in the same corner where I put it."

"So, your grandfather never saw the map. If he had, would he have recognized it for what it was?"

"Oh, I'm sure of it. The minute I found it stuck between the pages of one of the books, I knew it was different."

"Why?" He took a drink and watched her closely.

"The paper was thicker, more textured than any I'd ever felt before. I also noticed the map contained glyphs."

"Glyphs? As in hieroglyphics? Like the Egyptians?"

"Kind of. They were faded, but visible."

"Was that the border on the top and the bottom?" At her nod, he asked, "Do you know what it said?"

"Something along the lines of what the Spanish writing said about the legend of the five Mayan kings. At any rate, I began to wonder, so I took it to a friend of my grandfather's who suggested I take it to a paper expert and so on. The Mayan manufactured paper much the same way as the ancient Egyptians did papyrus.

"I made a copy so the original wouldn't get damaged any further during the research. The day Rod stole the map I received the final confirmation from a professor of ancient languages. The glyphs weren't just random drawings, but clearly stated what the map was about. And then, all hell broke loose."

"Why didn't you tell me this right off?"

"I wanted the map back. It was so rare, so priceless, that I knew what I had to do. For all I knew, it was the *only* original Mayan map in existence. In my idealistic mind I believed the map belonged in a museum. Call me naïve, but that's the way of it. I wasn't about to let that weasel Rod have it—not that he'd have a clue the *map* was real."

She ran her fingers through her hair and bit her lip as she tried to put her feelings at that time into words.

"I couldn't go after it on my own and all you were interested in was the treasure. I was afraid if I told you it was bunk, you'd say forget about the whole thing. I didn't trust you enough to tell you about the map. I didn't know *you*, not then.

"When I found out why you wanted the treasure, I felt like a rat. I almost told you on the plane. I wanted to tell you a dozen different times, but couldn't figure out how to do it. I left it too late."

She finished her beer and set the bottle on the coffee table, then snuggled into the cushions, her legs curled under her.

He stared, his mouth curving into a lopsided half smile. "A lot of things about that week puzzled me, the most glaring being the last night. You were wildly flinging clothes into your backpack, demanding that we leave. You were damned near hysterical, and *that* was totally out of character."

"On the plane home, I got to thinking about your determination to recover the map, your lack of enthusiasm, and then I remembered your comments and questions regarding the treasure. Plus y*ou'd* seen Rod and followed him. *You* knew where their camp was located and *you* didn't seem at all surprised when they burst in on us. Once again, I thought about your strange behavior. Why were you so anxious to leave? Then I made the connection. What if? Mission accomplished, right? You managed to get the original map."

She took a deep breath and let it out. "Mission accomplished," she confirmed.

"How?"

Alex spent the next fifteen or twenty minutes giving him a blow-by-blow description of her tailing Rod, the switching of the bogus map she'd carried from Chicago for the real one, and witnessing the thieves taking everything.

"Good God, no wonder you tossed him the copy," he exclaimed when she finished, a look of respect in his eyes.

"I couldn't let the real map be found. I knew you'd be angry. I just never realized how angry. I don't think I've ever seen a human being that furious before."

Quinn leaned forward and rested his elbows on his knees. He shook his head, then sat back to run his hand over his face and through his hair.

"I was angry all right and in no mood to hear any explanations. Of course, if I'd curbed my impulses, listened to you, and not taken off, I would have had us out of there in a flash." He paused and looked her in the eye. "So, where is the map?"

"In the hands of a prestigious auction house being authenticated all over again. The manager called me yesterday. He sees no problems and expects to sell it to the highest bidder in a few weeks. We're partners. Half of that selling price is yours."

"What happened to idealistic and museums?"

"You happened. You, your mother, and your grandmother. If a museum wants it, let 'em bid for it."

"How much do they say its worth?"

"It's hard to say, but I figure on a substantial return." She named an amount that had his jaw dropping and his eyes wide in disbelief.

"Holy Saint Shit!"

She laughed. "That's enough for your mother and grandmother to live like queens."

He chuckled with her. "Rod and Victoria had the biggest score of their lives in their hands for weeks and never knew it."

"Quinn, I've always been curious. Why weren't Rod and Victoria arrested for your grandfather's death? They never seemed to be shy about hiding themselves."

"The doctors said my grandfather died of a heart attack. There wasn't any evidence to the contrary. Rod was right. My grandfather died before he hit the floor. Proving deprived indifference or that their actions brought it on would be almost impossible considering his medical history. Of course, I'll never believe that, but I'm not the cops or a doctor."

"Which brings me to another question. What happened after you left me that night? Where did you go? What did you do?"

He tapped the bottom of his empty beer bottle against the palm of his hand and said, "Mind if I have another? How about you?"

She shook her head. He rose, walked into the kitchen, and returned with a new bottle, then sat down again.

Taking a long swallow, he placed it precisely on the coffee table and eased back into his corner of the sofa. He told her about his feelings of betrayal and how he realized he didn't need the map.

"I'm so sorry, Quinn. I just never knew *how* to tell you. What happened after you left?"

"The next morning, Miguel and I found Rod and Victoria's empty camp. They'd taken their clothes, the tent, some food, and that was all. It didn't matter. I knew where I was going."

"Their guides stole just about everything. Rod and Victoria each had a couple of duffle bags and I think I saw at least one backpack," she said. "How long did it take you to get to San Luis?"

"Less than two days. We moved fast. We got a room at a local inn. The next morning we crossed the footbridge, headed east, and guess what we found at X?"

"A small museum?"

"And a campground. How did you know?"

"Grandfather's book. He mentions it further along in the chapter."

He sighed and shook his head. "I'd originally told Jorge and Miguel we were doing research on a book about Mayan legends. When we got to the museum, Miguel knew all about it. He'd been there before. If I'd been honest, he would have told me the truth in the beginning."

"It seems we were all a little short on that commodity. What did you do next?"

"I asked a few questions of the curator. He said the museum was near an old burial site discovered in 1950. It contained a few artifacts, but nothing that could be considered great riches. I was all set to head back to Guatemala City when it dawned on me you must have known what we'd find."

"I know," she said unhappily. "I was trying to figure out a way to break it to you and chickened out each time. Then events moved so fast, I got run over. Did Rod and Victoria ever show up?"

"Yeah, the next day. I staked out the campground and waited for them. I had to see the expressions on their faces. It was worth the extra time."

"What was the reaction?"

"Stunned disbelief. Rod kept saying over and

over 'She said the map was real.' He looked as though he'd been, well, conned. Poetic justice, if you ask me."

"It's probably the first time a mark has ever fought back. I wonder how he liked being on the receiving end of a swindle."

"I doubt if he recognized the irony. By the way, he still walked funny. You did a real dance on him."

For only the second time in a week, she laughed. "It was spur of the moment. I never wanted to confront him at all, but when the opportunity arose, I jumped all over it. God, it felt good!" She leaned forward and whispered, "Just like an orgasm," and then laughed when he grinned. "What was Victoria's reaction?"

"She looked like she wanted to cry, if you can believe that. I know this is going to sound nuts, but I felt a little sorry for her. The look of defeat on her face went deeper than just disappointment."

"Did you talk to them?"

"No. I'd been watching the entrance to the museum and followed them inside. I stayed 'in the shadows and listened while they talked to the curator. Then they left."

"Did their thieving guides show up, too?"

"Not while I was there."

"I wonder how long it took them to realize the two maps they stole didn't match," Alex mused. "I also wonder where Rod and Victoria are now and what they're doing."

"Probably scoping out a victim for the next con. For all I know they're still in Guatemala. We'll never see them again. Unless Rod wants revenge."

"Don't worry. There's an alarm system in place now. What did you do after Rod and Victoria left?"

"Returned to Guatemala City. I paid Jorge and Miguel and flew here. I needed answers."

She rose pacing the limited space of the room.

"Quinn, I can't tell you how sorry I am about not trusting you. I wanted to and should have, but I just couldn't bring myself to confess. Our relationship had become complicated, and I didn't want to lose it or you."

Quinn also rose and stopped her agitated strides by placing his hands on her shoulders and forcing her to look at him.

"Alex, I missed you the first day on the trail. I missed your warmth, your smile, the sound of your voice, your stubborn determination, even your damned logic. The night I walked out, I admitted I loved you. I think that's why it hurt so much. I loved you, and you didn't trust me." He tightened his grip as his eyes bored into hers. "So, have I just made a fool out of myself?"

Alex almost melted. She threw her arms around his neck and burrowed into his chest.

"Oh, Quinn, I love you, too! I don't know how it happened. It just did. I knew it the day we made love behind the waterfall. It confused the hell out of me. You weren't what I was looking for at all." She sniffled and stood on tiptoe to kiss him. "For years, I wondered why my relationships never worked. I'd either get dumped or I'd end up being disappointed because the guy didn't measure up to what I thought were logical standards.

"Then you came along, and I realized I couldn't make a checklist for love. It's either there or it isn't." She paused, and then took the plunge. "So, where do we go from here? I think it's only fair to warn you that I want the whole enchilada—a home, a husband, and kids. I know that's not on your agenda, but could it be?"

Quinn didn't answer right away. Instead he kissed her a lot longer and harder than she had kissed him.

"It's what I want, too, Alex." He held her close.

"The day I almost drowned had me thinking about my life. I don't regret any of the things I've done, but suddenly, the next adventure didn't seem so exciting without you sharing it. I guess...that is...somehow...aw, hell, I'm not good at putting my feelings into words. I love you. I want to spend the rest of my life showing you how much."

"Well, if that's a proposal of marriage, the answer is yes," she said a bit breathlessly.

It was a good thing he'd wrapped his arms around her because her legs had suddenly become useless. If he let go, she'd fall at his feet.

He smiled and kissed her again.

"I think we just got engaged." A sober look came over his face. "I guess that means I have to get a real job. I'm not trained for anything useful."

"Well, let's be practical and logical," she said as he grinned at her. "Your grandfather has an unfinished book. You could send a partial off to a publisher, and then finish it."

"I never thought of that. I'll bet the old boy would have gotten a kick out of being published. But I don't know if I can write."

"We'll find out, won't we? I can help. After all, my grandfather was an author. Maybe it's in the genes. Besides, it'll give me time to sell the shop."

"What? Why? You love this."

"Darling, I want to run a business. It doesn't matter what kind. I chose antiques because I knew something about them and had an initial inventory that cost me nothing. I have something else in mind."

"Like what?"

"If you can stand Waukegan, we could live in my grandfather's house while you finish the book. Then, we can take a share of the proceeds from the sale of the map and form our own business—adventure tours. We'd charge people to live out their fantasies.

There are a lot of Indiana Jones wannabes, both male and female, who would love to part with several thousand dollars for a week of doing whatever their hearts desire. I can handle the business end of it, and you can schedule the tours. I'd even let you go on a couple. Hell, I may go with you," she said.

His hand slid down to squeeze her bottom. "Oh, you would, would you? You seem to have this all thought out."

"It's been a long week and a half."

He kissed her again, and then raised his head, giving her a quizzical look. "You're absolutely sure the treasure is a hoax?"

"Absolutely. Besides, silly man, you *did* find a treasure."

"Yeah? What?"

"Me, knucklehead."

He grinned, pulling her hips into close contact with his. The passion flared and surged over her like a tidal wave. A tiny fire burned deep inside. Unzipping her caftan, he slid his hand inside to caress her breast, his thumb massaging the nipple until it was hard. She clung to him, her heart pounding, slow and heavy. Her legs trembled.

"Lady, it's been a lot longer than a week and a half," he said with a throaty growl. "I'm tired of talking business and of practicality. In Santa Rita, you specified seven kids. Let's get started. Where's the bedroom?"

She laughed and waved a hand toward the hallway. "Right through there."

Quinn picked her up and carried her through the door.

Epilogue

Phoenix, Arizona
Six weeks later...

Rod Halston stared into his cereal bowl. In a foul mood, he had no interest in this so-called healthy crap Iris bought. His mind focused on other things like Alex's parting shot regarding impotence. Last night's date with a cocktail bimbo had not been a success in that department. Neither had the one last week or the one the week before that. He worried.

He glanced across the table at his sister, spooning the crunchy garbage into her mouth as she read the morning paper. Suddenly, she stopped with her spoon halfway to her mouth and an incredulous expression on her face. She dropped it into her bowl and laughed.

"What's so funny?" he asked in a disinterested voice.

"Here, read this." She handed him the paper. Her laughter built.

He stared at the article Victoria pointed out entitled, "Ancient Mayan Map Brings Record Price", and then began to read.

"Mr. and Mrs. Quinn Rafferty...highest price ever paid...*Mayan map*...Why that...that..." He was so flabbergasted he could barely speak. "We had it in our hands for weeks and never knew it! No wonder she followed me. Mr. and Mrs. Quinn Rafferty! The bitch didn't let any grass grow under her feet, did she? How did she and Quinn get it? Our guides took it." He didn't know whether to rage or cry.

Victoria laughed harder. "Who knows? Maybe they swiped it back from them. It doesn't matter. How does it feel to have a mark pull a con on you?"

"Stop laughing," he shouted. "It's not funny!"

No, it wasn't funny at all. Alex had kept the secret of the map from him in spite of his smooth talk and persuasive ways. The thought that the map might be important for something other than the treasure hadn't entered his mind. He couldn't believe it and certainly had never seen it coming. Alex? Uptight, logical Alex? He wanted to throw something, preferably at his sister whose laughter continued to peal. It was all her fault. Treasure he understood, but a *map*?

Gradually, Victoria regained control. "No, it's not funny, but it sure is ironic." She tossed her napkin onto the table and rose. "I've come to a decision, Rod. I'm going to find a job."

"It's about time. Iris is driving me nuts."

"No, you don't understand. A legitimate job. I'm no longer in the con business. I only wanted the treasure so I could cut loose and not have to live con to con. I'm a damned good secretary. I may never be rich, but maybe I can be happy. I'll live here until I can afford my own place. Who knows? I may even find a man who'll want to marry me and settle down."

Rod felt pole axed. His shoulders slumped and his breakfast sat like a lump in his stomach. She couldn't mean it. Not Vicky. She was just pulling his chain. He couldn't take any more shocks. He took a deep breath.

"You can't be serious, Vicky."

"Oh, I'm very serious. It's time for a change."

"But, what about me? How will I survive without you?" he whined.

Victoria smiled with a malicious expression.

"Rod, in the words of Rhett Butler, 'Frankly, my dear, I don't give a damn'!"

She marched out of the room, leaving Rod staring after her, his mouth hanging open in consternation and disbelief.

****

Waukegan
Three months later...

Quinn burst through the door of the shop with a suddenness that startled Alex. Ignoring two matronly customers, he pulled his wife into his arms, kissed her soundly and picked her up, twirling her around.

"Quinn," she gasped in embarrassed delight. "Behave yourself! What brought this on?" He kissed her again before setting her down.

"I just got off the phone with Zane Morrison. New Horizons Publishing in New York wants to publish Grandfather's book. I thought you might like to know," he said, grinning. "I can't believe how fast it happened. After I read what Grandpa had written, the rest just flowed. If it hadn't been for you, the whole project would've never gotten off the ground." He swept her into his arms, kissing her again.

"Darling, that's wonderful news," she whooped, hugging him. "But all I did was contact Grandfather's publisher. He set us up with Mr. Morrison. You did the real work. Tonight, we celebrate with champagne."

"Naw, let's do it now!"

She squealed in surprise as he slung her over his shoulder. "Quinn!"

Turning to the grinning customers, he said, "I'm sure you ladies won't mind returning in an hour or so, will you?"

He dropped Alex onto a Regency chaise lounge, then locked the door behind the laughing women,

274

flipped over the closed sign, and pulled the shades. He had that swashbuckler grin on his face, which never failed to turn her on.

Returning to Alex he pulled off his shirt and murmured, "I've been having fantasies about this particular piece of furniture for weeks."

She laughed softly and lay back in a provocative pose.

"Well, Mr. Rafferty, we will soon be in the business of fulfilling fantasies. We can call this research."

He leaned over with a wicked gleam in his eyes, and said, "I love research."

A word about the author...

I was born in Indianapolis, Indiana, but lived for many years in Memphis, Tennessee which I now consider home. I have two adult children and four grandchildren. At present, I reside in Ft. Lauderdale, Florida with my husband, Bruce, and two dogs, Lucky and Liza.

I've been a serious writer for six years and belong to RWA, Florida Romance Writers, River City Romance Writers, the special interest chapter of RWA, Kiss of Death, and Mystery Writers of America, including the Florida chapter. I achieved PRO status in 2004. I also co-chaired FRW's 2007 Fun In The Sun Conference.

Thank you for purchasing
this Wild Rose Press publication.
For other wonderful stories of romance,
please visit our on-line bookstore at
www.thewildrosepress.com

For questions or more information,
contact us at
info@thewildrosepress.com

The Wild Rose Press
www.TheWildRosePress.com

Other suspense-filled Roses to enjoy from The Wild Rose Press

DON'T CALL ME DARLIN' by Fleeta Cunningham. Texas, 1957: Carole faces not only censorship but mysterious threats and a fire-setting assailant. Will the County Judge who's dating her protect or accuse her?

~from Vintage Rose (historical 1900s)

SECRETS IN THE SHADOWS by Sheridon Smythe. Lovely widow Lacy had taken in two young children—and the rambunctious little angels wasted no time getting her into trouble with Shadow City's new sheriff...

~from Cactus Rose (historical Western)

SOLDIER FOR LOVE by Brenda Gale. An award-winning novel set on a lush Caribbean island. As CO of the American peacekeeping force, Julie has her hands full dealing with voodoo signs and a handsome subordinate.

~from Last Rose of Summer (older heroines)

TASMANIAN RAINBOW by Pinkie Paranya. A concert violinist grapples with remote ranch life, intrigue and the mystery of a missing diary, the peril of a flood in which all could be lost, and the undeniable attraction of the man who would do anything to protect his son.

~from Champagne Rose (contemporary)

THAT MONTANA SUMMER by Sloan Seymour. Samantha has everything but love. Dalton has only one thing on his mind: land. Neither wants to be a summer fling or be stalked by a mysterious attacker.

~from Yellow Rose (contemporary Western)

A CHANGE OF HEART by Marianne Arkins. Jake Langley returns to Wyoming to find more than changes at the family ranch. Discovery of a well-kept secret sets duty against heart's desire, changing hearts and lives forever.

~from Yellow Rose (contemporary Western)

DRAKE'S RETREAT, by Wendy Davy. Maggie needs a place to hide. Drake's Retreat, deep in the Sierra Nevada Mountains, is the perfect solution. But she has to convince the intimidating resort owner to let her stay.

~from White Rose (inspirational)